The PepperAsh Clinch

Franky Sayer

Published by Sirob Press

British Library Cataloguing in Publication Data.
A CIP catalogue record for this book is available from
the British Library.

ISBN: 978-1-9997108-0-4

Chapter One

"Woody can't get the barbecue to light," Max Podgrew reported to Elspeth Antworthy and her daughter Nora Stickleback who were busy in the kitchen at The Fighting Cock public house in Ashfield. Darkness had descended outside, as predicted at around half past seven on a late September evening, and most of the guests were gathering in the garden area. The sight of the vibrant bunting pennants fluttering in the light breeze had been replaced by twinkling coloured bulbs, lengths of which were strung around the perimeter of the car park and gardens.

The celebrations were in aid of the new landlord and landlady, Woodrow – Woody – Stickleback and his wife Nora, taking over the tenancy of the pub. Their son, Henry – a quiet lad, tall for his age, with Nora's dark hair – had celebrated his fifth birthday two weeks before. Henry had not particularly liked starting school but, after just a couple of weeks, had made friends with three other boys – Sidney, Bloo and Hopper. Nora had invited them, together with their respective parents, to the do this evening.

The party was not only for the new tenants of The Fighting Cock but was part of a community effort to help bring the good folks of the two villages, Pepper Hill in the west and Ashfield in the east, together. They had lived as friendly but separate entities for generations. However, the national government reorganisation earlier in the year of 1974 had altered civic boundaries all over the country. As these two hamlets already shared a church – St Jude's, located almost exactly midway between the two - it suited the local council that they be amalgamated to form one village. And this was not to everyone's liking.

"Well, I'm sure at least one person out there has the intelligence to sort it out!" Elspeth snapped irritably. "We're busy in here."

"Bloody good job she isn't our new landlady," they heard Max mutter as he returned to the garden. He was a quick-tempered farm labourer, who lived in the row of cottages close to the pub, of indeterminate age, but reason said he must still be quite young. And he gambled. Elspeth definitely did not approve, and she puttered under her breath,

"Bloody shame, you mean."

Although Nora heard her, she ignored the comment. They were buttering soft white rolls to go with the beef burgers and barbecued chicken portions, if they ever materialised. Woody was self-appointed chef with Max as his understudy.

"Maybe I'd better go and see what's happening," Nora said. She set down her butter knife and picked up the serving plate of prepared rolls. "I'll take these out; people can nibble them while they are waiting."

The tables had all been placed to one side of the lounge-bar, covered in brightly coloured cloths on which were laid the bowls of salads and platters of cheeses and crackers. These had been safely wrapped in cling film against the midges, gnats and thieving fingers.

"No, no. I'll go," her mother stated. "Put the kettle on, I'll be back in a minute, and we'll have a cuppa while they get themselves organised."

Everyone's invitation for this evening had included a request that they contribute something that was special to their particular family. Max Podgrew had brought one of his grandma's own recipe fruit cakes, thoughtfully sliced and wrapped; Poskett had donated packets of crisps and snacks from his shop in Pepper Hill. Nora noted with amusement that these were very near, on, or beyond their sell-by dates.

Elspeth spent a few minutes re-arranging everything on the table to her satisfaction. Six bottles of home-brewed, non-alcoholic wine had been donated by the Ervsgreaves, a pleasant but posh couple who lived in the last house along the road out of Ashfield towards Cliffend. Elspeth moved the bottles from their prominent position to a space at the back of the main table, hidden behind the notice that advised people to collect their drinks from the bar.

Music suddenly blasted from outside. Woody had installed a sound system during the afternoon, which included four speakers, one in each corner of the garden. Elspeth walked quietly to the door to have a look. Max was in charge of choosing the records, while Woody still struggled to light the barbecue – a barrel-shaped, custom-made model provided by the local blacksmith, who just happened to be busy elsewhere this evening.

Several people were hovering expectantly, but it

would not light: the lid over the grill had been left open and the intermittent drizzle during the day had drenched the charcoal.

"Don't worry," a jovial voice called above the disgruntled murmurs from the crowd. "Tip a bottle of Woody's best scotch over it and toss in a match!" This was met with raucous laughter.

Elspeth sighed sharply, turned around and marched back into the kitchen.

"I wish they would all stop acting like a load of kids," she muttered angrily to her daughter. "Before someone gets hurt!"

"I know," Nora squirmed. "But it's a good way to bring everyone together." Nora was tired of her mother constantly criticising her and Woody's new venture.

"Well, all I'm saying is that it's a shame that they can't get the coals to light!" Elspeth stated with satisfaction.

"I'll go and take a look," Nora said. She was a community-minded person, and really wanted to make a success of the pub, but sometimes she did wonder why she bothered.

"We'll both go this time." They walked outside just in time to see Max place a compilation LP onto the turntable. He then left the music station to help Woody, who smothered the coals with fuel and held aloft a gas lighter.

"Oh, for goodness sake," Elspeth exclaimed. "Of all the stupid things to do…" The remainder of her complaint was lost in the cheers as the barbecue finally flared into life.

Later, outside, with the music quietened to a

bearable level, family groups were sitting on the benches at the picnic tables eating their chicken legs, beef burgers in rolls and other nibbles; they had all diligently avoided the salad. Gnats and midges fluttered in the illuminated circles around the outside lights. Inside, many of the single men and women had congregated at the bar.

"So, d'you think you and Woody will be able to make a go of the pub?" Elspeth enquired, having swallowed a mouthful of chicken before discarding the remainder.

"We'll have a damn good try!" Nora exclaimed. Her plate was full but her appetite was vanishing a little further with each jibe from her mother. Hoping to change the subject, she commented, "Henry seems to have settled into his school okay. He is a little bit taller than most of his classmates, though."

"All the better for him to stand up for himself, then!" Elspeth stated with a sharp nod of her head. Nora sighed. This was not the happy event she had planned. Elspeth looked over to her, set her plate down then took her daughter's and piled it on top. She held out her hand, and said gently,

"How about a truce? I'll stop complaining about your choice of husband, if you jolly well cheer up, eh?"

Nora smiled. Yes, she loved Woody, but she also recognised that he had his problems.

"Okay. Truce, Mum." And they moved easily into a hug.

"Anyway, I've got something for you from a friend of mine who moved out to New Zealand years ago. She's a bit behind with the news, and she sent a big brown teddy bear over after I'd been telling her about you and Woody starting a family. She later said I told her you'd had a girl. Of course I didn't, but she's one of those people who are never wrong." Luckily it was too dark in the corner where they were sitting for Elspeth to witness her daughter's smile. "Anyway, it's still wrapped in cellophane, so you can pass it on to the next jumble sale, or friend's child, or whatever, if you don't think Henry will want it. Or maybe, if you have another baby, it might be a girl this time."

Nora flinched. Her most prayed for wish was to have a brother or sister for Henry, but four years of disappointment was wearing down her hopes. Elspeth felt Nora withdraw, and added softly, "Well, it's in the car. I'll fetch it for you later."

"Okay. And thanks. If you give me her address, I'll write a note back to her."

"Good girl," Elspeth said, patting Nora's arm. Looking around them, she saw that the party was going well. Groups were gathered, eating, drinking and chattering. Paper plates, plastic cutlery, glasses and napkins had been discarded all around the garden. "Right, young lady," she addressed her daughter in her familiar way. "Let's start clearing up, shall we?"

"Well done Mrs S," Max said as Elspeth retrieved his plate from under his beer glass. He was sitting with his mates, enjoying a cigarette. Elspeth swiped away a cloud of smoke.

"It's Mrs Antworthy to you, young man," she scolded. Max's response was lost as someone turned up the volume of the music.

Couples began to dance with each other, adults with children, partners with partners, sometimes with other people's partners. They spilled off the lawn and gardens, and onto the spare area of the car park. Most of the men and many of the women were inebriated, laughing and giggling like kids. The younger children had been whisked away by their mums, who had left the fathers in charge of the older ones and the teenagers.

A party album was playing, and the circular hokey-cokey dance morphed into a long line which Max led off in a curving, gyrating conga. The change in movement made him realise he was a little wobbly and, although he was okay doing the one-two-three steps, the side-kick was proving precarious.

The snake coiled around itself, limited by the reach of sound system. Then, to maintain the momentum and venture further afield, the revellers sang their version of *Dah-da, dah, dah, dah, da-dah dah; dah-da dah, dah, dah, da-dah dah; De-dah, dah, da; de-dah, dah, da* along in time to their dance. It quickly became a competition as to who could be the loudest and most out of tune. They then lost the music completely, which finished soon afterwards anyway, and moved beyond the boundary of the car park and down the road.

"Get back in here," Elspeth screamed into the darkness at her son-in-law, who had taken over leading the conga. Her voice travelled easily through the darkness, although Nora winced when she heard it.

"Right'o captain!" Woody replied drunkenly and swung the dancers into a very tight turn. The line cambered and weaved around the road, with little regard for traffic – luckily there wasn't any – or for the people who lived in the small holding opposite the pub. Other neighbours were either here at the party, or too far away to be disturbed.

Max thought the person behind him was gripping his hips a little too tightly; a quick glance over his shoulder was met with the florid face of a lady from Pepper Hill whom he was sure he'd seen in the bookmaker's in Cliffend. Surprise made him trip, and he took down several other people as well, to the cries of "Whoa!" "Hey!" "Ouch!" "You alright?" and "Gerroff!"

The front and rear ends of the conga ignored the casualties in the middle; they joined up and were led back into the pub car park, and then began weaving around the vehicles. But the rhythmic singing was beginning to fade, along with people's energy and enthusiasm. The sound system was emitting a hissing noise from the needle stuck in the ever revolving grooves at the end of the record.

Everyone suddenly stopped as an explosion shattered the night air.

From the ensuing silence, an inebriated voice asked, "You didn't leave that petrol can next to the barbecue, did you, Woody?"

Chapter Two

Reverend Quintin Boyce – Quinny, as he preferred to be called – arrived at St Jude's Church rectory in PepperAsh on the last Friday in June, during the very hot summer of 1976. The sun had been shining relentlessly since the beginning of May. East Anglia, being the driest region of the country, was suffering badly from drought; even the grass in the graveyard was stunted and straw-dry.

The taxi driver carried Quinny's suitcases through the front door and placed them on the floor in the hall. He was not due to arrive until the beginning of July, but he had informed the Bishop of Mattingburgh, Patrick Clement, that he would take up residence a week early.

"But the ladies of the parish are planning to give the house a thorough spring clean before you get there. They'll want to spruce up the church for the induction service as well," the bishop's voice rose in surprise at the news. "And the good folk of PepperAsh have arranged a welcome reception at the village hall in Pepper Hill on the Friday before you celebrate your first services."

This news confused Quinny for a moment; "Where," he asked the exasperated bishop, "is Pepper *Hill*?"

Bishop Clement ignored the question. He knew that, although Quinny was a very good rector, he was also a cantankerous old bachelor, very set in his ways and with no family to retire him to. Rumours had also spread at his previous parish, which he refused to deny, that he *didn't actually believe in God*. At that point, the bishop had decided a change was needed.

He was also aware that Quinny suffered from a form of depression; although this had never been official diagnosed, it was said – as with many people – to have stemmed from his childhood. Quinny's parents and siblings perished in a bombing raid during the Second World War along with most of their friends and neighbours. In fact, an entire suburb was decimated, including shops, schools and the town hall which held all the civic records and registers. There was a debate about Quinny's actual age; he thought he had been born in 1937, but this could not be verified, nor the date and month established.

After the bombing raid, Quinny's welfare became the responsibility of the local church and, through them, he was found a foster family. Thousands of other children all over the country – and indeed in other nations, both allies and enemies – were in similar positions. Although very young, Quinny knew his circumstances were not unique. He was bright and thrived at his new school; he gained a scholarship to a boarding grammar school which in turn led to a place at university and thence seminary, then on to a career in the Anglican church.

Meanwhile, on this bright summer's day, Quinny paid and generously tipped the taxi driver who responded with "Cheers." When the front door was closed behind him, he surveyed his new home.

The rectory felt dark and dismal, even on such a gloriously sunny day as this. But, for once, Quinny was feeling positive and hopeful: he decided it could be made homely and welcoming.

He walked along the hallway to a door that looked as if it should lead into the kitchen. When he opened it, sunshine cascaded over him and he smiled. But this faded when he bent down to inspect the contents of the fridge. It was empty: he wasn't expected until next week! His pleasant thoughts came to an abrupt end, but were then moved to curiosity when he heard a noise at the front door. He walked back into the hall as a key was inserted, followed by an exclamation of surprise that it was unlocked.

A group of three chattering ladies marched into the rectory, looking as if they were about to embark upon a grand cleaning session.

"Oh," the stout and substantial figure of the leader exclaimed when she saw Quinny standing in the hall. "We didn't think anyone would be here. Reverend Boyce, isn't it?"

Quinny recoiled at her sharpness, and his hand moved to the dog collar around his neck. He smiled and aimed his voice for lightness; he did not want to alienate people who volunteered for hard labour, especially if it was for his benefit.

"Yes," he said, "Please, call me Quinny – short for Quintin, spelt with two 'i's'. People always spell Quintin wrong. There's no 'e' and everyone always seems to want to use at least one, if not two. Quinny is easier."

He realised he was rambling; it was a habit he'd

formed when nervous. But he knew he must not, even on the first meeting – especially on the first meeting – show any signs of weakness.

"Quinny," she said with a downward thrust of her wattle-like chins. Quinny nodded. The two faces behind the ring-leader echoed her disapproval as they surreptitiously jiggled the dusters, mops, bucket handles and brushes they were carrying.

"Very well, Quinny. Is that Reverend Quinny? Or just Quinny?"

"Well, maybe Reverend when the business is formal. But, as I imagine you are here to help me settle in, I hope we can be more informal. How do you do, Mrs?" he asked, as he extended his hand.

"Ervsgreaves," she obliged. "I'm very well, thank you." She then turned and introduced the others, one of whom, it transpired, had had the foresight to bring tea, milk, sugar and biscuits!

"Excellent," Quinny enthused. "Please, go through to the kitchen. I expect you know where everything is."

As they sat in the kitchen enjoying a cuppa before starting work, Quinny became intrigued by their chatter.

"Yes, well, PepperAsh is of course two hamlets. Them idiots in charge..." the lady speaking, Miss Childs, waved her hand vaguely in the direction of the kitchen window, "...when they re-arranged the boundaries..."

"She's referring to the local government re-organisation which, I'm sure you'll remember, took place a couple of years ago," Mrs Ervsgreaves explained.

"…decided that Pepper Hill…" this time Miss Childs indicated towards the hall door, "…and Ashfield should be lumped together as one village!"

"Outrageous," the smallest of the three ladies whispered: Quinny was sorry to realise he had already forgotten her name – Mrs Marble, or Mabel something or the other.

"It's made worse," Miss Childs – Alice – explained, "because people from Pepper Hill have traditionally been buried in the half of the graveyard around the back of St Jude's, where the sun doesn't shine so much; but people from Ashfield are buried at the front!"

"Which just goes to prove that we are entirely different communities," the indomitable Mrs Ervsgreaves stated. She then added with satisfaction, "I live in Ashfield – the last house out on the way to Cliffend, or the first one in, one could argue."

Miss Childs scowled, then explained, "Pepper Hill, of course, has the post office and shop; and the village hall. Not to mention the airfield at the top. I live in Pepper Hill!"

Quinny almost had time to acknowledge this before the timid lady ventured, "Yes, but Ashfield has the pub…"

"Huh!" interceded Mrs Ervsgreaves. "And that isn't anything to boast about, is it? With the landlord being a complete drunkard!"

"That's unfortunate. Maybe I should visit him," Quinny offered. "And we can all pray for him. And for his family. Does he have a family? What is his name? And the name of the pub?"

"The Fighting Cock!" exclaimed two of the ladies together. They looked at their new rector with both amusement and embarrassment.

"Oh," Quinny said quietly. "That's unusual, isn't it? The name is normally The Fighting Cocks – a pair. I mean one is no good on its own, surely." He was baiting the good ladies to see how far their senses of humour and tolerance extended.

"Well, "Mrs Ervsgreaves pronounced. "There's no need for two cockerels to cause a fight in that pub. With Woody Stickleback in charge, he could pick a good enough fight with himself, and still lose!" She folded her hands across the top of her substantial bosom and nodded her head, which concertinaed her many-layered chin.

The silence that followed gradually made the ladies realise they might have actually been a little too judgemental. They all then had the grace to look remorseful and, to divert attention from their criticisms, raised their tea cups and sipped in unison. Quinny studied them carefully.

"Nora's very nice," Miss Childs stated, gulping, "She was very kind to me when I had a turn in the bank in Cliffend the other week. She was in the queue behind me, and took me home to Pepper Hill in her car, to save me catching the bus."

"And they did hold that lovely party when they first took over the pub," Mabel added.

"You mean the one where the barbecue exploded?" Mrs Ervsgreaves asked, then proceeded to tell the new rector the sorry tale.

Chapter Three

Two weeks later, the welcome reception and the ensuing induction service were over. Bishop Clement, who had conducted the latter, took a sabbatical, thankful that Quinny had not upset anyone so far. And now, with the rector's first Sunday service successfully behind him, he hummed as he pottered in his study.

Quinny was wondering why the bishop had made such a fuss about PepperAsh, warning that the two fractious communities did not really speak to each other. So far, he had discovered that the church had one warden from each hamlet; the parish council was made up of seven members, three from Pepper Hill, the slightly larger in land area of the two, and four representing Ashfield with its greater (by ten people) population. The parochial church council comprised three members from each (Mr Ervsgreaves being the treasurer), plus a gentleman who now lived in Cliffend but had spent most of his working life in Pepper Hill.

Quinny chuckled as he poured himself a glass of water. He would have made a cup of tea, but the weather was still insufferably hot outside: a high pressure area had settled comfortably over the country and seemed in no hurry to wander off elsewhere.

Quinny's kitchen window opened onto the large rear garden which was tended by the good gentlemen of the parish – mostly retired and, with a couple of exceptions, married to the band of ladies who cleaned and polished and cooked. Quinny despaired that none of his volunteers were under fifty – nor indeed were many members of his congregation. And there didn't seem to be any youngsters showing interest. But, he reminded himself, he was still new to his position, and he did not yet appreciate if this situation arose because the younger generation didn't care and were happy to leave it to the older ones, or that they were *not allowed* to take part in organising activities lest they upset anyone – or just made a mess of it!

Quinny sighed as he sat down and stared out at the parched grass which was his lawn. The radio was on and the presenter's voice slowly penetrated his thoughts. Although he had not been listening properly from the beginning of the programme, he quickly pieced together that the subject under discussion was to do with obsessions – or, more accurately, how to stop them.

"If something has become a habit, and is causing problems," the guest speaker explained, then immediately backtracked with, "I'm not talking here about serious medical or social addictions, you understand, I'm referring to irritating habits that you may wish to break. These might include cigarette smoking, or drinking just a little too much alcohol, or obsessive cleanliness, or even avoiding certain items – maybe to the extent of having to alter routes to work or the shops in order not to encounter them. Research has proven that a possible way to disrupt such habitual, obsessional behaviour is to cause a distraction."

Quinny humphed as he thought, *That's all very*

18

well, sunshine. But usually you're stuck with the thing that's causing the problem that makes you want to do whatever it is you consider a bad habit in the first place! Although thoroughly sceptical by this point, he continued to listen.

"It sounds simple – too easy, in fact," the detached voice stated knowledgeably. "But try it, please; don't be put off by its lack of complication or sophistication." *This chap likes the sound of his voice using long words,* Quinny mused. "Place a large rubber band – or elastic band, whichever one wishes to call them nowadays – onto your wrist. Make sure it's big enough not to cut off the circulation, though. Then just ping the band against the skin to stop the train of thought veering onto the action one is wishing to curtail. And, may I say, this has also been proven to work for mild depression."

"Mixing your *one* and your *your* now," Quinny sneered before dismissing the advice as patronising rubbish. But he could feel the incessant summer heat and the weight of his memories pushing him into blackness and despair. Maybe it was worth a try. And it was by no means the worst advice he'd ever received.

He knew he had a couple of large rubber bands in his desk drawer which originated from a bundle of envelopes posted through his letter box. He retrieved them and stretched both over his right hand and onto his wrist. His left wrist was already busy carrying a watch.

Quinny's wrists were not particularly big but the bands – one a dull red and the other standard manilla – were still a little tight. He rearranged them to lie flat against each other, then set about ignoring them.

But, every so often throughout the afternoon, he absentmindedly twanged one or the other, or both, against his skin, not because he was feeling depressed or angry in any way, but just to experience the sensation. And the sharp smarting *was* sufficient to remove all other thoughts - for a few moments, anyway.

By evening, Quinny was a little worried that this practice could be regarded as a heresy. He was respectful to his calling, he wore a cross - not a crucifix, but a small wooden one - around his neck under his dog-collar and shirt, hung from a spare, very long, black boot lace. But he quickly realised that the sting from pinging the bands was more efficient at warding off the dark thoughts than holding on to his cross. Then he wondered if this would become an obsession in itself.

With this in mind, he thought maybe he ought to hide the bands. But, when the doorbell rang a few minutes' later, he forgot about them, until his visitor asked, "Why have you got two rubber bands on your wrist?"

"Oh, that's where they went, is it?" Quinny improvised. "I wondered where I'd put them. Thank you." And he pinged both bands. Meeting his parishioner's questioning face with a bright smile, he asked, "Now, what can I do for you?"

Chapter Four

Henry Stickleback arrived home from Cliffend Middle school at 4.25 p.m. on a dismal Friday afternoon in February 1979. The inside of the bus's back windows were misted with condensation, but he could still see his friends pulling grotesque faces and gesturing as the driver pulled away from the bus stop. This was just part of his gang's ritual.

The astute nine year old Henry knew that one of the reasons Hopper, Sidney and Bloo hung around with him at school was because he regularly gave them bags of crisps. He helped his mum quite a lot; being an only child, living in a pub and spending most of his time with adults, he learned quickly that doing odd jobs here and there not only staved off boredom, but brought rewards.

"Thanks, son. Help yourself to crisps. Take some for your friends tomorrow," Nora would say.

Henry wondered if they really were his friends, though; he had heard them making fun of him, of his dad, and especially of their surname. When they didn't think he could hear, the lads laughed about how many spines they had on their backs: three, five, even twelve he'd heard one idiot suggest. But the jibe that really hurt him was that Woody had no spine at all. And Henry knew, even as he scrunched his way across the car park that afternoon, Woody would already be drunk.

Henry opened the big door into the lounge-bar of The Fighting Cock public house. The fire in the corner hearth roared, although the pub was not due to open for at least another couple of hours. Nora sat at the table nearest the bar, working through the week's invoices. The cleaner, Mrs Mawberry, was dusting and wiping down the surfaces. The fug of stale cigarette smoke hung just above the fragrance of furniture polish and coal soot. He closed the door carefully so as to avoid a cloud of smoke billowing into the room from the change of pressure to the chimney.

"Hello, son," Nora said with a smile.

"Hi, Mum." He then looked over to the lady with duster and mumbled "Hello Mrs..." He swallowed the name he couldn't recall, but his grin invited her to respond before she started emptying the contents of glass ashtrays into the bin she carried with her. She then gave each tray a slow and thorough wipe. Nora realised she was stretching this last job, hoping for a cup of tea, or something stronger, before leaving at around five o'clock; so far today Mrs Mawberry had not gleaned any gossip to pass onto her friends.

The drunken shenanigans of the landlord at The Fighting Cock were a constant source of amusement to the villagers of both Pepper Hill and Ashfield. Nora Stickleback was pitied and derided in equal measure, as Henry knew was true of himself.

Henry made his way from the lounge-bar into the kitchen, to find something to eat. He was feeling restless and tired, and he ached all at the same time. And he was constantly hungry. He had homework to do, but decided it could wait.

He wandered back through to the lounge-bar as

he finished eating the sandwich he had hastily made. The last piece of cheese slipped from between the slices of bread and, stuffing the remaining crusts into his mouth, he bent to pick it up. He did not intend to eat it, but to place it in the waste bin to prevent anyone slipping on it.

However, as he crouched down, he caught sight of a half-full bottle of whisky hidden towards the back of the shelf under the bar near the cash till. His curiosity was sparked: although the optics were easily reachable – everyone told him he was tall for his age, and anyway, he could always stand on something – he had not yet sampled any of the magic elixirs that changed his father's personality from grim and grumpy to happy and carefree.

Henry peeped up over the bar and found the room empty: both ladies had gone.

Nora realised that it would only be a matter of time before Henry tried a secret drink, but still prayed that he wouldn't. And she didn't think he would only be nine years old when it happened.

Henry was not aware of his mother's fears, but suddenly wanted the experience – he was, after all, a normal, inquisitive lad. He felt excited as he unscrewed the top. But he turned his head sharply away when the pungent smell was released.

Tentatively, and without breathing in, he placed the rim of the bottle to his lips and tipped it up. The weight pushed more whisky into his mouth than he had anticipated, and he swallowed a good shot before he could pull the bottle away.

The taste repulsed him. He coughed noisily as the liquor scoured the back of his throat and burned its way up his nose and down into his stomach. Shaking his head violently and jerking his shoulders, he spat out and spilt far more than he drank. Then he retched.

"There you are, young Henry," Woody slurred a few minutes later, when he discovered his son still hiding under the bar. Henry's head was spiralling and he felt very unwell. "Ah huh! So, you've found my secret stash, have you?" Henry quickly picked up a nearby cloth and pretended to be mopping up the spillage.

Woody reached forward, retrieved his bottle and took a generous swig. Henry noticed that the whisky smell from his father's breath was different from the stench all around him; it was warm and personal, obnoxious and menacing.

Soon they heard Nora's footsteps approaching. It was too late to escape. She found them both sitting on the floor in a whisky soaked pool.

Henry did not stay for the ensuing argument, but crept shakily upstairs. He stripped off and showered, leaving his damp and reeking school uniform in the bathroom to be washed. He assumed his mother had not suspected that he'd had any of the drink, but that Woody had spilt it.

He was in a deep sleep later that evening when Nora sat at the kitchen table and wept to herself. She felt her life was futile. Now not only did she have the constant worry of a drunkard husband, but also feared that Henry would soon follow suit.

Chapter Five

As Woody Stickleback's health and state of mind had deteriorated, Nora absorbed most of the duties involved in running The Fighting Cock. She was helpless to prevent his self-destruction: he needed to stop drinking, but he didn't want to. And there was nothing Nora could do. So she concentrated on work – the everyday serving, ordering, re-stocking, cleaning and paperwork and looking after their son Henry, whilst in the background, and unknown to most people, she just about managed to control Woody's behaviour.

Christmas 1979 was dull and dismal, and the rain-laden wind felt much colder than it was thought snow and frost would have been. Nora worked on, not even resting during the lull between the two festivities.

The New Year's Eve party seemed to carry on well into New Year's Day; luckily The Fighting Cock remained closed until lunchtime on the second day of January. By this time, the snow had arrived, swirling in on the north-east wind, bringing with it Scandinavian frost and ice. The landscape was slowly transformed into a rolling whiteness, soft to look at, hard to the touch, and sometimes blinding in its comfort.

On the fourth day of the New Year, Nora looked out of the pub's window; the benches and tables that customers used in the summer months had become mystical, curved-topped objects, strapped to the ground sometimes with long icicle-like stays. Her car had remained unused in the car park for several days; it suddenly looked as if it were a barnacle on the surrounding flatness, like an ornament on a cake that had been covered with icing.

Nora needed to go shopping, but she was not looking forward to venturing out. She had to buy a couple of school shirts and other items for Henry, whose new term started soon. Luckily, Henry worked hard at school and, although not a model pupil, he had not given her too many problems – as yet. And he did help out as much as he could at home, although Nora was constantly worried in case he decided to try a drink and ended up like his father. She thought that day had come last February, but now she was almost totally sure nothing had happened to set him on his father's road. She sighed, and silently thanked God.

The day was bright, but the air was sharp. As Nora walked across to her car in her wellington boots, her breath, once inside her lungs, stung before it quickly steamed back out. The sun sparkled and spangled over the crystals in the snow; although it made her eyes smart, it brought a promise of warmth and comfort for some time in the future.

Having brushed away the snow from the door and unlocked the car, she then swept as much off the roof and all the windows as she could reach before she climbed in. The car seemed darker than usual, with a grey-blue pall over the interior. She changed from her wellies to ordinary boots, settled and was pleasantly surprised when the engine started on the second turn of the ignition. She carefully edged the wheels onto the deep snow that surrounded her parking space, leaving behind an oblong patch of bare ground, and drove out of the gateway onto the road to Cliffend.

As she looked back, she waved at Henry, who was about to start scraping and clearing a path across the car park to the door for the regulars to walk on. The road surface had been spread with salt and grit but ice sheened on top again; she drove slowly, aware of her responsibilities at home and her need to keep safe.

Once in town, Nora quickly finished her shopping. She then found it hard to concentrate on the journey back to Ashfield. She tried not to hurry, but knew she needed to be home in time to open for the lunchtime session.

Climbing a slight incline in the road, which the car normally took with only the tiniest amount of extra acceleration, Nora suddenly saw the scenery beyond the windscreen swirl; she felt the muscles at her waist twist as the lower part of her body was wrenched around; she clung her top half to the steering wheel by her fingers. Adrenalin shot through her, causing the extremities of her limbs to tingle. All of this happened in the miniscule moment it took for the rear end of her car to flick around, the tyres no longer gripping the slippery surface, leaving her on the opposite side of the road and facing the direction from which she had just travelled. The engine stalled and she jolted to a halt. But the windscreen wipers carried on, stubbornly clearing the snow from the glass.

Nora was shaking badly.

Then she held her face in the palms of her hands, and her head slumped forward until it touched the steering wheel. Luckily the central horn trigger was not particularly sensitive, and it did not blast out. But she sobbed anyway. She just didn't think she could cope if anything else went wrong.

Suddenly, amidst the noise there was a knock on the window by her ear. A voice called,

"Mrs Stickleback? Nora? Are you all right?" Another voice asked,

"What happened?"

The driver's door was opened by a couple who were regular summer customers to The Fighting Cock. Mr and Mrs Ervsgreaves liked to sit outside on a Sunday evening and enjoy the view of the sunset beyond the River Potch and Ashfield Staithe. She did not know them well, but they worked tirelessly for the community, especially at the church.

"I don't know what happened," Nora replied shakily, sniffing back the tears. They helped her to stand up, encouraging her to move away from the car, now stranded and looking slightly pathetic amid the bright whiteness all around. "Thank you," she said as Mr Ervsgreaves handed her the clean white handkerchief from his breast pocket.

"Careful, my dear," Mrs Ervsgreaves, wearing a red hat, scarf and gloves set, advised as Nora began to move. "These roads are still so slippery. You'd think the council would grit them properly, wouldn't you. Are you okay, my dear? You're trembling. Let me get you into our car." Nora allowed herself to be led to their passenger seat and sat heavily down. "There, make yourself comfortable while my husband just checks that your car isn't damaged. Oh dear," she sighed as another vehicle approached. She waved her hands for them to slow down, and nearly lost her own footing.

The occupants of the second car helped to start and turn Nora's car, which Mr Ervsgreaves drove slowly back to The Fighting Cock. Nora found herself strapped in beside Mrs Ervsgreaves, who ensured she kept a safe distance behind her husband. She did not state that an inferior vehicle such as Nora's might inadvertently, without any help at all from the driver, decide to slide around again, thus removing any blame from Nora; she was implying that a solidly-built car, such as hers and her husband's, would travel along the icy roads without problems. Nora thought she meant well, though it was a very clumsy way of saying the incident was not necessarily her fault, but that of her car.

Later that evening, still trembling at times from the mishap, Nora admitted to herself that she could no longer manage all the everyday work at the pub, as well as look after her drunken husband and her ten year old son, without more help. She suddenly felt exhausted. But, so as to forget her other worries, she let herself be absorbed into the conversation at the bar.

"So, when d'you reckon Twelfth Night is then?" Max Podgrew asked, his complexion ruddy and his hands raw and red from working outside. Quinny had been the rector of PepperAsh for a few years now, but had not so far paid for a single drink. He stated emphatically and with the full force of theology behind him, "It's the night after Epiphany! And that's the sixth of January."

"No, it's the fifth," Stan, one of the regulars, interceded. Quinny turned slowly around on his stool and stared at him. The movement made Nora think about the twisting sensation she had experienced when the car had slid earlier; her muscles were still sore.

"Well, if you want my opinion," Max started to say, but was halted by a chorus of "We don't!"

"You're getting it anyway! The celebrations were well and truly over by New Year's Day, so the decorations might just as well have come down then!"

"Yeah, but you could say that of Boxing Day," Stan ventured. This time everyone turned around and stared at him. He picked up his pint, shrugged his shoulders and said, "I'm just saying!" Nora noticed with a silent smile that no one had asked for her opinion.

"I would like to've seen you climbing a ladder to take down the streamers on New Year's Day," Quinny commented to Max. "On second thoughts, no, I wouldn't – you'd've fallen off, the state you were in."

Chapter Six

The following morning, Woody was still in bed, and likely to stay there for most of the day. Nora waited until Henry had left for school before starting to remove the decorations. She had decided to throw out all the old trimmings, including the pathetic plastic Christmas tree, and start afresh next time.

Annie Tillinger and her husband, Derek, had moved into the Old Police House in Ashfield's sister hamlet of Pepper Hill just after they were married. The property had been sold when the local police authority decided a resident bobby was no longer required in the villages. Derek worked at an engineering company in Cliffend, called Tarskers. Their children, Rosalie and George, travelled to school on the designated bus, and Annie found herself at home on her own all day. She decided she needed a part-time job to occupy herself – plus, of course, any extra money she could earn would be useful.

She thought she would start this morning by asking Mr Poskett who ran the post office and shop almost opposite her house. She put on her decent coat – not her best, because that might give the impression she was too posh to serve in a village shop and do some of the lifting jobs she imagined this might entail. She waited outside the shop with Rosalie and George until the bus arrived. She waved as it left, but her children were too busy talking to their friends to notice. Then she ventured into the shop.

The bell above the door brought old Poskett out from the store room. No one seemed to know his first name, and there wasn't an initial in his shop sign to give any clues.

"Mr Poskett?" she asked, suddenly feeling quite nervous. "I was wondering if you needed anyone to help out, maybe just a couple of hours or so during the day. You see, the children are both at school now and I'm finding myself at a loose end. I wondered if there would be any chance of earning a bit of money?" She decided to include that last comment, in case old Poskett thought she was volunteering her services for free.

Poskett removed his wire-framed spectacles. Annie felt herself quake as she squinted in response, maybe hoping that empathy for his myopia would gain her a favourable interview. She was disappointed with his response.

Annie's next enquiry took her to Ashfield and The Fighting Cock public house, run by the Sticklebacks. Annie didn't have access to a car; Derek used theirs to travel to work. But there was a surprisingly regular bus service; both Pepper Hill and Ashfield were on the route from the coastal town of Cliffend in the east to the city of Mattingburgh in the west, and it was quite easy to travel between the two villages.

Over the sound of the cleaner as she vacuumed the carpet, Nora hadn't heard anyone enter – she had opened the main door to free the air inside of the smell of beer, cigarettes, smoke from the fire and the sweat of people. She was surprised to see

Annie Tillinger standing there when she eventually looked up.

"Hello. Sorry to disturb you, I can tell you're busy," Annie stated tentatively.

"It's okay. Good to see someone so early." Nora looked at her watch. "We're not open just yet, but I could do with a coffee now. Would you like to join me?"

Annie was caught off-guard. "Yes, that would be very nice." She hesitated but, as Nora straightened herself, she saw how tired the landlady looked and hurried on. "Actually, I've come to ask if you need help here, a cleaner maybe, during the day when the kids are at school?"

Nora smiled and reached her hand out and gently patted Annie's shoulder. "You must be an absolute mind-reader. My regular cleaning lady – Mrs. Mawberry, do you know her? She's hurt her back and is off sick, so I need some help at the moment. When can you start?"

"Now. I'll make the coffee. Today's free, if you want me to do a trial, Mrs Stickleback." Annie smiled back, relaxing, thankful that she had worn, under her second best coat, her third best jumper and skirt.

"Please, call me Nora."

Chapter Seven

Jim the postman had three envelopes to deliver to The Fighting Cock public house. He was very cheerful as he greeted Nora.

"Morning, Mrs S. Lovely day." It was mid-September, the sun was shining and he was wearing shorts.

"Glad to see someone's happy," Nora replied, glancing enviously at the Mediterranean suntan on his lower legs, his arms and face. Nora's skin remained white all year round; she couldn't remember the last time she had sunbathed. "Been anywhere nice?"

"Yeah," Jim replied, his smile widening as he handed her the post, "Majorca. Had to make the most of it this year – my last chance with that *Under 30 Only* company. I'm an old man next month – thirty-one! Huh, never thought I'd be thirty-one. 1987's a bad year for me. See ya." He left, and Nora – approaching her fiftieth birthday – felt very old indeed as she walked slowly back to the pub.

Henry was restocking the shelves behind the bar. He had celebrated his eighteenth birthday earlier in the month, and was now so tall that he towered above his parents. His hair was still dark, but the beard he had decided to grow since he came of age and his mother couldn't tell him to shave it off, was tinged with the ginger of her own father's colouring.

Nora looked at her watch, hoping Annie would

soon arrive. They always started the day with a cup of tea. She went through to the kitchen and filled the kettle with water. She then inspected the three envelopes; one contained an invoice, one was bumf, and the third was from her insurance brokers.

When Nora had married Woodrow Stickleback, her mother, Elspeth Antworthy, had insisted she take out a life assurance savings' policy. She had managed to meet the regular payments without Woody realising; the total being increased considerably when Elspeth's bequest was added and the policy updated some years ago. This matured on Nora's fiftieth birthday, 10th October.

Nora was astounded when she read the final amount, including all the interest. There was a form to be completed and returned to confirm her instructions for the money. She suddenly felt giddy, relieved and – to an extent – free. A broad smile lit her face. But she knew she had to be sensible. She sat down and re-read the letter.

For many years, Nora had dreamed of renovating the pub, upgrading the fittings, and refurbishing both the lounge-bar, and their private residence. But, with this money, she could possibly purchase the property freehold from the brewery, and run it without the restraints currently imposed upon her.

The night of the exploding barbecue, thirteen years before, had marked Nora and Woody taking over the tenancy of the pub from his parents. But Nora had never felt it was truly theirs. Now, however, she would be able to make the business her own; hopefully Woody would not interfere.

Just at that moment, she heard a clatter from the room above. When the kettle had boiled, she made a mug of tea for her husband; she would wait for Annie to arrive before she actually prepared theirs. As she climbed the stairs, she made plans: she would phone the brewery to check on her situation with regard to buying the pub. Then she needed to make appointments to see her solicitor and someone at the bank. But before she did anything else, she had to complete and return the form.

She sighed as she reached out her hand to open the door to hers and Woody's bedroom. Maybe she would wait until tomorrow before doing anything, just to allow herself time to digest the news.

A little more than a month later, overnight on the Thursday to Friday, a tremendous gale swept across the south east of England. This had not been forecast, and caused a massive amount of destruction; trees were uprooted, with some landing on roads and railways, buildings, cars and other structures; roofs blew off, chimneys were felled and power cables and telephone lines were brought down. By the following Monday morning, when most of the damage had been assessed, it was officially being described as a hurricane.

Switching off the radio as the newscaster finished listing rail services that were still disrupted, Nora rang her bank to make an appointment to see the assistant manager, Mr J. Jones. She needed some of the money from her insurance policy to purchase a new car.

"That gale blew an old beech tree down onto the bonnet; it's a write-off now," she explained. But Mr Jones did not seem to think this warranted his interest; he looked anywhere but directly at her. Nora felt insulted, and started to gabble. "We were lucky that the wind didn't do any damage to the pub. The news on the television showed a lot of buildings were destroyed. One of our regulars, who lives just up the road, had part of the roof and the chimney stack blown off his cottage. The insurance company will pay something towards replacing it – our car, I mean, not Max Podgrew's roof and chimney. But I want to buy something better – more powerful and substantial, reliable – not too expensive though because, with Henry now being on the insurance, the costs will all add up. And I need it immediately for the business."

Nora suddenly straightened her shoulders, sat upright and gripped the handles of her handbag. She was remembering her chagrin when Mrs Ervsgreaves and her many chins had criticised her poor car after she had spun it around on the ice. She changed her tone as she stated the total she required, impulsively doubling the previous amount she had calculated.

Mr Jones capitulated with a nod, and then picked up his telephone to call someone to make the necessary arrangements.

Chapter Eight

"Rosalie, you are sixteen years old. You keep telling me not to treat you like a child, so stop acting like one!" Annie Tillinger stated with controlled anger. But her daughter's blue eyes were filled with genuine tears. "Anyway, you won't be on your own. George is here." George hovered discreetly in the hall, listening to the argument but not taking part. "And Nora's coming to stay overnight."

It was the Tuesday after the Bank Holiday weekend at the beginning of May 1988, and Nora Stickleback was closing The Fighting Cock for a week while the pub was refurbished. The sale from the brewery had been completed surprisingly quickly and without complication.

Derek still had several days' holiday due from his work and so he and Annie had decided to have a short break. They contacted Perrona Dawn because, a while ago, someone in the pub mentioned the company did cheap rates for their river cruisers between Easter and the Bank Holiday at the end of May. The couple hired a boat for a Tuesday-to-Saturday slot and were looking forward to it.

But now, as she and Rosalie faced each other angrily in the kitchen of the Old Police House, Annie was regretting the whole idea. Rosalie was supposed to be revising for her GCSEs, and was being extremely difficult about her parents going away, which Annie blamed on a mixture of hormones and exam nerves.

"Nora'll be too busy seeing to the alterations at the pub!" Rosalie sniffed. Her expression then changed, and she asked, "Is Henry coming too?"

"No, Henry's staying there with his father." These two factors were a relief to Annie, which immediately made her feel even more guilty.

Annie's other concern about the arrangement was that her daughter had what used to be called, when she was a teenager, a *crush* on Henry. Annie could see that he had grown into a good-looking young man; more than three years older than Rosalie, Henry was mature. He was quiet but responsible; somewhere during his older childhood and younger teen years he seemed to have taken over the patriarchal role in his family.

Henry's father, Woodrow Stickleback's liver was failing. His skin had a permanently jaundiced tinge – even the whites of his eyes were yellow and bloodshot. His hair, what was left, was grey and spikey, and he was extremely thin. At one point, Annie had asked Nora if perhaps he'd had a stroke, but Nora was adamant that the doctor had assured her that his appearance, together with his slurred speech and impeded movements, were all caused purely and solely by his drink problem.

After Easter, Woody had been in Mattingburgh hospital for three weeks. He was home again now, but looked so dreadful that Nora had told him to stay upstairs out of the way.

This morning, though, Annie continued to try to reason with Rosalie. "Nora said the pub will be in such a mess for a few days that she'll be glad to get away in the evenings. I'm sure the break will do her as much good as it will us. And, anyway, you don't need your dad or me here to tell you to do your studies. Or to get your uniform ready, and go to school. Or to clean up after yourself."

Annie drew a breath before her mouth launched into the familiar complaint which her brain was telling her not to actually say. "George doesn't need us to follow him round all the time. He can sort himself out, and he's two years younger, so why can't you?"

"But Mum, the exams start soon. You can't go and leave us now!"

"It's only for a few days, for goodness sake. Don't you think we deserve a holiday as well?" Annie retorted. She noted that Derek seemed to have disappeared, leaving her to deal with Rosalie's tantrums. Again.

"Rosie, we'll be okay. I'll do my bit," George said, at last entering the kitchen, and the disagreement. He hated his parents using him as a shining example; neither did he think it was fair of them to go away at the moment. Even he, as the stereotypically annoying, insensitive *little* brother – he was a good deal taller and broader than his *big* sister – could see that she was anxious about her exams and wanted the comfort of their parents nearby.

George was not noticeably cleverer than Rosalie but, by not panicking and quietly getting on with things, he was gaining better marks at school than she had. And he had a different attitude towards life: if he knew that homework or tests were due, then he concentrated and got them over with.

Rosalie, on the other hand, worried and fretted about things until her mind whirled so much that any extra work she did was rendered useless by the stress. George often tried to calm her, but his efforts just seemed to upset her more. Her words were now spat at him rather than spoken.

"Don't call me Rosie, George! My name is Rosalie. That's Rose-a-lee. ROSALIE!"

"All right, all right." Annie shouted. "Just calm yourself down, young lady!" She was beginning to think that the holiday was a waste of time; she would now be too anxious to enjoy her time away.

Eventually, Rosalie capitulated. "I'm sorry. Mum," she whispered as she hugged Annie. "I didn't mean to be selfish. I'll just miss you."

"I know. But it's only for a little while, and it'll give you a chance to..." she tried to remember some of her daughter's more annoying habits, but suddenly nothing seemed to stand out; struggling, she blurted out "...do your make up at the breakfast table, leave your laundry on the floor..." Then, triumphantly, she remembered, "...not wash up properly and leave sugar in the bottom of the cups."

"Yes, but I don't take sugar, so it isn't my fault, is it?" Rosalie retorted, feeling more secure arguing a point with which she often made a stand.

Eventually, Annie and Derek were satisfied that everything was okay; they finished their packing and stacked their suitcase into the car. But their journey to Cliffend was fraught with problems. The near-side front tyre suddenly seemed a little deflated. It was not exactly flat, but Derek had to unload the boot in order to retrieve the spare wheel and the tools in order to replace it. Once on their way from Pepper Hill to Cliffend, a drive that usually took between fifteen and twenty minutes, they caught up with a tractor which they were forced to follow nearly all the way to town.

When they finally arrived at the Perrona Dawn complex, the marina car park area was full. Derek deposited Annie outside the reception entrance with their case and drove around the nearby side streets in search of a space. As he locked the car to walk back, he hoped that if he inadvertently stole someone else's spot, the disgruntled resident wouldn't sabotage his vehicle while they were away.

As he carried their case through the main holiday complex building to the marina, Derek whispered (so that the representative couldn't hear) "You know, I think some of the chaps Nora's got working on The Fighting Cock were involved here when *Dawning Day* was taken over by *Perrona* and the new centre was built."

Annie looked around critically, scrutinizing the details and hoping ease of cleaning was taken into account in the designs. Judging by what she saw, she concluded glumly that it was not.

The couple were extremely relieved when Derek finally started the engine and eased the boat, delightfully named Peach Dream, away from the jetty, out of the mooring lagoon and onto the River Potch. As they chugged inland, Annie sat up on the deck watching the town recede and countryside take its place. The motion was soothing, and at last she began to relax. The afternoon sun was still warm and she closed her eyes.

Annie had arranged to telephone Nora in the morning, just to make sure Rosalie had settled: she refused to call this evening and, to prevent any communication being possible, she and Derek had planned to moor at Ashfield Staithe, which – although miles from civilisation – was ironically just in view across the marshes and up the hill from The Fighting Cock.

Chapter Nine

Annie had prepared the spare bedroom at the Old Police House for Nora to sleep in while she and Derek were away. Having been used to rising early, Nora couldn't lie in, even for one morning. She had been in the kitchen for only a few minutes when the telephone rang. Her immediate thought was that something had happened to Annie and Derek. She quickly picked it up.

"Hello," she said tentatively into the receiver. Wearing a light tracksuit, George appeared in the doorway, followed by Rosalie who, standing barefoot and still wrapping her dressing gown around her, was dwarfed by her younger brother. She was shivering and George instinctively placed his arm around her shoulders as they both waited to hear the reason for such an early phone call.

"Mum?" Nora thought Henry's voice sounded uncharacteristically thin and distant.

"Henry, what's the matter? Are you all right?"

"Mum?" With the repetition, Nora heard her son's voice as it had been years ago: young, uncertain, vulnerable.

"Henry? What's wrong?"

"Mum, it's Dad. He's shouting. He's been sick. There's blood in it – a lot of blood. I think he got to the booze last night. I locked the door to the stockroom, but he got through. I'm sorry, Mum."

Nora was shocked. She thought Woody had learned his lesson; one more binge, he had been told, and his liver would, in layman's terms, give up.

"Okay, Henry." She looked up at Rosalie and George's faces. "I'll be right over." After a pause, she asked Henry, "Have you phoned the ambulance?"

"No. I'll do it now," her son replied, suddenly spurred into action. He cut the connection with Nora and immediately dialled the emergency services. When Nora arrived at The Fighting Cock, an ambulance was in attendance. But they were too late. Woodrow Stickleback had died.

An hour later, the phone at the Old Police House rang again. Rosalie was upstairs, so George answered.

"I don't want you two to worry," Nora started to explain quietly, unable to rid herself of the vision of her husband's gaunt and lifeless body: the shocked expression on his face, the yellowing skin sporting stunted grey stubble stretched over his bony chin. She swallowed hard against the bile. "But Henry's dad has just died." Her eyes were dry, but she blinked as if to clear the image.

"Oh," George didn't know what to say. His limited life experience had not yet equipped him for this. "Can we do anything?" he asked, remembering the phrase other people used in such situations.

"No, well, yes. Er, just carry on as you normally would – go to school, that sort of thing. Look after Rosalie."

"Okay," George replied. "We can catch the early bus from here to Ashfield and stop off with you until the school coach comes."

Rosalie was brushing her hair when she came into the kitchen as George replaced the receiver.

"Who was that?" she asked, although she was fairly sure she knew the answer.

"Nora," George replied as he handed a mug of coffee to Rosalie. "Woody died – not sure of the details. I said we'd go over before school."

"Thanks," Rosalie said as she took the drink. "Poor Woody. Mind you…"

"Don't, Rosie," George interrupted. Good, solid, fourteen-year-old George. "Don't say he deserved it, or that you're surprised it hasn't happened before now, or anything like that. It's not fair on Nora, or on Henry."

Rosalie looked at him. She had been so busy growing up herself recently that she had forgotten George was also still only an adolescent. He had just begun to shave, and she could see where he had missed a patch; the golden stubble glistened against his soft skin. He had always seemed so mature and sensible, but she knew he must have fears and insecurities of his own. He had been so embarrassed a year or so ago when his voice began to deepen: occasionally it broke to a squeak in the middle of a word or sentence, making his face flame so red that even she dared not tease him.

"How's Henry?" Rosalie asked compassionately.

"We can find out soon. Come on – get yourself ready, we've only got ten minutes before the first bus comes."

Rosalie and George alighted at the stop outside the pub car park in Ashfield; they filed across the gravel and through the open door. The lounge-bar was almost unrecognisable with the interior fittings stripped, all the furniture removed and some of the floorboards up. The windows were wide open, as usual in the mornings. Two workmen stood by the unlit fireplace in the corner, quietly occupying themselves, obviously aware of the tragedy that had just taken place.

In the kitchen Henry was making breakfast – toast and tea. Neither he nor Nora was particularly hungry, but at least preparing a meal gave him something to do.

"Hello, you two," Nora said. She suddenly seemed diminished, her shoulders were hunched and she looked cold. "I'm sorry…"

"No, no, don't be sorry." Rosalie rushed in and took Nora's proffered hands. "It's not your fault and, as Mum rightly said before she left, I am old enough to look after myself – us both – really," Rosalie quietly turned to Henry. "Hi, Henry, how're you doing?"

Henry looked up. His face was pale above the reddish beard he sported; a deep crease line seemed to have been stamped between his brows. His eyes looked as if he was forcing himself to stay awake and his hands shook.

"I'm, er… I think…"

"You're in shock, mate," George stated. "Can't believe it, I guess."

"No, well. It's…"

"I'll make us all a fresh pot of tea, shall I?" Rosalie offered, for want of knowing what else to say or do.

They sat around the table, sipping tea and ignoring the toast, while Nora explained,

"Woody has been taken to the Cliffend hospital; there was no need for me to go, they'll ring if a post mortem is required. Henry will have to give a statement at some point, but they said that could wait until he feels up to it." She smiled at her son, but he tilted his head downwards. "The police were very kind – everyone was."

"Have Mum and Dad phoned yet?" Rosalie asked as she squeezed Henry's hand.

Nora hesitated before replying, "No." She looked as if she was trying to work out why Rosalie would be asking this. Then she appeared to remember, and added, "I expect they'll wait 'til they can moor by a phone box – I'll probably hear from them lunch time." Nora fell silent. She guessed Annie and Derek would return as soon as they heard the news. At least, she hoped they would: she felt she needed her friends.

When Maurice Spelter had been appointed manager of Cliffend's Perrona Dawn marina and leisure complex, one of the London directors had described the location as "The knee cap of the rear leg of the sitting dog that is Great Britain." Maurice had laughed at this but, looking at a map, he could see how that conclusion had been drawn. He enjoyed his job and tried to make each holiday the company provided a memorable and pleasurable experience.

Today, which happened to be the third anniversary of his moving to Cliffend, he received a telephone call from the police that would tarnish the memories of his tenure. Mr Spelter waited a few minutes before ringing through to his secretary and asking her to bring in the details of the previous day's boat hires.

"Thank you," he said as he took the folder from her. He flicked through until found the boat, Peach Dream, and checked the hirer's name. Further down the form he found that particular couple's contact – Nora Stickleback.

Chapter Ten

Reverend Quintin Boyce did not believe that the number three held any particular significance in the world, other than denoting the Holy Trinity, and the number of days it took him to eat a whole loaf of bread. All the same, he placed that number of elastic bands on his right wrist – each one a slightly different shade of brown. It was then he received the telephone call from Nora to say that her husband, Woodrow Stickleback, had passed away.

Quinny did not drive although he had taken lessons in the early nineteen-sixties, just after he had been assigned his first position as curate. But he seemed unable to judge distances with the speed at which either he or other cars were travelling. He couldn't feel the size of the vehicle he was in charge of, had no spatial awareness, and was constantly bumping into things; neither could he co-ordinate himself enough to use his foot to operate the clutch whilst changing gears with one hand and steering with the other. The head instructor at the driving school recommended Quinny not pursue the activity; he would have placed some kind of warning on any future licence applications if he'd had the means to do so. Instead he had written a candid but kind letter to Quinny's bishop at that time to explain.

Quinny accepted the situation – exploited it, some concluded. In more urban appointments, he had been quite happy to use public transport; if he arrived late it was the fault of the bus or train. Even here in the wilds of PepperAsh, with over a mile between the two hamlets of Pepper Hill and Ashfield, he used the buses, and anyone else he could persuade to give him a lift. The entrance to the small car park at St Jude's Church and the rectory was not an official bus stop, but most drivers would pull in if they could see Quinny waiting, in the same way they would stop when they saw him walking along the road, as would Poskett from the shop, and the postman, and many other regular travellers: they might not attend church, but they considered this their Christian duty.

And, if nothing else was available, Quinny always had his bike. However, in total contrast to their view of giving him a lift, it was his experience that many drivers seemed to think they scored points in some celestial pay-back game if they tried to knock a man of the cloth off his wheels.

Luckily, today Quinny had not had to resort to pedal power, but managed to cadge a ride with the postman, Jim. He spent the morning at The Fighting Cock, talking to Nora and Henry. Unfortunately, though, he'd had a meeting arranged for just after lunch, but was back at the pub later.

By this time, Nora had been informed that there would not have to be a post mortem as Woody was under medical treatment at the time, and the cause of death was obvious. Cliffend's funeral directors, Maude and Griffin, would be in contact soon regarding the funeral and, for a positive distraction, Quinny suggested he and Nora look through the hymn book for something suitable to sing.

The workmen ripping out the interior of the next room were trying not to make too much noise, but occasionally the crashes, drillings and hammerings made them both jump. Nora drifted into silence several times and Quinny realised she was listening to them. A radio was on and one chap was whistling an accompaniment; Quinny was surprised at how well he held the tune.

Nora was remembering once having sung a hymn that included words about forgiving *our foolish ways*, and wondered if this would be a little too glib, given the circumstances. The telephone rang. She looked up at the rector.

"Would you like me to get that?" he asked, half rising from the chair before Nora nodded.

"Hello," Quinny wasn't certain if he should say the pub's name or his, so he fiddled with his rubber bands and said neither. The voice on the other end identified himself as Mr Maurice Spelter, the manager of the Perrona Dawn leisure complex in Cliffend. He asked if a Mrs Nora Stickleback was there and, if so, could he speak to her.

"I'm afraid she's just had a bit of a shock," Quinny explained. He turned slightly away and lowered his voice. "Her husband died this morning. You're speaking to the parish rector, Reverend Boyce. Is there anything I can help with?"

There was a pause, then the man on the other end of the call drew a deep breath.

"In that case, I'm really sorry to have to bother her at a time like this," he said, "But Mrs Stickleback's name was given as contact for a couple who hired one of our boats yesterday – a Mr Derek and Mrs Annie Tillinger? Would you happen to know them, Rector?"

"Yes, I do know them. Why?" Quinny felt a coldness stirring in the pit of his stomach.

"I'm afraid I have some more bad news," the man said quietly. "There seems to have been an accident on board, and – well, the police are still at the staithe – Ashfield Staithe."

"What sort of accident?" Quinny asked anxiously. Nora raised her eyes from the hymn book and stared at him.

"I don't know all the details, but could you, or Mrs Stickleback, please contact them – the police? I have to go to the staithe myself now."

"Right, okay. I'll, er, I'll speak with Mrs Stickleback, then make my way over there. Thank you."

Quinny replaced the telephone receiver and looked across the room to where Nora sat at her kitchen table. The sounds from the lounge-bar had ceased.

"What is it?" she asked apprehensively. "Something about Annie and Derek?"

Quinny sat down next to Nora. Taking the hymn book from her hands, he held them. Her fingers were cold, and her eyes still glistened with tears for her husband.

"That was a Mr Spelter from Perrona Dawn. He'd got your number as a contact for the

Tillingers."

Nora shifted on the chair. Her life had taken a catastrophic turn this morning, and she felt somewhat removed from reality at the moment.

"He just said there'd been an accident on board their boat, and that the police are there – Ashfield Staithe."

Nora was quiet for a moment before saying, "They said they were going to moor somewhere where there wasn't a phone so Annie couldn't check up on the kids every half hour. But what kind of accident? What's happened?"

"I don't know. The man asked if you could ring the police – presumably the Cliffend station. I'll wait if you like to see what they say."

Quinny's fears for the number three – the second and third elements of the trilogy – were suddenly real. He looked around, then asked, "Where's Henry?"

Chapter 11

A detective sergeant attached to the case contacted Nora early in the afternoon. He introduced himself but, as he spoke quickly in a soft Welsh accent, she could not catch his name.

"Can you meet us at Cliffend hospital, Mrs Stickleback?" he said and before she agreed, he carried on, "This afternoon, four o'clock? I know that doesn't give you long, but if you could make your way to the mortuary, it's in a separate building at the back of the main block. We need someone to identify the bodies. I understand the couple's children are both still under eighteen and, as your name was given as contact, we'd be grateful if you could do it. There are some papers to sign, too. And," he eventually stopped talking for a moment to clear his throat. Nora thought that, if she had been quick enough, she would have asked questions, but he soon continued, "It'll be better at the hospital than if the bodies were in situ – on the boat, if you see what I mean. I'm sure you can understand that we need to be, er, sensitive."

And then he paused properly, obviously expecting a response. But Nora was silent, the horror of seeing her husband that morning still fresh in her mind. She did not want to imagine this, wherever it was deemed appropriate to take place.

"Mrs Stickleback? Are you still there?" the detective sergeant enquired.

"Yes, yes," Nora stumbled over her reply. "Yes,

I'm sorry. I was just trying to take it all in."

"Of course. Have you got any questions?"

"No, I don't think so. Hang on, yes. What did they die of?" Nora immediately realised her wording of the question sounded tactless. "I mean, what was the cause of death?"

DS Aimsley understood that people did not always think before they spoke when stressed; he also knew that many, sometimes vitally important, details were given unexpectedly in these moments. But there was nothing sinister here, just routine checks; he feared the coroner's verdict would cite misadventure.

"The pathologist's preliminary report indicates carbon monoxide poisoning, but it isn't definite yet. There will be post mortem examinations on both bodies, and tests will easily identify if this is the cause. The vessel will have to be examined as well, and all the appliances on board checked. It will take a while to come up with the reports. But we should have some answers in a day or two."

All Nora could think to say was "Thank you."

When the call was finished, she explained everything to Quinny. He listened, nodded, and twanged his elastic bands, occasionally making himself jump with the ferocity. In order to prevent herself from telling Quinny how annoying his habit was, Nora went upstairs to change her clothes.

Ashfield Staithe was approximately four miles from the Perrona Dawn marina in Cliffend and about half that distance from the Fighting Cock public house; it was just visible, on a clear day, from the southwest facing bedroom windows. Nora glanced out in that general direction. Looking over the top of the cottage and small holding, Tidal Reach, situated opposite the pub, down along the pastureland across the marshes, she could just see Ashfield Staithe.

The only vehicular access from Cliffend to the staithe was along a narrow dusty track that ran between the river wall on one side, and the marshlands on the other. Luckily, the weather had been dry for a few days; if there had been any amount of rain, the track's surface would have been covered with mud, and almost impassable.

Nora picked up her hair brush and absentmindedly glanced out of the window again. She could just about see an ambulance being driven slowly away from the staithe and back towards town.

Nora reached into the wardrobe and selected a jacket – her navy one with gold buttons, which she had not worn for a while. The hook of the hanger caught on cellophane poking down through the slats of the shelf above. Before she could prevent it, the large, ugly brown teddy bear that her friend had sent from New Zealand for Henry fell on top of her. She picked it up and looked at it. After a moment, she pushed it back onto the crowded shelf, wishing she could hide in a cupboard, and remain there for years with no one bothering her.

Her reverie was broken by a knock on the bedroom door. The police liaison officer had arrived to take her to Cliffend hospital.

Downstairs again, she asked, "Henry, will you

wait here for Rosalie and George?" As she waited for his response, Nora was surprised by how proud she suddenly felt of her son.

"What shall I tell them?" Henry asked; although distraught, he was trying to maintain his self-control and be strong. "I, er…"

"Henry shouldn't be left to pass that kind of news on," Quinny said gently. "You go with the police, Nora, and I'll wait for the bus with Henry."

Quinny had been taught how to break bad news, to deal with the consequential outpourings, to ignore the reactionary rantings, and to offer words and actions of support. Although not the worst news Quinny had ever had to impart during his years as a rector, he was struggling to find the best way to tell two teenagers that their parents had died, so soon after learning of the death of their dear friends' husband and father.

Later, Quinny was still cursing the number three as he gently sat Rosalie and George down at the table in the kitchen of The Fighting Cock public house, Ashfield.

Henry watched from the doorway through to the lounge-bar. He felt cold and empty, an outsider in his own home, and there was nothing he could do to make the situation better.

Chapter 12

Nora and Henry both stayed overnight at the Old Police House with Rosalie and George, although everyone was restless and no one slept. They returned to The Fighting Cock the following morning, as soon as Quinny and a family liaison officer arrived to be with the Tillingers.

Nora settled down with the telephone, contacting family, friends and associated business people to pass on the sad news of Woody's death. She graciously accepted their condolences, and ignored the underlying, unspoken remarks that this news was not a surprise. She promised to let them all know the details of the funeral, as soon as these were finalised – and, yes, there would be a 'do' at the pub afterwards – if the renovations were finished in time. Out of all the calls she made, only three numbers were unanswered, she left messages for two and ignored the other, a King's Krisps and Snacks' rep: she hoped they would hear the news sooner or later.

On the Thursday afternoon, Nora went back to Pepper Hill. Henry stayed at the pub to be with the workmen as the refurbishments continued. Both Quinny and the family liaison officer declined when she asked if they would like to stay for lunch.

Later, Nora offered to go through the process of contacting the Tillingers' family and friends. Rosalie and George agreed, grateful that they would not have to explain. They sat next to each other on the sofa in the lounge; Rosalie was huddled into a large, moss-green cardigan which Nora recognised as having belonged to Annie.

Her mind drifted back to the clinical coldness of the mortuary at the hospital. She purposely did not remember details of the visit, the journey in the police car, the liaison officer's name or that of the attendant, nor the various papers she had signed – everything twice, once for Annie, once for Derek.

But she knew she would never forget their faces; lying there, in the same chilled room, partitioned from each other; both appearing just to be asleep – peaceful. The only abnormal feature had been a slight pink tinge to their complexions. In a strange, detached part of her mind, she noted how different they had looked to Woody. And she envied them for being able to be together.

Nora shivered, then drew the telephone and Annie's address book across to the table and sat down. Whereas her hands had been steady when dealing with her own situation, she realised she was shaking now.

"I'll make a pot of tea, shall I?" George volunteered, anxious to be doing something. "At least that might warm you up," he added, indicating towards the cardigan.

By the time Rosalie held the mug in her hands, her fingers were pale and her nails blue. George sat back down next to her and, mindful of the hot drink, gently eased her towards him. Although he was desperately hurt by his own loss, he would have gladly taken the entire burden if it set Rosie free from her pain.

George had been there when his sister and mother argued as his parents prepared themselves for their holiday; unlike his father, he had not crept away – Derek did not like conflict – but had stayed to support Rosie. He was glad they had made their peace before the holiday had started; he could not begin to think of the guilt she would now be feeling if they hadn't.

Rosie was only sixteen, and, although two years older than George, he felt she was less able to deal with life than he. George could forget everything else while he concentrated on just one thing. But his sister could not; her mind always held on to other happenings around her, which robbed her of total attention, and made both learning and coping difficult.

Nora watched them on the sofa together. She was very worried about Rosalie, but was also concerned about George; although he had not descended into the periods of silence that both Rosalie and Henry had, he hadn't yet spoken of his loss. Nora sighed, then said,

"Right, I'd better get on, then."

"Thanks," George acknowledged. Rosalie sipped her tea; the other two cups on the table, one each for George and Nora, remained untouched. Nora rang the first telephone number; it belonged to a care home in Glasgow where Derek's mother resided. The lady in charge advised Nora to speak with a Shirley Pessham, Annie's sister, who lived in Australia, she being the only other person they had any details for, beyond the Tillingers and their children.

"But Mum and Aunty Shirley haven't spoken for years," George said when Nora relayed this. "They fell out when Dad made a joke about convicts being transported to Australia."

"That's an historical fact, why would it upset your aunt?" Nora enquired.

"Turns out her husband's great-grandfather *was* sent there for stealing. They found out when they started to look into their family tree."

Nora eventually found Shirley's number in Annie address book. She dialled in trepidation, conscious of the fact that a call half way around the world in the middle of the day would undoubtedly be expensive. But, in the circumstances, it couldn't be avoided.

The call was answered almost immediately by a harsh female antipodean voice saying "G'day." Nora explained that she was a family friend of Annie and Derek before imparting the sad news.

"Oh," was the initial response. "Right, well I suppose I'd better come over and sort it out – TERRENCE!" She had screamed the last word very loudly without removing the receiver from her mouth. Over twelve thousand miles away, Nora was nearly deafened. Although a hand was then placed over Shirley's mouthpiece, Nora could still hear her muffled voice speaking.

"I heard most of that," George said when Nora finally replaced the receiver some ten minutes later.

"Yes, I expect most of PepperAsh heard it as well! Anyway, I presume now we just have to wait to hear of their travel arrangements." Silence followed as they digested the news, then Rosalie suddenly asked,

"Where's Dad's car? Is it still at Perrona Dawn? And their clothes, and the things that they took with them?" Nora shook her head slightly, looked around and, when she realised the answer was not to be found in the room, she picked up the card left by the police liaison officer and dialled the number.

Shirley and Terrence Pessham arrived at the Old Police House in Pepper Hill just before noon on Saturday.

"I'll take charge now," Shirley stated as she walked into the lounge. Rosalie and Nora were still tidying up, expecting a telephone call from the visitors asking to be collected from the train station at Cliffend. Instead, the Pesshams had taken a taxi. "Which room are we in?" she asked as she looked up towards the ceiling. Rosalie shrugged and glanced over to Nora.

"I haven't sorted anything out yet," Nora stated while Rosalie quietly slipped past Terrence and out of the room.

"Well, a fine welcome this is, and from my own family!"

"I'll leave you to it," Nora said in her most offended, very English voice, which contrasted sharply against the new arrival's squawk.

"Well, aren't you going to stop and help?" Shirley blasted. "Some friend you turned out to be!"

Nora halted, turned around and glared at

Shirley's tanned and wrinkled face.

"Well, excuse me," she fired back, placing her hands angrily on her hips. "But I have a funeral to organise as well. My husband died the same night as your sister and brother-in-law. And, as you've just announced that you're in charge now, I'm off home." Nora picked up her handbag and car keys. As she walked from the lounge to the hall, she saw Rosalie sitting dejectedly on the stairs. "Come on," she said quietly. "You can come back to the pub with me; you'll be left in peace there."

Rosalie gratefully followed Nora. She was in the car by the time Shirley stormed out of the door and tried to catch their attention. And that was the first time Nora had seen Rosalie smile for several days.

Later that afternoon, Quinny called into The Fighting Cock to finalise an outstanding detail for Woody's burial. He stared around the newly refurbished lounge-bar. The walls and ceiling had been repainted, covering the previous nicotine-stained cream with a light shade somewhere between blue and green. He peered at the optics on the wall behind the cash till, and the shiny brass pump handles that matched the gleaming foot rail being fitted on the floor around the bottom of the bar. He and Nora were sitting on a scattering of plush new chairs, and he stifled a sneeze from the smell of paint and upholstery. The freshly installed banquettes that lined some of the wall spaces were still bound in polythene and, in the corner opposite the fireplace, were stacked the remaining new chairs, tables, and pouffes.

"There's only the carpet to be laid now. The fitters should be here in an hour or so. They said it won't take long to do. And they'll move all the furniture into place as they go," Nora gestured towards the pile. "It's made of a new blend of fibres, supposed to be hard-wearing, guaranteed fire retardant, resistant, or whatever. It's blue, dark blue." Nora realised she was rambling.

"Oh. Right," Quinny murmured as he looked down at the floor; the previous tiles had been cleaned and prepared, but the scuffs and stains still showed. Wishing to change the subject, Nora asked,

"Have you met the indomitable Shirley Pessham, Annie's sister, yet?"

"Oh, Yes. She's quite a, er, challenge," Quinny tactfully replied with a grin. "I understand Rosalie came back here with you."

"Yes, she said she'll wait for the bus and catch George before he goes home. I've told them I'll run them back later, after they've had their tea. Or they can stay here tonight, if they want – you never know, they might feel like helping me to restock – it'll give them something to do. I'm still aiming to re-open tomorrow. Henry's in the cellar; there's only a few odd jobs left to do, and a load of rubbish to go to the tip."

"How's Henry taking everything?" Quinny asked, nodding his approval.

"Just getting on with it, I think. A bit quieter than usual. Mourning in private – you know what youngsters are like."

"And George?"

"Well, George is different. He's looking after his big sister. He went into town this morning – said he wanted to pop into the library. He's annoyed at his aunt's interference. Obviously he's too young to take charge – but heaven help Shirley if she upsets Rosalie when he's there!" Nora sighed. "Have they decided anything yet – you know, a funeral or…?"

"Cremation," Quinny stated as he fiddled with the elastic band on one of his wrists. "She said something along the lines of 'they'll be cremated, let the kids get on with their lives'. She didn't think it was good for them to have a grave to tend for the rest of their lives!" And he jumped a little when the band snapped back onto his skin.

At that moment, they became aware of Rosalie walking across the gravel car park outside towards the bus stop to meet her brother.

Chapter 13

Nora was pleased with the pub's refurbishment; the builders and decorators had seen the tragedies in the Tillinger and Stickleback families unfolding and, as their own contribution, had worked hard to ensure everything was at its best. In return, everyone who had helped was invited to the opening, which took place on the Sunday.

It was a subdued affair: plans had originally been made to advertise the event on the local radio, in the Cliffend Herald and with posters around the area; celebrations were to include a barbecue and a band playing live music. The mention of the barbecue reminded the older regulars of the party held when Nora and Woody first took over the tenancy of the pub, and many comments were made about repeating the performance of the barbecue exploding.

But, in the end, the evening was marked in a suitably dignified manner; customers received a free drink and nibbles, and were happy to mingle and talk quietly, congratulating Nora on the décor and trying a few of the new beers on offer.

Rosalie and George had stayed with Nora and Henry at The Fighting Cock ever since their aunt and uncle arrived. Nora shuddered as she recalled Shirley Pessham's harsh voice on the telephone yesterday demanding that the youngsters return to the Old Police House. Nora had not felt like arguing, and said it was up to them. They had chosen to remain. Nora's invitation for Shirley and

Terrence to attend the opening was met with derision. And so far they had not appeared, for which Nora was grateful.

Not wishing to encounter their aunt, nor be involved in the re-opening, George had wisely suggested he take Rosalie out for the day; a bus left Cliffend for Mattingburgh mid-morning and they caught it from The Fighting Cock car park. Nora waited with them and, when the bus came into sight, she discreetly passed money to Rosalie, knowing she might accept it whereas George would not.

"Use this to buy a proper meal lunchtime," she said. "There'll be somewhere nice open you can go, even on a Sunday."

Rosalie looked down at the notes before tucking them into her bag. "Thanks, Nora, you're very kind. I…"

"Just look after yourself, and that brother of yours," Nora ordered as she kissed Rosalie's cheek.

"Thanks. We'll be back later this afternoon."

Nora reflected that they hadn't said what they planned to do for the day, but was sure they just needed this time on their own. She wandered slowly back to the pub, rubbing her hands, wishing she could do more for them, and for Henry.

As she pushed open the lounge-bar door, she was again astonished at the transformation. The upholstery on the new chairs and benches was a deep blue-green sturdy velvet-type fabric; the carpet, quickly laid yesterday, a dark blue colour that would absorb most of the stains, but unfortunately showed up the crumbs and fluff.

This carpet offered a talking point when embarrassment ended other conversations; it gave off a peculiar smell, said to be a new kind of fire-resistant treatment that had been applied.

"We'll all be high on the fumes, if it doesn't go soon," Max Podgrew commented, to which others agreed while swiping the tough surface with the soles of their shoes, as if this would scuff away the stench. "And Stan," he added, "don't light up in here, will you? Or we might all explode!"

Although she did not know the cause, Nora thought the laughter from the group at the bar was refreshing. She was standing near the redundant till, glancing around and hoping Annie would have liked the re-styled room; her friend had helped to choose some of the furniture and fittings, and Nora felt it was a kind of tribute.

A healthy number of people crowded in; groups and individuals were arriving while others left, creating a living, breathing ebb and flow. Despite hiring two extra staff for the day, Nora and Henry were kept very busy serving drinks, collecting and washing glasses. After an hour or so, Nora paused for a moment, then rang the brass bell at the bar.

"Thank you all for coming today," she said; despite her efforts, her voice sounded thin and insubstantial. "As you can see, the refurbishment has been completed, despite one or two upsets."

A voice at the back of the crowd, murmured "Good on ya for carrying on, gal!" and two or three others echoed "Hear, hear." Someone added, "Nice carpet, I could use any off-cuts you've got left." A woman hissed, "Shut up, Stan!"

Nora paused for a moment, swallowing hard and avoiding the eyes of all those gathered in front of her. When she had composed herself again, she continued,

"I don't want today to be sad, but I would just like to remember absent friends – Annie and Derek, and Woody." She fingered her wedding ring and, glancing at Quinny, saw her actions reflected in his rubber bands. "And I know you will all do everything you can to help the youngsters – Henry, Rosalie and George – to come to terms with their losses..."

"And you, Nora. We won't forget you either," Stan said from the back. "To absent friends. And to those left behind. God bless them all, isn't that right Rector?"

Quinny raised his pint and those assembled followed the gesture, either repeating Stan's toast or echoing it in their own words. There was silence while everyone supped.

"Thank you," Nora said, blushing. "You are all very kind. And of course, it goes without saying that you will be welcome back here for Woody's wake after the funeral."

There was a quiet spell in the pub later that evening. George and Rosalie were back from Mattingburgh, both stubbornly remaining at the pub, despite their Aunty Shirley's insistence that they return to the Old Police House. With three customers at the table closest to the fire, Nora was taking the opportunity to sit down with a gin and tonic while Henry checked the stock on the shelves.

"I need to go into Cliffend tomorrow morning," Henry advised as he walked over to Nora. Rosalie, who had drifted to the table as well, asked,

"Can I come?"

"Don't see why not," Henry replied, secretly pleased that his plan of telling his mother within Rosalie's hearing had worked.

"Don't you think you ought to go to school?" Nora asked cautiously.

"No, my form teacher told me he'd sort out some revision papers for me to look at. He said it'd be okay to stay off until after the funeral – cremation, or whatever Aunty Shirley has decided. I can't concentrate on school work anyway. I don't know how I'll get through the exams."

"Don't worry about them," Nora stated, already taking Rosalie's side. "If need be, you can re-sit them next year. There's no hurry, and don't let anyone bully you."

Rosalie tipped her head downwards and studied her fingers. "Everyone keeps telling me what's best for me – do this, don't do that. But no one asks me what I want to do. I can't tell who's bullying me and who's genuinely trying to help," she said, in a quiet voice.

"We'll help," Henry was quick to answer. "Mum and me'll look out for you. and for George."

"Oh, George can stand up for himself!" Rosalie stated despondently. "He's got his own future to plan. He's cleverer than me; he won't stay around here when he's finished school."

"Well," Nora began hesitantly, "Let's just get the next few days over with, then we can have a think about school and studying and all that. Anyway, Henry, what are you planning to buy in town tomorrow?"

"I need a new suit," he stated. "I haven't got anything smart that fits." Henry passed the six foot mark before he had left school, and hoped he had now finished growing upwards; he wouldn't mind extra muscle, though, to help assuage his lankiness.

"Oh, okay," Nora commented, thinking it was a shame such a momentous occasion as Henry spending money – he had been a skinflint, even as a child – was brought about by bereavement. "Would you like me to come along?"

"No, thanks Mum, we'll be fine – that is, if you're serious about coming, Rosalie?"

"Yes, please."

They then felt the atmosphere change as the door opened. Reverend Quinny and Max had returned, arguing as they entered.

"Good. Right, well that's that settled," Nora commented. "Excuse me, I'll deal with this pair." And she stood up. Henry tried not to notice that she finished the rest of her drink in one swallow.

Chapter 14

Cliffend was chilly, despite it being May; the cold wind was blowing straight in off the North Sea. Henry parked his mother's still relatively-new car along the side of the road at the end of the cliffs which gave the town its name. Taking Rosalie's hand, they walked quickly to an established gentlemen's outfitters in the High Street. The sign above the window stated Knatwich & Tacks.

"They can't really be the owners' names," Rosalie whispered to Henry as they approached.

"As far as I know they are. Anyway," he turned and smiled at her. "I can't laugh at anyone for having a comical name, can I?" He opened the door for her and noticed she was smiling too.

Once inside the shop, they looked along the rails of suits. Rosalie gasped when she read the price labels.

"Henry," she whispered hoarsely. "You're not spending that..." and she pointed at a figure, "...on a suit, are you?"

"I want a good one," he replied quietly, having recovered from the shock himself. "I might need it again one day."

"You can wear whatever you like to Mum and Dad's cremation," Rosalie stated miserably. "I'm wearing jeans!"

"No, you're not," Henry said. "You just want to annoy your Aunty Shirley by saying you will."

"Well, she's getting on my..."

"Can I help you, sir?" an assistant asked from

behind them.

"Yes," Henry replied. "I need a new suit, for my Dad's funeral. Dark, but not black. Grey, plain, no stripe."

"Certainly," the assistant said in a sombre tone, although smiling slightly that such a young gentleman should be so decisive in the sad circumstances. "My condolences, sir. Shall I measure you? Then I can show you what we have in stock. Or did you require made-to-measure?" The assistant's eyebrows quickly rose.

"Not on this occasion," Henry replied astutely. "There won't be time, the funeral's next week. Maybe when I get married, I'll give you more notice."

The assistant met the irony with good grace, and smiled, first at Henry then Rosalie, although she was looking through a catalogue and missed the exchange.

Nearly an hour later, having tried on at least half a dozen suits, Henry finally made a purchase. A slight adjustment was needed, and Henry arranged to collect it the morning before the funeral.

When they left the shop, Henry suggested to Rosalie that they have a coffee in the café opposite the post office. "There's a good view of the street from the window seat, and it's nice sometimes just to sit and watch."

Settling down with coffee and a slice of chocolate cake each, Henry asked,

"So, what did you and George get up to yesterday, while Mum and I slaved over a hot bar?"

"We just went for a walk around Mattingburgh. Ended up at the cathedral. We had a look round – didn't go to the service or anything. But we lit candles. Don't know what good it's supposed to do, but I did feel better for a while sitting and watching the flames burn. They've got a café-thing – refectory, I think it's called – in a crypt underground; it's like an enormous stone cavern, with arches holding the roof up, and uneven steps down. We had a full Sunday dinner there, would you believe? They even asked George if he'd like a glass of wine to go with his meal! I mean, *George?*" She scowled at the indignity. "He's only fourteen. And they didn't ask me!"

"So, what did he say?" Henry was intrigued.

"He said, 'No thank you, my companion isn't old enough to drink.'" They both laughed so much that other customers in the café began to stare at them. "I mean, how could they think he's old enough and I'm not?" Still chuckling, they finished their cake.

"Neither of you are," Henry stated cautiously.

"Well, no. But that's beside the point! And then he ate my Yorkshire pudding, and three of my roast potatoes – he's such a pig sometimes!" she said fondly. "Then we just came home – I mean back to the pub – neither of us wanted to go *home*." She blushed, then changed the subject, "So, what were you and that chap serving in the shop talking about?"

"Oh, just about suits and what people buy them for."

"Funerals," Rosalie sighed thoughtfully. "And

weddings."

"Well, I think this one might be *suitable* for both."

"A *suitable suit*?" she countered lightly.

"Yes, it's a good colour. Sombre, serious, business-like." He purposely avoided the word *sober*, but added, "It fits well – well, it will, with an inch or so taken in at the trouser waist."

"It fits okay now, but give it a couple of years and you'll have expanded."

"No, no I won't! Well, maybe in the muscle department."

"Well, you're not wearing it to our wedding," Rosalie stated playfully. "You can definitely have a made-to-measure job for that!"

"Oh? I thought this one would be okay. Shouldn't the groom be serious, and sombre – maybe no need for business-like, but..."

Henry stopped abruptly, having listened again, this time inside his head, to the words Rosalie had spoken. Rosalie's face, pale in recent days, was reddening; a frown of realisation drew her brows together. But a smile was forming and she suddenly looked like the Rosalie of old.

"So, you are going to marry me, are you, Henry Stickleback?" Henry didn't reply; it was his turn to blush. "I'm not sure I want to be Mrs Stickleback, though. I think I'll keep my own name, thank you!"

"Oh, so you *will* marry me, then?"

"Not sure yet. Let's wait and see how the next few days pan out, shall we?" She tipped her cup and looked at him from above the rim.

Chapter 15

Woodrow Stickleback's funeral was held early on the Wednesday afternoon, a week after his passing. The death certificate stated he died of cirrhosis of the liver, caused, no doubt Nora concluded, by years of heavy drinking.

Henry's new, dark-grey suit made him look very grown-up, and despite the sad occasion, Nora was proud of her son. When they climbed out of the black limousine and stood up, she linked her hand through the crook of his arm, ready to follow the coffin into the church. And she remained holding on, even for the part of the service when they were seated. A few times, Henry was aware of her discreetly raising a handkerchief to her eyes, and he squeezed her free hand with his. He hoped, prayed, that when today was over, they could start a new life, without Woody and the insecurity his behaviour had brought. Henry realised that dependency upon alcohol was an illness, in the same manner as asthma or gout. But it hadn't stopped it blighting their lives and leaving them open to ridicule.

There were not many people present at the funeral; even so, Quinny noted someone managed to sit in the creaking pew four from the front on the northern side. Henry looked around, nodding to cousins he had not seen since childhood who were almost unrecognisable; two of his old school friends, Hopper and Bloo attended (the other, Sidney, was on remand in Mattingburgh awaiting trial for GBH). They looked uncomfortable in their best attire, and both felt guilty for having spoken badly of Henry's father in the past.

Rosalie had asked Nora and Henry if they minded if she didn't attend. They said it was okay either way but, if she didn't, they encouraged her to stay at the pub, rather than be dragged home to Pepper Hill to help her Aunty Shirley. George told them all that he would go to school as normal; no one contradicted him.

"And may his soul now rest in peace, Amen," Quinny concluded the sermon. He stepped down from the pulpit, moved to the coffin and recited the commendation. The wake was held at the pub, of course, and Henry noted there were more people here than there had been in the church.

Once back behind the bar, and having discarded his suit jacket and his black tie, Henry handled the customers with ease, neither fast nor slow, but steady and with a few words of gratitude to each. The banter was friendly and criticism of Woody was kept to a minimum, especially within earshot of the Sticklebacks.

"Keep busy, son," was a piece of advice given by many regulars, happy that this was sound and solid, because they could see it was exactly what Henry was doing. Max repeated the phrase with a wink each time he pushed his beer glass towards the tall young man. Henry knew this was everyone's way of being supportive. And much of the drink was given free, far beyond the amount Nora had calculated for the occasion. With this and the opening day, their takings would be down considerably this month, but neither Henry nor Nora cared.

"We'll have to swallow the loss, just this once," Nora declared as she checked the till roll.

"We can call this Granny Elspeth's treat," Henry stated.

"Yes, that's a good idea. And I think, sad to say though, she would have been glad to see the back of Woody!" Nora smiled at her son as tears formed in her eyes; he had not really known Elspeth – she moved far away after that first night – but she was sure they would have liked each other. "Did I ever tell you how angry she was at our opening party when Woody left the petrol can…"

"…next to the barbecue when you were all doing the conga round the car park?" Henry laughed. "Several times, Mum!"

"I wasn't doing the conga!" Nora exclaimed indignantly. "Your granny and I were busy tidying up. Mind you, I wish I had been," she finished wistfully, pretending to mime the dance as she hummed the tune quietly to herself.

Later, when proceedings were slowing and people began to leave, Nora felt she needed some peace and quiet – time on her own, away from the noise and smoky atmosphere of the pub. She slipped away back to St Jude's Church to visit the grave. It was early evening and the air was still, the only sounds being birdsongs and the occasional vehicle travelling along the road between Ashfield and Pepper Hill.

A wide path led from the gate to the church door; half way along, Nora stepped onto a track leading across the front to the Ashfield half of the graveyard. This footway was the width of a lawn mower and, even in the shadow cast by the bulk of the church, she was amused to see grasshoppers leaping out ahead from under her feet.

The mound of earth was covered with turf, and Nora could smell the soil. She had asked mourners to send donations to a liver cancer research fund, rather than bringing flowers. Although Woody's liver failure had nothing to do with cancer, Nora felt this would be more appropriate than giving the florist in Cliffend too much business – old Smithy, the proprietor, had openly criticised Woody within Nora's hearing.

But there was one wreath, starkly colourful against the replaced turf. It was labelled *from Dear Wife and Loving Son,* and had been placed over the spot where Woody's heart would be, deep below. Nora felt an empty sadness as she crouched down and smoothed the petals on the lilies and roses; but, like Henry, she was sad at the waste rather than the loss.

Whilst discussing the details of the funeral with the undertakers, she and Henry had spoken about erecting a head-stone later, but she did not really wish to see an empty space left on its face just waiting for her details; the grave was double depth, but she wasn't certain where or how she wanted her mortal remains to be disposed of. She still had too much life to live to think about that.

"I would recommend you call into the funeral parlour in about six months' time, Mrs Stickleback," Mr Maude, or was it Mr Griffin? –

they both seemed to look the same – had stated.

Here at the graveside, Nora felt the warmth of the sun shining and, rather than returning to the pub where Henry was very capably hosting the remains of the wake, she thought, not of her own bereavement, but of the two young Tillingers who were at this moment also suffering.

Chapter 16

The cremation service for Annie and Derek Tillinger was due on the Friday, some ten days after the tragedy. Mrs Pessham had not engaged Maude and Griffin, Cliffend's funeral directors, but had gone further afield to Fenstone to a new company called Betching's.

Bizarrely though, Shirley had asked Quinny to conduct the service. He had called round on Thursday to check everything was going as planned.

"No wailing and weeping, mind you," Shirley instructed him, while determinedly not offering any refreshments. "Here's what I want!" And she handed a list to him – not waiting for his comments, but exclaiming, "God, it's cold here, why don't you *Poms* have any heating in your houses?"

Luckily, neither George nor Rosalie was present to witness to their aunt's rudeness; they were still with Nora and Henry at The Fighting Cock. Quinny did not know what would happen to the Old Police House when Shirley and Terrence returned to Australia after the service; although Rosalie was sixteen and legally old enough to live on her own, the reverend doubted her maturity to cope at this time of bereavement. And, although Quinny thought George was probably mature enough, he was too young.

With a sigh, Quinny glanced down at the piece of paper. It was headed *Service of Thanksgiving for the Lives of Annie Beatrice Tillinger and Derek Tillinger.* Dates of birth appropriate to each, plus that of their deaths, were printed underneath in brackets.

Quinny was not really concentrating on the writing in front of him, his mind had spun him back to the day when he was a child and people gathered around and looked down on him. They were all wearing black, but he was in a jumble of borrowed clothes; his shorts were too long and his grey socks had fallen down to expose the raw skin scratched by the sharp-edged rubble. Their words raced through his mind, the fact that they thought it was a miracle anyone had been pulled out alive. That had been a dull, drizzly day.

The day of the Tillingers' cremation was bright and sunny. But, as soon as Quinny arrived at the crematorium, he witnessed an ugly argument in the foyer. Rosalie, wearing a plain, dark green dress, was holding Henry's hand. Nora had accepted George's arm in much the same way as she and her son had accompanied each other two days previously.

"Right, well, we'll have you all in order here, if you don't mind," Shirley announced, her voice harsh in the sombre surroundings. She stepped forward as if to physically separate George and Nora, telling them,

"You, George, you're with me. And you, Rosamy...mary – whatever – you're with Terrence!"

"Oh, no!" George stated with a force that halted the self-appointed boss. "And," indicating to Rosie,

"If you can't even get my sister's name right, then *fucking well shut up!* Leave us alone; let us get on and do things how we want! And you can clear off back to Oz as soon as *this...*" his gesture encompassed the assembled people and the crematorium "...is over!"

The two black-suited funeral directors in attendance looked askance at the young man who dared to swear on such an occasion; both, however, thought if the antagonist had been a relative of theirs, they would have wanted to do the same.

At that moment, the hearses approached, one behind the other. Everyone's attention returned to the solemn matter at hand – everyone's except Shirley, whose face had turned a thunderous red, rage visibly shaking her. Terrence wisely guided her to the rear of the gathering.

The arrival of the two vehicles, and the presence of two coffins, reinforced the enormity of the loss the two deaths represented – not just as two individuals, but as a couple. As parents.

Derek, the elder of the deceased, was carried into the chapel first; Annie's identical coffin – if a fraction smaller – followed. Nora and George fell in with the bearers' slowly measured steps behind Annie, then Henry guided Rosalie, holding her tightly around her waist, his strength supporting her as her shoulders started to quake.

Quinny's voice sounded strong from the head of the procession and, with great dignity, the cortége paced the distance from the door to the front of the chapel.

They all stood respectfully motionless as the two

coffins were transferred onto a special double-width catafalque. The mourners were ushered into their pews, Shirley and Terrence being last to take their places.

Quinny turned to face the congregation. The undertakers drifted silently and gracefully to the back and out of the door; he looked around the inside of the stark crematorium chapel – the *gathering hall*, as they had tried to make him call it. It was intentionally non-denominational, non-faith specific, neutral and heartless.

And beige.

Quinny hated beige. He looked down at the order of service sheet; the readings were not biblical text, but sentimental poetry. There were no hymns, "My sister and brother-in-law weren't what you'd call *churchy* people, so I don't want any hypocrisy," Shirley had told Quinny. Instead recordings of a couple of songs were to be played through the chapel's hi-fi system.

When settled into the seats, George found himself nearest to the aisle in the front row. Rosalie was next to him; he held his sister's hand and she did not object when he whispered, "It'll be okay, Rosie."

Henry held Rosalie's other hand – he had heard George's assurance; he would not dare to shorten her name, and he wondered what it was that George was saying would be okay.

Nora felt alone at the wall end of the pew. She wanted to comfort Rosalie and George, but realised George could, as Rosalie had informed her last week and proved just now outside, fight his own battles. And Rosalie's, by the looks of it.

Nora silently vowed that, when today was over, she would have to concentrate on herself, and Henry. Shirley had not arranged for a get-together after the cremation, but Nora had spread the word that everyone would be welcome at The Fighting Cock, now hosting its third event after the refurbishment.

When she stepped over the pub's threshold later, she was met with a party neither she, nor the Tillingers, could ever have imagined. Friends of both families had combined and organised a buffet and clubbed together for a few rounds of free drink.

Shirley and Terrence tactfully disappeared without saying goodbye.

Chapter 17

Rosalie Tillinger's soul felt a little lost. Four weeks had passed since her parents' deaths. Her GCSE exams were looming – eight subjects, but she could not concentrate on anything. Other than the loss of her parents. And her growing feelings for Henry.

Confused as she was, she thought she might be falling in love. Thoughts of Henry were the only thing to lift her heart when the leaden pain of her parents' deaths gripped her. She pictured his face, remembered his touch when he wound his arms around her, protective and secure. And all the time he was dealing with his own bereavement.

People warned her it was a distraction, or a reaction to her loss; she argued that the same could be said for Henry. Nora seemed to encourage them; at least she did not discourage them. And sensible George thought it was good for both of them; it kept Rosie occupied. He himself was making enquiries for a holiday job with the engineering company, Tarskers in Cliffend, where his Dad had worked.

One of the foremen, Graham Boston, had known Derek Tillinger and was able to put in a word, initially for a cleaner on the shop floor. George was still only fourteen years old and the foreman warned him there was a limit, due to insurance, union directions, health and safety, and the like, as to the type of work he would be able to do. George didn't mind; he just wanted to keep busy. During the interview, he asked pertinent questions, and it was recognised that he was not afraid of hard work.

Graham warned that the wages would be a pittance, but George explained, without disclosing too many details, that an interim payment had been made on his parents' life assurance policies. Their solicitor, Ambrose Brideman, as executor of their wills, had dealt with the finances. It had become almost an unspoken agreement that George and Rosalie would remain living at the pub with Nora and Henry; Rosalie had another eighteen months to wait until she was technically an adult and Nora didn't like to think of them there on their own.

"We're off to Cliffend early on Sunday, Mum, if that's all right." Henry said to Nora after closing time and the last customer had left on Friday night. Rosalie and George had been watching television earlier in the evening, but had both drifted off to their rooms at some point. Henry shut the glass washer door and set the programme. His mother was standing at the doorway through from the bar to their kitchen, her hand hovering over the light switch.

"I'll just lock the front door," he told her as she strode across the room.

"I've done it, and checked it," Nora replied in mock exasperation.

"I know, I know." He came back and stood beside her. She relinquished the light switch and he flicked it off then shut the door on the darkness.

"Any special reason?" Nora asked as she filled the kettle and set it to boil.

"Sorry?" Henry replied, not really listening.

"Why you want to go to Cliffend on Sunday morning?"

"Well, Rosalie said she would like to go and have a look round the car boot sale in that little park near the town hall. I thought I might see if there's anything to stand on the mantle-piece in the lounge-bar – to add to the new décor," he laughed. "The gate opens to the public at eight o'clock. I said we'd need to leave here about seven to get a parking place and be first in the queue."

"Seven o'clock?" Nora queried incredulously. "She'll never be up and ready by then."

"Yeah, well I did wonder about that," Henry responded.

Nora studied her son's face. It was obvious to anyone who thought about it that Henry was in love with Rosalie. He was a hard-worker, mature for his age, not very imaginative, but thoughtful and polite. Nora was a little concerned that Rosalie, who had always been a scatterbrain and flighty, was taking advantage of level-headed, solid Henry.

But then, she remembered the nights between Annie and Derek's deaths and the funeral when she heard Rosalie weeping in the spare bedroom next to hers. Nora had listened as Henry crept in to comfort her. There was a condom vending machine in the pub Gents'. Nora trusted her son was being sensible – if indeed they did... But she did not really want to think too much about that, and she knew he would not take advantage of a vulnerable young woman.

But she could not be as certain of Rosalie's

motives and intentions. The promise to her friend Annie to take care of Rosalie and George while they were away still resounded: but the presumption then was that the couple would return after a few days; now the pledge echoed heavily and stretched into eternity. And, even when she tried to tell herself that the youngsters' private lives were none of her business, she knew that, to a degree, they were.

"Okay, then enjoy yourselves and don't spend too much money!" Nora replied light-heartedly. "And if anyone's selling strawberries, you could bring a couple of punnets home."

Chapter 18

The car boot sale phenomenon was only in its second season in Cliffend. The Cliffend Herald, the local weekly newspaper, had carried an article after the first event of the year, which stated that, in view of the likelihood of rain this weekend, the sale had been moved to inside the town hall itself.

When he looked out of his bedroom window, Henry was pleased to see that the weather was dry. He was then surprised to find Rosalie already up, dressed and in the kitchen when he came down.

"Breakfast?" George asked. He was sitting next to his sister at the table, both were eating cereal.

"Thanks," Henry replied distractedly as he started to shake cereal into his bowl. He noticed Rosalie was wearing the new skirt she had bought when they were in town together last week. She looked stunning – blonde hair creatively untidy, only a trace of make-up and a neat figure. She had lost a little weight since her parents' death, but she didn't like people drawing attention to it.

Nora was the last to arrive at the breakfast table. They chatted as they ate, and to a casual observer, they looked like a normal family.

First to finish, Rosalie rose from the table and said, "Right, I'll be back in a minute." She rushed out of the room and upstairs to finish getting ready.

"I think you might need a coat of some sort, the forecast is for rain," Nora called after her, hoping she didn't sound too patronising but thinking that Rosalie's skirt was rather short.

Eventually Rosalie and Henry left. George cleared the table and dried the dishes as Nora washed.

"I dread to think what they'll come home with," Nora remarked then repeated the gist of her conversation with Henry on Friday night.

"Oh," was the only comment George could make, smiling to himself.

As Rosalie and Henry left the pub car park to travel to Cliffend, they saw a *For Sale* board being driven into the ground in the front garden of the smallholding opposite.

"I didn't know estate agents worked on Sundays," Rosalie commented.

"I didn't know *that*," and he indicated Tidal Reach, "was being put up for sale," Henry stated, a little offended that he had not heard anything about it from gossip in the bar.

"Why, you're not interested in buying it, are you?" Rosalie turned her head to study it as they passed. The cottage was of the typical flat-fronted style, but not too small and, unlike most similar ones in the area, the first floor rooms did not have dormer windows. There was also quite a lot of land with the property.

"Hadn't thought about it," he said quietly, obviously thinking about it now as he also registered the dark grey clouds hanging above the town they were driving towards.

The rain had begun by the time they reached Cliffend. Henry managed to park in their usual place at the top of the cliff, and they walked quickly towards the town hall.

The sale was being held in the large main entrance area. The atmosphere was damp, overcrowded and bustling: muted conversations, banter and instructions echoed around the dusty walls; the parquet flooring quickly became damp and muddy, and a cold draught accompanied customers in. A sudden shiver ran through Rosalie, and Henry turned towards her.

"Here, have my jacket," he said, slipping if off and wrapping it around her shoulders: he had thought to wear a warm sweatshirt over his shirt. She slid her arms in and gathered it thankfully to her. She thanked him with a smile, then began to glance around her.

"Look." She pointed to a man in the corner who was removing his goods – none too carefully, Rosalie thought – from a supermarket trolley, and placing them on the floor in front of him. "He's being a bit rough with those, isn't he?" And, in confirmation, he dropped a vase. It didn't break, but it did give off a dulled snap.

"Oops," Rosalie giggled. Although Henry thought it was good to hear her laugh, he placed his index finger to his lips.

"Maybe we'll come back and have a look when he's set up properly," he whispered.

As they manoeuvred through the crowd, the distinct smell of polish and wood and generations of people holding papers drifted into Rosalie's imagination, bringing with it a memory of herself as a youngster in a school uniform – most of which was too big for her – standing with her friends for a formal photograph. But the tableau vanished when Henry said,

"Come on, let's go and get something to eat." He pointed to a sign hanging from a ladder near the stairs which read *Refreshments*, an arrow underneath pointed to a door a little further along the corridor.

"But we've only just had breakfast," Rosalie exclaimed.

"I know, but I'm still hungry."

"You're always hungry! You and George. You could both eat for an army!"

"Young men's prerogative," Henry stated, repeating the word he'd overheard used in the bar a few days before, and hoping this was within the correct context.

Inside the canteen, Henry steered them to a table in the corner. He then went to the counter and returned a few minutes later with bowls of hot soup and buttered rolls. Rosalie looked at him in dismay. He had noticed that she had not really eaten much earlier. He now commented casually,

"These are quite big helpings, so I'll finish what you can't manage. You know what Mum says about waste!"

"It smells nice," she stated as he placed the soup in front of her.

They ate in silence, except when Rosalie admonished him for leaving breadcrumbs in his beard. When they had finished, Henry struggled to form the question he needed to ask. His leg jiggled up and down as he leant his elbows on the table.

"So," he started with. "How are you doing, I mean how are you *really* doing?" Rosalie looked up.

"About the same as you, I guess," she murmured.

"But my situation is different. Mum and me, well, we'd kind of expected to lose Dad at some point. The last time he was in hospital, they told him to give up the drink altogether, or it would kill him." Henry shuffled in his chair, which suddenly seemed too small for him. "I was angry at him for sneaking downstairs and drinking when I was there on my own. Did Mum tell you that he'd stolen her keys? All the drink was locked in the store room; the bar was empty because of the refit. But he still managed to get to it. She says I didn't leave the door unlocked, although I wouldn't be surprised if she's just saying that so I don't blame myself."

"It still wouldn't have been your fault, even if you had. And our circumstances are completely different, aren't they?" Rosalie rested her hand on his, and wondered how she could explain without hurting either of them too much. "My Mum and Dad died suddenly – one minute there, the next minute gone." She stopped speaking and swallowed hard. "We can't compare, really; we're just all left without them. You've only got your Mum now, and I've got George."

"You've got me," Henry said hurriedly. Rosalie looked at him. He seemed so much older than nineteen – wiser and able to cope. But then, so was George, and he was still only fourteen. Maybe she was at fault; perhaps she was the immature one.

"Thanks," she smiled at him, squeezed his hand as a tear sneaked out of her eyes, making her sniff, which she thought was very unattractive. As a distraction, she lifted her head and glanced around.

The canteen was busy; some people carried strange shaped parcels and bags, others spoke in conspiratorial tones, pointed and indicated towards the exit door. The sound of a baby crying close by startled her; all the other tables were now occupied and a queue of customers was lining up at the counter.

"Right well, we'd better go, or people will be gate-crashing our table," she said suddenly. "We came to have a look round the sale, didn't we? What is it you're hoping to find?"

"Not sure really," Henry replied as he stood up, realising again how tall he had become. "Something to put on the mantelpiece in the lounge-bar, to fit in with the new decorations, I think."

Chapter 19

Henry placed his arm protectively around Rosalie's shoulder as he steered them towards the door. All the space around the sides of the entrance hall had been taken. There was constant movement as people bustled and voices bounced off the stark walls. Some customers rummaged through the goods for sale even while the stalls were still being set out; at others, vendors simply looked on, bored with the routine. A rather belligerent young woman was haggling with a middle-aged gentleman at a pitch mid-way along the wall. Rosalie thought it was unusual that he was offering to buy all her wares for £20.00. The woman had a loud voice and, intrigued, she and Henry were drawn towards them.

"Piss off, you mean old bastard. If you think you can bully me into parting with this lot," and she swept her arm in a semi-circle to include the stacks of pots and crockery on the floor in front of her, "for less than a ton, then you're screwed." And, to emphasis this, she wound the point of her index finger at her own temple.

Henry looked down at the heap: most of the things seemed worthless. But among them were a few colourful pots, not all flawless but full of character.

"Leave it, it's just rubbish," Rosalie whispered, not wishing to be involved in an irate conflab.

"Hang on a minute," Henry replied. "Look at these!" And he indicated towards two tall ceramic mugs. Both were cream glazed, and embellished with gold lining on the brim and bases, and along the side of the handles. Decorating the body of the mugs were colourful, almost life-like cockerels. Henry bent down between the disputing buyer and seller, and carefully picked them up.

"These would be ideal!" he whispered in Rosalie's ear.

"What?" Rosalie hissed back.

"They would really brighten the place up – you know, one at either end of the mantelpiece!"

"Is your Mum really going to want a lot of junk standing around? I mean, she's only just decorated."

"But they're brilliant. Cockerels, you see? The Fighting Cock!" Henry's voice had risen in excitement.

"If you don't stop saying *cock*, I'm going to walk away and leave you!" Rosalie scowled. "Everyone's looking at us!" And she glanced around her, daring on-lookers to comment.

"No, everyone's looking at those two arguing," Henry stated, nodding towards the stall holder and the man. "I'm going to buy them. If Mum doesn't want them, I'll use them myself."

"Okay, okay," Rosalie shrugged. "Let's have a look at them then."

Henry stepped closer to the window behind the vendor and held the mugs up to the light. They seemed to be a pair although the pictures were very slightly different – this, together with the texture, suggesting they were hand-painted, and each had a smaller version on the back.

The cockerels themselves looked ready for combat with their bright, fiery red combs and wattles contrasting sharply with the cream of the mugs' background; the feathers on the bodies had been picked out in orange and yellow detail; the tails and wings, fanned and held high, sported black plumes with iridescent blues and greens. The prancing feet and splayed wings gave the birds movement, and the open beaks proclaimed their arrogance.

He handed one of the mugs to Rosalie and they inspected them thoroughly. The handles were sound, there were no obvious chips, but one vessel had a thin crack at the base.

"I'll give you a quid each for these," Henry said when the woman paused. She had dropped her asking price for the dealer to "£50 for the lot!" Henry looked down at the jumble and wondered if he had been too generous.

The man sneered and said, "A pony."

"Or one pound fifty for the two," Rosalie intervened.

"Done," the woman snapped at the young couple and held out her hand without looking in their direction. Rosalie quickly retrieved her purse from her bag and produced the exact coinage – she didn't want to risk distracting the woman in order to receive change. Henry held onto his prizes.

"Not you, you mean old bastard," the woman aimed back at the man. "£45. No less. And you have to pack 'em all up."

As Rosalie paid, Henry beckoned her away.

"Come on, let's get back home," he urged as

they walked towards the door. Outside the rain had stopped and the sun was now shining down onto the glistening, somewhat slippery pavement.

"Thanks," Rosalie whispered to Henry.

"What for?"

"Just, well, everything. Soup, crumby rolls, talking, buying those, those …"

"These?" Henry enquired as he held aloft his booty. "Here, you have that one," and he handed the perfect one to Rosalie. "And I'll have this."

"I thought they were for Nora, or for the pub at least," Rosalie said.

"Yeah, well. Mum'll be happy anyway."

Rosalie accepted her gift. Then she remembered she had paid for them anyway. First, she slapped Henry's arm. Then she kissed his cheek. Luckily, he sensed the second was imminent, and bent slightly forward, otherwise she would not have been able to reach.

Chapter 20

When Henry and Rosalie returned to The Fighting Cock, Nora was setting up for the lunchtime opening. They found George sitting in the corner of the bar near the fireplace with the day-to-day accounts' ledgers closed and finished in front of him; he was making a list in a notebook.

George helped Nora and Henry around the pub, partly in recognition of the hospitality he and his sister were receiving, and partly because he liked to keep busy. He was versatile and had learnt quickly how to connect the barrels, clear the pipes, check the pumps, replace the optics, maintain the stock and operate the glass washer. Also, and much to Nora's delight, he understood her book-keeping system.

Nora insisted that she didn't want anything in return for their keep. She was pleased that Henry had company of more or less his own age, and she felt she was fulfilling her promise to her friend, Annie, by helping to look after them. And they brought life and energy to the pub, despite their own, individual bereavements.

Nora had no time to grieve herself: she had lost the man she loved many, many years before Woody actually died; but she had kept her marriage vows *in sickness and in health* and *'til death do us part* and had faithfully looked after him.

Her mind was also occupied with thoughts of Henry's future, especially if his and Rosalie's relationship became serious. She too had seen the

For Sale sign up at the small holding opposite the pub. And she could still just, *just* afford to buy it. She hoped to be able to speak with them both about it later. Meanwhile, customers needed serving.

"Swot," Rosalie chided George as she sat down opposite him. "What are you working on there, then?" He was using their father's pen, a heavy silver and electric blue ball-point; it hadn't been expensive but was pleasing to hold, and as a present from Annie, it had been Derek's favourite.

Slowly, Rosalie and George were sharing out their parents' possessions, and George had gladly relinquished Annie's jewellery to his sister. Her favourite item was a gold locket. Inside, it held two tiny photos, one each of her and George. She wanted to replace these with pictures of Annie and Derek, and she would not wear the locket until then, but kept it safe.

Rosalie watched George finish writing. She thought that, each time she saw her younger brother, a little something had changed: the shape of his jaw, the fact that he needed to shave – if not every day then nearly. Although he was not quite as tall as Henry, he was broader across the chest and shoulders; the muscles in his arms greater despite the fact that Henry did more physical work. Later today, he had planned to clean and tidy up the gardens, the benches, and all around the car park.

"Tarskers," Rosalie read the name written at the top of George's page. Below he was listing questions and notes. "So, how did you actually find out about this job, then?"

"I happened to see Mr Boston in town," George replied. He laid down the pen, and looked up at her, happy that she was showing an interest. "D'you remember him, the chap Dad used to work with?" But he regretted mentioning their father as soon as he saw Rosie's face blanch. He reached out his hand and gently touched hers to say he understood. He continued, "Well, he said there might be a job there for the summer holidays and he'll see about getting me an interview. He said not to get my hopes up, though, because I'm a bit young to start a proper apprenticeship. I'm just putting down some ideas, questions to ask..." But he could see the focus had vanished from Rosie's eyes. He abandoned the subject and asked,

"Bit wet getting to the car boot sale, wasn't it?"

"We ran from the car to the town hall. Everything was set out in the big entrance area – you know, where we all had to stand for our photos after the school won that Achievements' Award?"

"I think I was still at middle school then. But I know where you mean. Did you buy anything? I mean, I hope you didn't come home with any more junk – your room is so full now."

"*And untidy*," Rosalie heard her mother's voice add. She banished the words. George both looked and acted like their Mum. Rosalie was more like Derek, except that he had been a quiet, methodical person and she knew she was noisy, disorganised and easily distracted.

"So, what did you get?" George persisted.

"These," Henry said as he walked through from the kitchen with a cockerel mug in each hand. He held them forward as he approached the table, and George took one from him.

"That one's got a crack in the bottom, here," Rosalie pointed out. "Near the edge. But it won't break." George fingered the fault and seemed about to test her last comment when she added, "Well, it won't break if you don't force it!"

"That's the trouble with you engineer-types, isn't it?" Henry stated with a smile. "You want to test everything to destruction."

"No, we just want to know how things work," George retorted with equal good humour.

"Mugs don't work," Rosalie interjected.

"Yes, they do," Henry stated with heavy irony, his mood suddenly changing. "It's freeloaders who don't work and let others carry them."

"Thinking of anyone in particular?" Rosalie asked, then added, "Oh! Sorry, I didn't mean…"

"Gosh, look at those," Nora tactfully interrupted as she took the other mug from Henry's hand. She ignored the conversation she had half heard as she approached the table. She would do anything to make Henry appreciate that their hard work had built a good business. Woody was unwell, not a skiver. One day she was sure he would see that. It was just that no one knew what had made her husband ill. She hid her sadness, smiled and said,

"Did I hear you say mugs don't work? Well, let me tell you, they most certainly do! They hold tea. Or coffee. Who's going to put the kettle on while I unlock the front door and let in the hoard of

Sunday lunchtime customers."

"Fiver says Max is first," she heard George bet the others.

"Quinny," Rosalie countered.

"He won't be out of church yet," Henry stated, glancing at the clock. "It'll be Stan."

Nora smiled at their banter. "It's a good job Max can't hear you lot, or he'd open a book." She turned the key, released the bolts, and opened the door, then said, "Hello, Max. Have you been waiting long?" Before Max replied, she heard George whisper,

"You two owe me a fiver."

"I haven't got any money, I bought these," Rosalie explained as she pointed to the two mugs.

"You were robbed," her brother stated handing the one he was holding back to Henry.

"No, the stall holder was robbed. I offered a pound each, but she was still arguing with another chap when Rosalie offered her one pound fifty for both."

"And the language she used on him as we left!" Rosalie added.

"I think some of that was directed at us," Henry stated, trying but failing to be serious. "Right, tea everyone?"

"Mine's a pint," Max hailed as he crossed to the bar behind Nora.

"What, a pint of tea?" Rosalie asked as she followed Henry out to the kitchen, gesturing towards the cockerel decorated ceramic mugs.

"No, a pint of Best," Max muttered unamused. He then asked Nora, "What've you been feeding those kids on to make them so cheeky?" Nora took a glass from under the bar and began to draw Max's beer.

"To be honest with you, Max, I'm just so grateful to see them laughing, after the few weeks they've had."

"Humph, well yes, that's a good point," Max conceded. And he turned towards the open kitchen door and said, "Proper romantic, I'm sure."

"You never know," Nora smiled as she held out her hand for Max's money.

Chapter 21

"I'll have coffee," Henry said. Rosalie was retrieving the ordinary cups from the cupboard when, holding out the two cockerel mugs, he added, "And we can use these."

"They'll need a good wash first," Rosalie exclaimed. "They're filthy inside."

"I don't want to ruin the pictures," Henry replied as he studied the different paintings of the prize cockerels.

"But you don't know where they've been! Or who's been using them, or what they've been used for!"

Henry looked quizzical. "They're mugs," he stated. "People drink drinks from them. What else would they do?"

Rosalie stepped back and looked at Henry with exasperation. There had been no irony in his voice, and she wondered how – working as he did in a pub – he could sometimes be so naïve.

"Maybe they kept paintbrushes in them," she suggested mildly. Henry tipped the mugs and, for the first time took a proper look inside. He was startled to see the ingrained dirt and cobwebs – one had captured a small fly which now lay upside down, dead. Up until that point, he had been so engrossed with the outsides that he hadn't thought of their practical uses. Rosalie continued, "Or pencils, or toothbrushes, or their false teeth, or planted pansies in them – I don't know, something unhygienic! Why don't you put them through the glass washer? That'll sterilise them."

"Best not," Henry responded quietly.

"Why?" Rosalie countered impatiently.

"'Cause it's for washing glasses, not mugs," Henry stated prosaically.

Rosalie gave a noise through gritted teeth to vent her frustration; it sounded like a cross between a scream and a growl. Henry ignored her. She stamped her foot and stomped back into the bar.

"Lovers' tiff?" Max asked Nora as Rosalie flounced past to join her brother, who was still working at the table by the fireplace.

"Ooooh! Henry really does annoy me sometimes!" she told him.

"Where's my tea?" George asked, ignoring her histrionics.

"Ask Henry!" she snapped.

In the kitchen Henry ran a bowlful of the hottest water the cistern could provide, squeezed in detergent and mixed it until the bubbles domed and miniature rainbows shone. He then submerged the two mugs and swizzled the water around with the wooden end of the washing up mop.

Henry then went upstairs and changed his clothes while waiting for the hot water to do its job. Half an hour later, having made all the drinks, he appeared in the lounge-bar.

"You could put us out of business," Nora chided as she accepted her drink in a cup and saucer. He had made George's tea in an ordinary mug, and George said "Cheers," as he took it. Henry then handed Rosalie the better of the two new mugs, looking at her and smiling as he explained,

"I soaked them in very hot water for a while, to get rid of all the muck or germs in them."

Rosalie smiled at Henry. His shoulders were hunched, which was unusual for him. His face looked a little crestfallen and, as if to prove that she knew her sensuality had power over him, she broadened her grin, and was rewarded when his expression sparkled in return.

"Thanks, Henry. I was only teasing you, messing around, like."

"Even so, you had a point," Henry conceded. George looked at them with critical eyes. He may be younger than either of them, but he could see how his sister was using, and abusing, poor Henry. And he shook his head slightly in disbelief that his old mate was allowing her to do so.

Henry caught George's disapproval and raised his eyebrows as he took the first sip of drink from his new mug.

"Argh!" he bellowed, then spluttered.

"Whatever's wrong?" Rosalie enquired.

"I, er, I made tea – at least, I thought I'd made tea. But I've put coffee in as well." Henry took another sip. He savoured the taste, chewed at it a little, then pronounced, "Actually, it doesn't taste too bad. Needs more sugar, though. Hang on." He returned from the kitchen after a few minutes, holding up his mug triumphantly. "Got it right now." And he took another swig. The thumb of his hand holding the mug's handle was clamped onto the top of a dessert spoon, the bottom of which was pinning down a tea bag. "It just needed a bit more coffee, and I've left the tea bag in. And put lots more sugar in too!"

"You've got to be joking, Rosalie exclaimed. "Tea *and coffee?* Here let me try." Henry offered the mug to her. She took a sip while he still held on, guessing her reaction. She did not disappoint.

"Urgh!" she choked. "That's revolting!"

"Here, let's have a go," George urged, his voice suddenly breaking into a squeak on the last word. Henry handed the mug to George.

"Oh my God," George puttered. "Rosie's right. It's awful! You aren't going to drink that, are you?"

"Too right I am!" Henry replied indignantly. He raised his drink to salute Rosalie and George. They picked up their respective mugs – Rosalie's containing only coffee, but quite a lot of it – and returned the gesture.

Henry tipped back the liquid. It was so bitter that it drew his teeth together, thrusting his lower jaw outward as he recoiled, pulling his chin deep into his neck and his shoulder up towards his ears. As the sensation scoured over his tongue, he shuddered and concluded they were right. It was revolting! When he finished the mug, he smacked his lips, wiped the back of his hand across his mouth and sighed like a seasoned drinker. And he smiled.

If he stuck to this beverage, at least he knew he would never be drunk.

Chapter 22

Horror flooded through Rosalie. She was burning hot, and her heart was beating at such a speed that her chest throbbed in pain. She felt as if her head had suddenly become enormous while the hall she was in was shrinking. The chair beneath her began to rock, and the roaring noises in her ears faded before rising and pulsating again.

She looked around; the exams were being held in the school's main hall. Students were sitting at rows of single desks all placed at the precise distance apart, sterile and condemned to honesty.

Her contemporaries all seemed to be behaving normally. Timothy was sucking lozenges – he had developed a sore throat and was *allowed* cough sweets; Dave held his pen between finger and thumb and wobbled the ends up and down, back and forth until it finally spun out of his grip and clattered onto the floor: it was his usual trick when bored. Phoebe and Nick exchanged one of *their* looks; although they thought they were discreet, the entire year knew they were a couple. Others displayed a range of emotions from alarm to calmness, some were blasé – nonchalant, even; others looked serious, earnest, or carefree and self-satisfied. Only a few sported Rosalie's glazed-eye, terrified look.

She began to panic; her breath came and went in short, sharp stabs. She wanted to get out. A tingling spread rapidly across the surface of her skin, causing the hairs to rise; the sensation settled in an urgent need to empty the contents of her stomach. As her muscles cramped, tears of pain filled her eyes.

Then the slow, insidious fear crept in, paralysing her limbs and preventing her from sitting straight, from even thinking. She tried to pick up her pen, although the exam would not begin for several minutes as yet, but found her fingers would not respond. Her breath was now so loud that she thought she might be crying, but she couldn't be sure.

"Rosalie Tillinger," one of the invigilator's voices cut across the quiet. "Are you alright?" The woman rose from her bench on the dais at the front of the hall. As she passed the lines of isolated students, everyone slowly turned and looked. The scene swayed in and out of Rosalie's focus, and her own voice was inaudible to her as she whispered her reply,

"I think I'm going to be sick." But she did hear the muted sniggers and whispering around her. She hoped the other students weren't being deliberately cruel, especially not her friends: nerves and adrenalin might have momentarily robbed them of their compassion. Or maybe it was a case of the strong individuals in the group falling on and vanquishing the weakest. This thought brought a fresh wave of nausea.

"Silence!" the second invigilator barked, the word echoing around the cavernous hall, which was more suited to its purposes of hosting sports events than accommodating academics. The man had been handing out papers, and his voice startled Rosalie, coming as it did from immediately behind her. "Take Miss Tillinger to the medical room, Mrs Ferdinand."

Rosalie swallowed the bile that had risen. She feared that she would not be allowed to continue. She knew she could miss one exam and marks for that would be made up of an average of the other parts for that subject. But there was always a stigma to this process: explanations had to be written and authenticated, special circumstances needed to be validated and, where appropriate, a doctor's certificate would accompany the paper to the marking centre. These documents would not be difficult to obtain in Rosalie's case; her form teacher had been advising her since her parents' deaths not to sit her exams this summer but to wait until next year.

Rosalie had stubbornly refused to listen. Her revision had been patchy, but she believed that, *on the day*, she would be okay; her results may not be brilliant – they probably wouldn't have been anyway. But at least she would not have to waste a whole year repeating her studies.

In the medical room, she leant over the bowl the school nurse had produced. She knew now that she would not be sick, but obediently sat still, accepting a handful of tissues and the comforting rub of her shoulder.

"Rosie, what's wrong?" George's voice suddenly interrupted her trance as he burst into the room, followed by Mrs Ferdinand.

"I'm okay," she murmured as he sat down beside her. "You shouldn't be here, George. The exam's about to start."

"I don't think you'll be sitting any exams today," Mrs Ferdinand stated.

"No! No. I must," Rosalie became agitated, thrusting the bowl towards George. "I've got to get back." She tried to stand up, but George, nearly a foot taller than his older sister, stood first and caught her wrist, preventing her rushing out of the door.

No one else would have been able to use physical restraint, but siblings were different: they would not accuse each other of assault, at least these two wouldn't, Mrs Ferdinand decided. And this was how she explained why she had fetched George to help.

"Listen, Rosie..." George held on tight as she squirmed.

"Don't call me *Rosie*," she replied automatically, slapping his shoulder before conceding and leaning into him.

"Rosalie. Sorry. Listen. Sit down for a minute," he urged. She sat. She listened. Mrs Ferdinand spoke:

"You are not well enough to take the exam. Myself and the other invigilator will verify this, as will the school nurse." Mrs Ferdinand gave a nervous smile. "And I think it would be best if George took you home."

"No! I don't want to go home!" Rosalie began to cry.

"She means back to the pub. Nora and Henry will be there, they'll understand." Assuming responsibility, George asked Mrs Ferdinand, "Can you ring them?" He recited the telephone number. "I'm sure one or the other will come and pick us up. That's okay, isn't it, Rosie?"

Rosalie looked at him. He had lost as much as she had – Mum, Dad – and he must miss them just the same as she did. But he didn't seem to be suffering this numbness, this despondency, this feeling of the futility of everything. When she didn't respond, he repeated the question.

"Yes," she nodded eventually.

George despaired. He wanted to look after Rosie, but he also needed to return to his own lesson. While he concentrated on maths' formulae, he could blot out the squeezing pain of losing his parents; he could turn from resentment at having to take over domestic and family duties into an alliance with Derek and Annie; he would remember and use the things they had taught him. Yes, he missed them. God, how he missed them. The Old Police House was a shrine to their struggles and sacrifices to give him and Rosie a good start. But they were not here. And he was.

"Come on, Rosie. We'll wait outside."

"Okay. But *don't call me Rosie!*" she remembered to snap. He ignored her. After a pause, she added, "What about your lessons?"

"Maths this morning, double English and Music this afternoon. Maths will be okay, we were working on our own through some examples anyway. We're just reading through something or the other for English at the moment." Rosalie looked away, feeling a mixture of guilt and relief. George continued, "And I can't imagine what they expect me to do for Music – as you know, I'm tone deaf, don't play an instrument and am totally not interested. Unless it's *The Pythons!*"

Rosalie managed to smile. *The Pythons* band consisted of six nubile sisters, ranging in age from sixteen to twenty-one, this only possible by there being two sets of twins; each played a different instrument, and all were indistinguishable by either looks or voice. George – along with the rest of the teenage male population of Cliffend High School and the whole world beyond – was smitten.

Brother and sister left the school through the front entrance door. This was strictly forbidden and, as the headteacher, Mr Morsley, watched from a distance, he held an arm out towards Tammy, an over-zealous prefect on her way to point out the rule.

"Let them go, just this once." He could not fathom whether the outwardly grieving Rosalie was affected more by their parents' deaths, or the quiet, self-controlled George. Either way, he predicted trouble. George was losing his youth, growing up too quickly. He foresaw Rosalie not turning up for the rest of her exams, and having to repeat this year. He dreaded the conversation he would have to have with her and her guardian, Nora Stickleback. He remembered Henry Stickleback as a pupil – mostly quiet, not too much of a problem; always seen sharing packets of crisps.

Chapter 23

"Is that Mrs Stickleback?" Mr Morsley enquired when the female voice on the other end of the phone simply stated, "Fighting Cock."

"No, it's Mrs Mawberry, her cleaner. I'll just get Nora for you." She managed to make *Nora* and *for you* rhyme, and he was still chuckling about this when the landlady herself spoke.

"Hello?"

"Hello, Mrs Stickleback. It's Mr Morsley, from Cliffend High School."

"Oh, yes. Hello," Nora responded cautiously.

The summer term had ended two or three weeks ago – Nora had lost track of the exact date. She frowned now: it was her belief that all teachers were on holiday throughout August, and contact from the Head now could not bring good news. Mr Morsley cleared his throat.

"Is everything all right?" she asked anxiously.

"Yes, yes. Fine. I, er, just wanted a word about Rosalie Tillinger. Is she still with you?"

"Yes." He could hear the smile appear in her voice as Nora replied. "Yes, and for the foreseeable future, I would imagine. Nothing is official, but I seem to have become their temporary foster mother – if teenagers need such a thing." And, because of her promise to the Tillingers, she now thought of Rosalie as her daughter, and of George as her younger son.

Before the summer term had concluded, George, with Mr Boston's help, had secured a holiday job

117

with Tarskers; he caught the bus to Cliffend each day, much as he had when at school, and returned in the early evening. He had commandeered the small back bedroom at the pub during his Aunt Shirley and Uncle Terrence's visit to the Old Police House between the deaths of their parents and the funeral; it was now very firmly his, and filled with most of the moveable contents from his room at Pepper Hill. He and Rosalie only returned there to collect various things, and occasionally to continue a token effort of sorting out their parents' possessions.

Rosalie, unlike the industrious George, was drifting through her summer holiday. She did help with the housework, which Nora found a blessing; and she worked shifts in the pub – collecting glasses and tidying up – but usually only if Henry was close by. Nora encouraged them to go out, then despaired when they returned from a foray into local jumble sales and junk shops for cockerel-related items – the latest being a very large and ugly bird, masquerading as a bronze door stop.

When Henry was busy and Rosalie was on her own, she seemed to alternate between reading teenage romantic novels and listening through headphones to cassette-taped music played on her Walkman – sometimes managing both at the same time. Nora was puzzled as to how she could do that.

"Good, I'm glad," Mr Morsley said. "I just wanted to suggest that maybe Rosalie thinks about applying to Clifftech for September. She might be better off studying and retaking her exams there, rather than returning here and having to join a class of students a year younger than herself, most of whom, of course, she will know; she may feel a little self-conscious. She might benefit from different surroundings and a new learning environment."

Nora felt relieved and, after a moment's thought, said, "Yes, that might be a good idea,"

Cliffend College of Further Education, or Clifftech as everyone called it from the days when it was a technical college, was quite close to the high school and on the same bus route, which was convenient for travel.

"They're holding an open day at the end of August," Mr Morsley continued. "You could both go and have a look round, see what you think. Anyway, let me know."

"Yes, I will – we will – have a look I mean, and I'll let you know how we get on," Nora stuttered, thinking she already had enough to do. But if it would help Rosalie, she was sure they could make time. Looking after three teenagers and a public house was exhausting, despite the help she received: it was hard sometimes to physically fit everything in.

"How is George?" Mr Morsley enquired.

"He's fine," Nora replied. "He's started at Tarskers – doesn't say much, but Mr Boston is keeping an eye on him."

"If only all my pupils were so keen to work!"

"I'll need to talk to you at some point about combining his practical training and continuing in full time education – I know he still has two years to go, but he seems very keen to stay with Tarskers – it holds a connection with his Dad: he used to work there." Nora was concerned, but not unduly. Mr Boston had promised to speak with the school and outline the scheme he had devised for George.

"Right, well, I'll wait to hear about that. And I'll leave the other matter with you. Goodbye, Mrs Stickleback."

Nora said "Bye," into the phone, feeling as if she had just been dismissed – and by a headmaster.

"Who was that?" Henry asked when he came into the kitchen a few seconds later. Nora explained.

"I'll take Rosalie to have a look round the college, if it helps," Henry offered. "Oh, by the way, Craig phoned. He can do his usual shifts – I don't think his offer of a free holiday worked out after all." Nora smiled and shook her head thinking that if Henry were like Craig, she really would be worried.

"Anyway, I'd better go and open up." Henry stated.

Chapter 24

Despite the misery of the past few months, Henry still enjoyed the camaraderie, the joshing and the good-humoured banter in the bar. He and Craig worked well together, and Rosalie brightened his world whenever she was around.

Later, with the last customer gone, the tidying up and restocking complete and Craig dispatched until the evening shift, Henry and Rosalie sat outside at one of the picnic tables. The sun was extremely hot in that particular spot and Rosalie positioned her legs to catch the rays. She snuggled her head into Henry's shoulder and closed her eyes.

"Don't let me fall asleep and burn my legs, will you?" she warned.

"Sorry, can't hear you, I've dozed off myself," he replied. He was happy and content, feeling that here, in this moment, with the girl he loved, was where he wanted to be for ever.

The following day, Nora had not particularly felt like dressing smartly, styling her hair and applying the right amount of make-up so as not to look tartish, but like a sophisticated business woman who was both serious and fun. Achieving this had exhausted her and, during a lull in customers, she sat on a high stool while Henry took a break.

Henry had now perfected his method of brewing his special tea/coffee concoction. He used the cockerel adorned ceramic pint pot with the crack at the base; he'd given the perfect one to Rosalie, although he knew she didn't use it for coffee or tea, but displayed it in her bedroom.

Henry's mug held almost a pint of liquid, and retained the heat so that it was not completely cold by the time he reached the bottom. The belligerent-looking cockerels painted on the outside – the larger on the front and the smaller on the back – looked about to raise their first cock-crow of the morning, and they somehow seemed to watch as Henry prepared his drink.

In first went the teabag, followed by three heaped teaspoons of instant coffee. The boiling water was poured over these while he stirred vigorously – with a dessert spoon. Next, he poured in milk until the hot liquid reached the correct colour; and lastly he piled in the sugar – three dessertspoons of white granulated.

When he brought his mug and a normal cup and saucer for Nora through from the kitchen to the bar, Max was there.

"Ordinary tea for you, Mum," he said. Max peered into Henry's mug and announced, not for the first time,

"By God, lad! That'll put hairs on your chest."

The conversation was thin; there was no particularly interesting news to share. Max ordered his second pint, commenting,

"It's a shame you can't get pictures of those cockerels for your pump handles. These old hunting scenes look a bit miserable against your mug."

"Don't put ideas into his head," Nora said good-heartedly. Henry didn't respond, but added pump handles to his mental list of items to shop for. After a while, Max said,

"Cheer up, lad. You and your Mum both look knackered."

"Charmed, I'm sure," Nora snapped sarcastically as she slid off the stool. "I'll go and serve these customers; I expect they'll have better manners." And she walked to the other end of the bar. As she drew the second of three pints, however, she decided that Max was right – about Henry looking tired anyway; she wondered how much time he spent at night with Rosalie. She didn't restrict their activities, but was glad they were discreet.

"Here, lad," Max beckoned; Henry leant over the bar towards him. "I can see that it's difficult for all of you at the moment." He paused, which allowed Henry to nod in agreement. "Why don't you talk to your mother about getting some extra help? I know you've got Craig, but he's a bit of a fly-by-night, isn't he? Anyone can see that you're all doing what you can, but with George back at school soon, and Rosalie off to college, you might need someone more permanent."

Henry stood back up, feeling a kind of enlightenment when the solution – even if he hadn't been aware that there was a problem – was so obvious. He inhaled deeply, held his breath, then eventually released it, saying,

"Okay. I'll speak to Mum. I guess you have someone in mind?" And Max nodded.

Three days later, Polly Merton, twenty-five years old, well-groomed, tall, smartly-dressed, perfectly mannered, gay, and with very good references from The White Fox Hotel in the Lake District, walked into The Fighting Cock and said to Henry, who was behind the bar at the time,

"Uncle Max says you're looking for a barmaid-cum-general dogsbody. Well, here I am. I can start immediately. But I have to leave at four-thirty to meet the estate agents in Cliffend. Shame I can't afford the place opposite!"

Chapter 25

It was usually the taste of brick dust that woke Quinny. Or the sound of someone crying, "Mummy. MUM! DAD!" He knew it was his voice as a child, not yet old enough to go to school. Him. Quintin Boyce.

He was calling from under the rubble after the bomb had dropped. It hadn't exploded, but their house collapsed anyway, weakened by the many previous raids. Quinny had been rescued – quite quickly compared with other survivors, who had endured long hours of cold and pain and hunger and thirst before help arrived. Inevitably, for some, aid came too late. And he felt guilty about that.

Quinny had been standing near the back door when the air raid siren had sounded. He had hesitated, wondering whether it was safe to run out into the garden and pick up his wooden train – a battered engine with a coal truck and one carriage, all painted a ghastly orange with red wheels. However chipped and dented and dirty it was, it was *his* – Dad had made it especially for him, as opposed to it having been handed down from his older brothers or cousins.

Everyone else in the house had run into the hall, ready to file down to the shelter built in the cellar, where they would wait patiently until the bombing above stopped. Questions continually haunted him, causing his lack of engagement with the world. Had they hesitated before going down because he was not with them? Or were they just not quick enough? Had it been his fault? If he had been there, and not gone back for his toy, would they all have been killed anyway, him as well? Or would they all have been saved?

He could not speak of these things; at the time, the people around him – the adults, who looked after him and were wise in all things – talked as if he could not remember. He did not correct them. How could he retell what had happened, or explain his guilt? He soon learnt that many others experienced worse. Maybe that was one of the reasons he trained for the priesthood; he thought he could empathise.

He thought of Henry, Nora, Rosalie and George, and sent a prayer up that they would one day be free of the torment and live long, happy and healthy lives.

Swallowing the imagined grit in his mouth, Quinny pinged his rubber bands. One of them was orange – the colour of his beloved train. He never saw it again; as far as he knew it had perished. He twanged the band again, and again, until his wrist was very red and sore, and a hammer inside his head thudded against his skull. Then he stood up from the armchair where he had been dozing, and sought solace inside the church.

St Jude's Church and its appointed rectory were constructed of local flint; the nave was built in the twelfth century, and the first rector was recorded on the memorial scroll as taking up his post in 1203. He bore the unlikely name of Mellsƒon (the 'ƒ' actually transcribed as an 's') i'Mattsƒonin. Quinny had neither the time nor the patience to research this but continually hoped someone would tell him the meaning.

The church's round tower had been added a century or so later; it being a feature of the Eastern Counties. The chancel, porch and other cosmetic appendages were added through the years. The interior had been painted white in the 1960s in stark contrast to the dark wood of the pews, pulpit and rood-screens. Flowers made the place look pretty – enormous vases with every colour bloom imaginable. The smell of polish and swept-away dust cleansed him.

Quinny liked the simplicity and quietness: the church was a comforting place to be, cold in winter of course, but pleasant for most of the year.

He sat in the creaking pew and dutifully said his daily office. Slowly, the prayers chased away the nightmares, and he began to feel refreshed and at peace. The day was warm and outside birds sang brightly, as though it were spring and not late summer. An occasional car passed along the road, but it seemed so distant that it did not interrupt the serenity.

When Quinny was ready, he slowly stood up, bowed to the tabernacle and crucifix, turned and walked down the aisle towards the door. He looked up to the vaulted ceiling then back to the plain white walls and finally to the tower beyond the font in front of him. He tried to imagine how a newly-wedded couple would feel as they saw this view, taking the first steps of their married life together; the organ music swelling the air with a triumphant march, and their friends and family standing to watch them pass, wishing them well. He shook his head at the sadness, and left.

The ionised air outside made him feel dizzy and worsened his headache. He then became aware of an urgency: he had been asleep for at least a couple of hours before walking over into the church. Now, the pressure on his bladder was building painfully and would soon reach its limit. He knew it was too late to return to the rectory to use the toilet there, and so he looked around, deciding to follow the mown path amidst the taller grass to the rear of the church – the Pepper Hill half of the graveyard. He found a yew tree to stand behind and apologised to the residents below nearby, assuring them that he meant no disrespect.

With his back to the view, the flow commenced: the relief was indescribable, and he felt his headache easing instantly. The hot, yellow liquid poured out, steam arising as it stung the ground, splashing and puddling a healthy distance from his shoes. It smelt, even outside here in the fresh air, hot and acrid.

Suddenly, he heard a voice call out, and twisted his head around in panic, desperately trying to keep his body facing the tree.

"Ah, there you are." Quinny hadn't finished. And he didn't think he could stop now even if he tried. Bishop Clement was striding across the long grass and graves towards him.

"I'll be with you in a moment," he called back. But the bishop kept walking. Then, when he obviously noticed, he said,

"Oh!" An awkward silence ensued, during

which the bishop withdrew around the side of the church. He was absorbed in the inscription of a headstone when Quinny finally caught up with him and apologised.

"I should have given you warning I was visiting. But I just want to run an idea past you, Quintin," the bishop began amicably, his tone instantly alarming Quinny.

"Please, Bishop Clement, call me Quinny – everyone else does."

"Oh, okay, Quinny. It's less formal than Reverend Boyce or Quintin, isn't it? Fifth child, and all that, eh? Were you the fifth child?" he asked superciliously.

"I have no idea," Quinny replied, thinking he really didn't wish to discuss his heritage. "My family were all killed during the blitz, no one ever told me about them." He swallowed another few grains of imaginary brick dust. "I don't even know my own birthday, Bishop." His mind was still fraught from the memory of his dream, and he hoped his rudeness would prevent further questions. "So, what is it that I can do for you?"

"Well, as you know," Bishop Clement commenced, drawing them both to a halt under a splendid chestnut tree, ignoring Quinny's discomfort. "The diocese is having to rationalise its administration and…"

"You want me to retire?" Quinny asked in alarm.

"No, no. Far from it," the bishop cajoled. "No, actually what we want is for you to take on the parishes of Bexnith and Nortisbourne."

Quinny stared at the bishop in disbelief. These two parishes were adjacent north and northeast to Pepper Hill. They had a church each, St Mary's and St Michael's, both of which were in considerable disrepair with very small congregations to support them.

"No," Quinny stated emphatically. "No."

"I must ask you to consider. It would mean an increased stipend, of course. And expenses."

"No." Quinny was not even shaking his head: his entire stance had grown rigid and unyielding. "No!" he repeated again, just in case the stupid old fool in his black frock-coat, purple shirt and gleaming white dog collar did not quite understand the answer.

"Well, it's either that, or we bring in a new rector to take on all three parishes – someone younger, more dynamic."

"Someone who can drive, twang a guitar and doesn't drink beer down the local pub but sups wine in the local wine bar?" Quinny's hand was searching for the elastic band on the opposite wrist. His fingers gripped it so tightly that the tips had turned white. Instead of pinging it against his wrist, however, he began to twist it, making it stretch further and until it really hurt. "Wears sandals without socks, says 'Hallelujah!' after each sentence and generally enthuses everyone into action?"

"Well, yes, something along those lines. But without the sarcasm, of course."

"Of course." Quinny's rubber band finally snapped, and so did his patience. Bishop Clement continued to stare at the defiant rector, until Quinny remembered the golden rule of dealing with bullies – no, *not the stand up to them and give as good as you get* one; the *do exactly the opposite to what they expect* rule.

"Okay then, Bishop," he said, as a sweet and anything-but-innocent smile crept across his face. "Okay. Add two more parishes to my benefice. Or bring in someone new to do all three. Either solution suits me fine. Now, if you'll excuse me," and he looked up at the sun swilling its yellowness high above them in the sky, "I need a pint. So I'm off to the pub. Can you give me a lift? Don't know how I would get on with two extra parishes, not being able to drive and all that. How would you resolve that problem, eh, Bishop? Grant me a car and driver? *Gratis*, of course."

Chapter 26

Towards the end of August, Nora suddenly realised that George would soon be returning to Cliffend High School for the autumn term. She could see that he had grown quite a lot during the summer holidays and, at breakfast one morning, she asked about his school clothes.

"I'll probably need a complete new uniform," he replied. "Most of it was getting too tight or too short by the time we broke up in July."

"Shall I meet you in Cliffend, then? And we can have a look around, make a start on getting you kitted out. I'll write a list." She thought she could remember what she had bought for Henry, despite his last year at school having been four years ago. She frowned and wondered if she had kept anything that might be of use to George now.

"Okay," George said without enthusiasm, "but it'll have to be in the lunch hour." He was very serious about his work at Tarskers, although when asked he did not elaborate on exactly what he did.

"We won't be able to buy everything in just an hour, and make sure you have something to eat, George. You'll have to take more time off than that," Nora insisted. She immediately sensed George's resentment, although his reaction was to raise his head above his breakfast plate and nod once, before stating,

"I can sort it out myself for school, if you're busy here."

Although independent in most things, George

was secretly glad that Nora had offered to help; he missed his Mum so much that the ache was like being eaten from inside; he was not clever with descriptions, but the best he could do was liken it to the effect of acid on plastic.

He could see Annie in front of him now; she was short, had grey strands mingling with her dark hair, wore practical but comfortable clothes, and was very strict about their manners. But the details of her face were fading, although he kept his memory sharp by studying the photograph he had of both her and Derek. Well, he would, if Rosie hadn't taken it to have two miniature photos made up for the locket.

Nora felt a little exasperated; if she had offered to take Rosalie shopping, there would have been no hesitation. She began to realise how fortunate she had been with her own son. Henry, despite the problems his father had caused, had with only a couple of exceptions been quite placid and sensible – maybe some people would call him dull. Luckily, Rosalie thought he was interesting enough, but sometimes she didn't even want to think about that.

"No, now that we have Craig and Polly, I can make time. Can't you take the afternoon off?" Nora asked. "I'll ring your boss, what's his name, Mr Boston?"

"No, no. It's fine. I'll have a word with him."

George did not want Nora to speak with the foreman; in truth, at only fourteen years old, he should not have been working nearly full shifts, but he was keen to learn and had a healthy respect for safety rules – more so, he suspected, than most of the adult employees. He worked with Mr Boston most of the time, and a couple of other chaps kept an eye on him if the foreman was called elsewhere. "Don't worry, I'll arrange for time off."

The following day, George met Nora at the café opposite the post office in Cliffend High Street at 12.30. Nora bought lunch, soup and sandwiches.

"I'll have to cook a meal for everyone this evening anyway, so this will do for now." She had forgotten that George was used to providing his own mid-day meal; she began to feel that, while he did not exactly resent her attempts to look after him – imposing an authority over him that he did not need – George was very capable of fending for himself, possibly even more so than Henry, who was older.

"We'll start at Knatwich & Tacks for the basics," Nora said when they left the café. "At least two pairs of trousers, I reckon. A blazer – we can get your school badge sewn on there too, it'll save us a job. Shirts, say, five, no six to be on the safe side – what neck size are you?"

George shrugged: when not working, he had spent most of the summer in T-shirts, jeans and trainers – overalls and steel-toe-capped safety boots had been provided for him at Tarskers, together with a hard-hat, the brim of which had made an indentation in his hair. He knew he had grown, but couldn't have told anyone his measurements – unlike Rosie, who was quite proud of her vital statistics and slim figure. He was thinking she looked better now than she had a couple of months ago. He missed Nora continuing, and had to ask her to repeat the first sentence.

"Don't worry, they'll measure you up properly. What games and PE kit do you need?"

"Same as last year, I guess," George replied numbly, remembering the rigmarole twelve months ago when Annie had frog-marched him and Rosie into town.

They'd had to buy their uniforms from the department store; Annie and Derek hadn't been able to afford two sets from a bespoke-tailored outlet. George felt a flicker of resentment. He didn't want to wear clothes that were a standard above what his parents could have afforded, unless he paid for them himself. But he knew Nora would not let him do that. And, although he was aware that Nora had access to funds from his parents' legacy, he didn't want to hurt her feelings, despite the fact that she was injuring his.

"I don't feel right about this," he said suddenly stopping in the street. "I'll leave it today, if you don't mind."

Nora could see she had misjudged the situation; she had tried to take over. She studied him for a moment, standing in the sun shine of a hot August lunchtime. She saw, objectively, a young man, more mature in both body and mind than most teenagers his age, but with an incredible sadness over-shadowing him. He would not look directly at her and hurriedly turned his head to find something else to focus on.

"Anyway, I really need a shower before I go trying on clothes in a shop," he said, with sudden hope. "I didn't think about it earlier, but I'm a bit, you know, sweaty from work this morning."

Nora flushed with embarrassment, and replied,

"Yes, of course. I'm sorry. Look, I'll take you home, now. We can come back tomorrow, or whenever."

"No, it's okay. I've got things I need to do here in town anyway." He stepped forward and kissed Nora's cheek. She could not detect any of the body odour he had just complained about, but was almost relieved at being released from her duty. "I'll make my own way back later," he said. "Thanks anyway. I appreciate you wanting to help." He side-stepped then turned and nearly collided with another pedestrian before hurrying away.

Chapter 27

Later, back at The Fighting Cock, Nora excused herself to Henry and Rosalie, saying she needed a little time on her own. The trip into Cliffend to meet up with George had exhausted her, and she honestly did not know which of the two was more relieved that they had not gone ahead with the shopping. She silently vowed to sort it out later.

Her window was open a little way because the room was quite hot; the sun still shone in. Despite this, Nora shivered.

As she settled onto bed, she could hear Rosalie and Henry talking as they sat at the picnic table outside. She wasn't purposely eavesdropping – if the youngsters had thought about it at all, they would have realised her bedroom was directly above them – but she did remain very still and quiet as they spoke. They were clearly talking about her.

"Things didn't go too well with George, then?" Henry asked.

"Don't know what happened. I haven't seen my *little* brother since this morning," Rosalie replied, a dejected tone sounding in her voice. "But your Mum did look a bit tired when she got back, didn't she?"

Upstairs, Nora was lying on her side. She tried to smile, but felt her cheek dragging against the cotton of the pillow case; she didn't have the energy to lift her head, and her lips fell downwards again. Her thoughts turned to Polly, who was downstairs managing the bar while she rested, and Henry and Rosalie chatted outside.

Polly Merton, with her trademark revealing décolletage, was serving the rector as Nora drifted into sleep.

"Old Max Podgrew isn't really my uncle, you know," Polly told Quinny. "And he isn't as old as you think he is. Anyway, I think he has a *lady-friend*." Quinny raised his eyebrows, waiting for her to reveal more – words that is; more flesh on display would have been too much for him to cope with. And as the moments passed, he found he was unable to prevent his gaze settling onto Polly's chest; the blouse she was wearing – a *top*, the ladies called them nowadays, he'd gathered – was low enough for a large hint of cleavage to be visible. Quinny knew she was gay and had a partner; he rubbed his eyes. He didn't mind an attractive face and figure on a bar-maid; his vocation did not demand his celibacy, and he thought he wouldn't have minded if a young lady had taken an interest in him when he was younger. But they hadn't. He placed his pint onto the beermat and fidgeted with one of the elastic bands on his wrist.

Max then came in, walked up to the bar, greeted Quinny and nodded to Polly for his usual.

"When you're ready, love," he added. He turned to the rector and said, "Now, she's a sight for sore eyes, isn't she?" Quinny grunted then finished his pint. "What's up with you?"

Quinny couldn't pinpoint what was wrong: nothing in particular; anything at all; everything. He was uneasy. The heat of the summer, the general dissatisfaction of his life, the fact that the bishop had caught him answering a call of nature in the churchyard could all be the cause of his restlessness. And suggesting that he take over two more parishes had almost seemed like a punishment. But Quinny had since seen the vacancy being advertised in the clerical paper, and he hoped the bishop had changed his mind. Nevertheless, the threat had unsettled him.

"Could do with another of these!" he said, indicating to his recently emptied glass. Polly delivered Max's pint, the froth still bubbling and a stream of precious beer cascading down just in front of her thumb. Quinny felt his mouth water. Polly raised her eyebrows and smiled as Max indicated for a refill for the rector.

"Cheers," Quinny said to both of them when his pint arrived, trying not to stare at Polly's alluring bust-line again.

"What's happening at St Jude's, then?" Max enquired. "Someone said the bishop was at your place a few days ago. He hasn't finally fired you, has he?"

"Not yet," Quinny replied enigmatically, smiling into his glass. "Although I can always hope he will soon, I suppose."

Chapter 28

Nora re-thought her tactics for George's school uniform, and quietly sorted through some of Henry's old clothes that she had stored away. With a mother's critical eye, albeit a substitute one in this case, she managed to gauge George's various sizes, surreptitiously glancing in his discarded shoes on one occasion, and on the pretext of hanging up a jacket, checking the label on another, T-shirts and jeans when she washed them and guessing the rest. She would, of course, have preferred George to have tried the items on in the shops before she bought them but, as she told the assistant in schools uniforms' section of the department store in Cliffend,

"At that age, it's hard to pin them down. And they don't want to be dragged along to the shops to buy clothes."

"It's no problem, madam," the assistant replied. "If anything doesn't fit, just bring them back and we'll exchange them." This customer looked a sensible sort, she deduced; there would be no need to recite the company policy for garments to be returned as new, not in the worn condition some people tried. Besides which, there would be a tidy commission for her from this sale. The boy must be having everything brand new. "I expect you're hoping this will be the last complete uniform you have to buy for him before he leaves school; it's certainly the largest sized blazer we stock." She was keen to engage this woman, who had written a cheque and was now searching for her bank card with which to substantiate it: her face looked familiar. And the name, Stickleback. Then she remembered. There had been an article or two in the *Cliffend Herald* earlier in the year. The pub in Ashfield. The landlord passed awayrecently; and there was something to do with a couple tragically dying on board a river boat. The Fighting Cock, that was the pub; her and her husband had been out there a few weeks ago. But didn't the son work there? Surely he was too old for school uniform.

"Problem is," Nora explained as she handed over the card and cheque, "This is all for a lad I'm looking after; if it was my own son, I would've just hauled him along. It's a delicate situation. I just want to get everything quickly and quietly, all in one go. No fuss." The assistant handed over the receipt.

"Thank you, madam. Well, as I said, if you need to change anything, bring it back. If we haven't got it in stock, we can order it." Nora picked up the two large carrier bags emblazoned with the shop's name, thanked the assistant and hurried out to the car park.

Back at the pub, Nora left all the new uniform – shirts, trousers, shoes, a brand new tie, everything – in George's bedroom. "Let me have the blazer back as soon as you can, I have to sew on the badge. And, if you could just try everything on before the weekend, so I can change anything that doesn't fit. And you'll be ready for next week." Nora explained in front of Rosalie, hoping she could recruit her as an ally.

141

"Yeah, come on, George. Let's go do a fashion show."

"I'm not trying things on in front of you," George said, slipping easily into the indignant sibling role.

"I'm not asking you to *change* in front of me," Rosalie stated with mock horror. "Just show me that it all fits." She clutched at his arm and hauled him to his feet in full knowledge that he could escape if he wanted to do, but to pull free would probably hurt her. And he would not do that.

Upstairs, with Rosalie banished to the landing, George tried everything on, carefully unwrapping the packets and then hanging up the garments as he took them off again.

"I need some more clothes hangers, Rosie," he called through the closed door.

"Right, I'll go and ask Nora."

Satisfied that he was completely alone, George quickly found the various price tickets – these had been left on in case the items needed to be returned. He made swift calculations, and was staggered at the total cost. He suddenly felt very weak, and was sitting on the edge of his bed when Rosie returned.

"Can I come in?" she asked as she knocked, not waiting for an answer. "Here," she said, thrusting an armful of hangers towards him, then exclaiming, "Oh," when she saw him. "Having a *moment*, are you?" And she sat down beside him, the unevenness of their weights on the mattress making her lean into his side. "Gets you sometimes, doesn't it? It's the ordinary things

Mum and Dad did for us that affect me the worse – you know, clean undies ready to put on, my favourite soup, Mum buying that magazine for me that Dad always said was a waste of money."

George slipped his arm round his big sister's shoulders and nodded. They remained there quietly for a while, both thankful for something they could not put into words, but both deeply, deeply sad. Eventually breaking the silence, George stated,

"This lot cost a fortune, you know. I'll have to repay Nora. I've got savings from my wages, but I don't think it'll cover it. We'll have to get some money from the solicitor. Uniforms are the sort of things we can have an allowance for, I'm sure."

"It's okay, George. It's all been sorted." George frowned in question. "Nora just has to tell Mr Brideman how much she spends and he gets her a cheque – she probably has to produce receipts and that sort of thing, though."

"Oh," George replied, thinking this made sense, and annoyed that he hadn't realised. "What about you? I mean, I get given all my books at the beginning of term, but you'll need some things when you start college, won't you?"

"Yeah, Henry's taking me out next week. We start the Monday after you, so there won't be so many kids about in town when I do my shopping."

George smiled. "Kids?" he asked.

"Yeah, kids. You know, getting in the way, being annoying. Big kids as well as little kids. And of course, *big kids*…" she tapped his shoulder, "…are the worst of all!"

Chapter 29

When Henry Stickleback was fifteen years old, he had wanted to be sixteen so that he could legally have sex; it was all his group of mates – Bloo, Hopper and Sidney – could talk about, although at that time they had no idea of how to make it happen. Girls were strange creatures who fascinated and enthralled them, then taunted and tormented in equal measure. Henry was popular, he was good looking, the tallest of his contemporaries, and not overly talkative; girls liked a boy who would listen, apparently.

Although at various times his friends plagued him to take alcohol to school for them, he refused outright for two reasons: firstly, he would have to steal it, and he did not intend to add to his mother's worries by breaking her trust in him and secondly, he saw in his father the problems drinking brought. Instead he kept up a plentiful supply of crisps. But still his mind returned to sex. Girls sometimes accepted a packet of crisps – prawn cocktail seemed to be their favourite. Nora noticed the popularity of that particular flavour, and the rate at which stocks disappeared being disproportionate to the amount she actually sold. She shrugged when she saw three packets in the top of Henry's school bag one morning; she ordered double the usual quantity from the wholesalers next time.

As Henry's sixteenth birthday approached, he also thought about motorbikes. He wanted to buy one as soon as he could. He had saved quite a lot of money from his allowance over the years, but he wasn't sure if he had enough – he knew there were expenses beyond the purchase price: road tax, insurance, a crash hat, petrol and leathers; he wasn't completely stupid.

Henry's sixteenth birthday coincided with the first day of the new school year, his last at Cliffend High. Even enduring the embarrassment of L plates fixed front and back, he pictured himself riding a shining new machine to and from school. He planned to go out in the evenings, meet up with the lads, and find a girlfriend.

Maybe he could even make Rosalie Tillinger from Pepper Hill notice him, although she was a bit young – when Henry reached sixteen, she would still only be thirteen. Henry had secretly admired Rosalie for as long as he could remember, but his mates thought she was stuck-up, so he didn't mention her to them.

Henry broached the idea of having a motorbike with his mother.

"I would be able to help you more, go into town for things for you," he faltered, realising he had not thought his case sufficiently through.

"No," Nora stated. "You are not having a motorbike. Sixteen is too young."

"But Mum, I've got some money saved up," Henry pleaded, the whine in his voice reflecting the very lack of maturity Nora was highlighting. But she didn't want to point this out and embarrass him even further; he was a good son, and although not academically brilliant, he was honest and helpful. And he hadn't started drinking, for which she thanked the Lord, but constantly kept watch for signs.

"I'm sorry, Henry. But the answer is still no. Save your money for next year when you'll be old enough to learn to drive a car."

"Your mother's right, lad," Woody had concurred. Nora had not realised he was standing behind her. And, for once, he appeared to be sober enough to support her. She had been grateful, and had given him a rare smile.

Henry had walked away from them and went upstairs to his room. He was angry, and annoyed that he lived out here in this dingy pub in a desolate village where nothing ever happened: he wanted to be with his friends. But he was dependent upon the buses for transport. Plus, he was still only sixteen; old enough to smoke, but he didn't want to; he could get married, but not unless his parents agreed. It irked that he still had to wait a year to learn to drive a car, and two years before he could vote, leave home of his own accord, and – which, if he were honest, grieved him most – serve behind the bar in the pub.

The Friday following this conversation, Nora handed Henry that week's edition of the Cliffend Herald newspaper. The photograph on the front page showed the mangled wreckage of a motorcycle, the rider of which had been killed.

"Colin Mayfield was a year older than you, wasn't he?" Nora asked as Henry tried to read the article. When she said the name, her son's hands started to shake and he felt sick.

"Yeah, I think so. Why?" The article did not give many facts and, after a quick scan, he asked, "What happened?"

"Police think he was going too fast. He'd just overtaken a row of cars that were slowing down – they were stopping for that new pedestrian crossing on the road leading up to the cliff, you know the one?" Henry nodded. "The lights turned red, and a group of children started to cross the road. Luckily, he must've suddenly seen them, or he would've ploughed straight into them. Anyway, apparently, he pulled in but he couldn't stop in time. He hit the back of a stationary car, and went over the top. He landed on the road next to the crossing. He was wearing a crash-helmet, but the bike followed him over the car, and ended up on top of him. It crushed his stomach and chest, and broke several ribs, punctured his lungs, and ruptured his spleen. That's besides his broken collar bone, fractured arms, legs and goodness only knows what else. It says there…" Nora pointed to the print "…that he died at the scene."

Henry swallowed hard. Just because someone else had been stupid didn't mean he would be. But he did not say this to his mother because, before he could open his mouth, she said,

"I tell you what, because you've been such a great help to me over the years here in the pub, to show my appreciation, I'll pay for you to have driving lessons as soon as you're seventeen. And I'll also put you on the insurance for my car so you can use that, until you can buy something of your own, of course."

Henry smiled, almost, and whispered, "Thanks."

"In the meantime, you'd better study hard and pass your exams." Henry started to protest, but Nora held up her hand. "I'm not expecting top grades; just do the best you can. A pass is a pass, in my book; I'm not worried about *A-stars*, or whatever! I know you think you won't need qualifications to work in a pub, but you never know what might happen in the future. "

Henry also wanted to leave school as soon as he could to help his mother; in fact, he was nearly seventeen before he finally left behind the fetters of education with seven modest GCSEs. Nora was satisfied, and made his employment permanent.

Henry passed his driving test within a month of his seventeenth birthday. But, by then, he wanted to be eighteen, so eager was he to grow up. He could see his youth hampering his latest ambition: he could not legally serve behind the bar at The Fighting Cock until he was eighteen.

When Henry finally turned eighteen, his father had just been discharged from his second stay in hospital with alcohol-related cirrhosis of the liver.

And the year that followed proved to be the worst in Henry's life so far.

Today, Sunday, 4th September 1988, however, Henry celebrated his nineteenth birthday, hoping the time from now onwards would be better. The last car boot sale in the town hall had been held the previous weekend, and today Henry could enjoy a lie-in instead of getting up and trawling through dozens of stalls looking for anything vaguely cockerel-ish. With these thoughts in his head, he rolled over and went back to sleep.

The pub had been busy at lunchtime. Nora gave him an envelope containing a card and a generous cheque. He smiled at the words she had written. *You're a good son, Henry. You deserve the best! All my love, Mum.* There was just one X; only one was needed.

"Thanks," he said quietly, aware that his face was reddening.

"Where're Rosalie and George?" she asked as she replaced glasses on their shelves.

"Not sure about George, but Rosalie's still in bed." Nora raised her eyes to the ceiling as if to see through the plaster above their heads. "I thought she'd be up by now, but I don't think she slept very well last night."

Nora was about to ask for further details, when Polly approached them.

"Here," she said. "This is from me," and she slid a large, distastefully pink envelope onto the bar, held his face in her hands and planted a red-lipsticked kiss on his surprised lips. "Happy birthday, big boy!" She patted his chest, winked at him, then spoke in general, "I'm off to service the loos – chap over there," and she pointed to the last customer, "was just complaining that we're nearly out of loo paper. D'you know if anyone's in the Gents'?"

Chapter 30

Rosalie was not, in fact, still in bed at The Fighting Cock public house in Ashfield. She had crept out earlier to go to Pepper Hill, to the Old Police House, leaving a note on her pillow telling of her whereabouts, and saying she would be back by lunch-time. She didn't want Henry to give her a lift, nor did she wish for George to offer to accompany her: she just wanted to be on her own.

She set off to walk a little way along the road towards Pepper Hill, hoping the bus would pick her up even if she wasn't at the official stop. They did for Quinny, therefore she was sure they would for her too. But she had misjudged the times. The summer timetable finished the previous week with the Bank Holiday, and the bus from Cliffend to Mattingburgh on Sundays now only ran every four hours; she had missed the first one by a good forty minutes.

In the end, she walked the entire route – just over a mile. Not far really, she thought. It was a pleasant day and there was little traffic, autumn was beginning to curl and colour the leaves, and many of the flowers on the verges were now only seed heads. A slight breeze that still held a shadow of summer warmth ruffled both the grasses and her hair, and she appreciated the connection. As she passed St Jude's mid-way she could hear distant voices singing a hymn and although she only knew a few of the words, the sound was comforting.

The Old Police House in Pepper Hill felt still and lifeless when she entered. She locked the front door behind her; she had never done so when they all lived here as a family – Mum, Dad, George and her. She walked silently to the kitchen, took a glass from the cabinet, turned on the tap and ran the cold water for a few minutes; the stream fell noisily into the steel sink before splashing back up at her. She filled the glass and took a sip, although she was not really thirsty.

She tried to move around quietly which, when she thought about it was ridiculous; it was her home, she could be as loud as she wished. She could even live here if she wanted to. But she did not want to: the heart had vanished from the place, and she thought it would never be warm here again.

People told her to look forward to the future, not back at the past. It was not always that easy. But she had discovered that, if Henry could be in her future, she might manage to carry on. Otherwise everything seemed just too futile to bother with.

Henry.

Rosalie smiled at the thought of him. Tall, dark-haired, his beard with a red tinge; he was kind, kissable, and she felt a shiver of excitement inside every time she saw him – especially when he looked at her. The smile widened and her face softened and, for a while she dreamed of Henry – his touch, his voice. She imagined how it would be if he kissed her, held her as a lover rather than some kind of foster sister, or someone he was trying to keep at arm's length. She began to picture what it would be like to be closer, to undress him, to have his hands on her skin. All over.

At this point, she shook herself. Although infinitely better than dwelling on losing her parents, she felt that now was not the time to daydream about such matters.

Rosalie carried her glass of water up the stairs. She opened the door to her old bedroom and stood in the middle to look around. The room was soundless, it contained no life, but it did hold a faint aroma of a distant fragrance. During her last fleeting visit here she had dabbed a little of her favourite perfume on. She must have left the stopper off: the scent had evaporated. Rosalie was not upset as she held up the bottle, it belonged to someone from the past; it did not suit the person she was now. She sighed, and the sound whispered back to her, reminding her that she had a purpose in coming here today.

As well as applying her perfume when last she called in, not only had she picked up a few clothes and other personal things, she had hidden Henry's birthday present and card, which she had managed to buy one day when she was in town alone.

Sometimes it was difficult to do the things she wanted to – go shopping, for instance – on her own. Henry would offer her a lift into town, or George would want to accompany her.

She would not have minded if George had been with her on the day she had bought Henry's birthday card and present. But she didn't want anyone there for the other little job she had done.

The lady in the photographers' shop had been

very helpful and, as Rosalie explained why she wanted miniature copies of the faces on the picture printed (no, unfortunately, she did not have the negative), she was charged a minimal rate, and the assistant fixed them into place as well. She thought it was very kind.

She looked around her room, trying to remember where she had put the roll of boys' wrapping paper she had bought for George's birthday in February. It suddenly came to her, and with that, the tape and scissors spread on the floor beside her bed, she opened the door to her bed-side cupboard and took out Henry's present, still protected by wads of tissue paper. Slowly, she unwrapped the layers then held it up to the light and smiled.

"I really hope you like this, Henry," she said with almost a warning in her voice.

Rosalie remained motionless for a while after she had finished, her self-confidence seeming to suddenly vanish. She wanted to see Henry. But the gift she had bought for him now seemed a little mean, compared with everything he and Nora were doing for her and George.

Eventually, she drank the rest of the water, tidied the things she had been using then unhooked a shoulder bag from her door. Placing the package carefully inside, she walked back downstairs, returned the glass to the kitchen, listened for a moment to the house's silence, then left by the front door, quietly turning the key in the lock as she went.

Chapter 31

Polly's very high heels clicked towards the door which opened into a lobby, revealing three other doors; to the left was the Ladies', directly ahead was the Gents' and to the right, the store room from which Woody had stolen the whisky that killed him. Polly unlocked the storeroom and collected her rubber gloves and some of the cleaning paraphernalia, plus an unopened packet of toilet rolls. She then made her way into the Gents', not bothering to knock.

"Sorry, Max," she said, sounding extremely unrepentant. She placed her cleaning gear on the shelf by the hand drier, then wedged open the door. Max was standing near the vending machine attached to the wall next to the double urinal unit. "I thought I saw you come through earlier, haven't been here all the while, have you?" she joked.

"No, no. Just paid a second visit. You know," and he lowered his voice, "men's problems. Oh no, perhaps you don't know, do you?" Max began to look flustered. Polly could not prevent a smile, the truth being her partner would no more use the Gents' facilities than she would.

Max continued to fumble with his trousers, but he wasn't, as she first thought, zipping up his flies; he was trying to push things into his pocket. The bottom of the opening ripped and a packet dropped onto the tiled floor.

"Oh, look out, Max. You've dropped your condoms." And she bent down, giving Max a full view down her front, while the man who had just walked in captured the benefits from the rear. "Planning to get lucky tonight, are you?" she asked wickedly, enjoying watching Max's face changing from puce pink to deathly white.

"Excuse me," the new arrival coughed. "If you aren't *actually cleaning* in here, I'll, er, just use the cubicle."

"No problem, sir," Polly said brightly. "I'll give you a minute – oh, here," and she ripped open the cellophane and dragged out a new toilet roll. "You might need this. Someone said it's running out." She turned to Max and whispered, "So it's you who's been using all the condoms, is it? We all thought it was Henry! How many have you got in there anyway?"

"None of your bloody business," Max's voice was rising. The occupant of the cubicle cleared his throat. Max pushed Polly aside and departed. He walked straight through the lounge-bar towards the door and left.

"What's wrong with him, then?" Quinny asked. He had just arrived, a regular from church having given him a lift to the pub. Nora picked out a glass for him, wondering how the reverend managed to do as little as he appeared to, yet still be at the centre of, and know about, everything.

"Don't know," she commented, indicating to the pumps, to which Quinny nodded his reply. "I think he came from the direction of the Gents'. Oh, wait a minute, though. Polly just went in there."

"Maybe she embarrassed him," Quinny said thoughtfully.

"I did more than embarrass him," Polly stated as she joined them. "I just caught him emptying the *condom machine*." She emphasised the last two words, then glared in the direction of the door, folded her arms and said, "Huh! Dirty old man. I said he had a lady-friend, didn't I?" her voice growing louder. Curiosity forced some of the other customers to turn around and look over towards the bar.

"How old is he?" Quinny asked.

"About fifty, I think," Polly replied. "He looks a lot older, though. Probably because he works outside – you know, all that sun and wind on his face making his skin wrinkled." Polly shuddered.

"Younger than me, then," Nora said quietly, more to herself than to the others. Nowadays, she felt so exhausted all the time that she could have added a couple of decades to her actual age.

"Even so, *Max* has just emptied the condom machine!" Polly repeated.

"I thought it was Henry using all the condoms," Nora said with apprehension. Quinny and Polly glanced at her, shook their heads slightly then looked away again. "I do hope he's being careful," she added, believing by their faces that they knew something she did not.

"What d'you mean, Mum – You hope I'm *being careful*?" Henry asked. Nora had not realised Henry, who had been in the kitchen, had just returned to the bar. But the others had. Exchanging mortified glances, Polly then widened her eyes at Quinny, to tell him not to interfere.

"Just chatting, lad," the rector said, ignoring

Polly's unspoken advice. "Just, you know, concerned, that's all." He raised his glass to his lips and supped.

"Concerned about what?" Henry demanded.

"That you are taking precautions," Nora said quickly. "You and Rosalie. You know!"

Henry looked at them in horror and disbelief. Polly – newcomer, gay, all round friend to everyone – had brought gossip to the bar which had enticed his Mum – the one person in the world who was meant to trust him, a trust that he in turn reciprocated, and the bloody rector – who was, Henry believed, bound by confidentiality – were discussing his and Rosalie's supposed sex life! And on his birthday! His face burned in fury and indignation. He did not want them to see how hurt he felt. He gathered all his self-control and said softly,

"I thought you knew me better than that, Mum." He quietly left the bar, walked through to the kitchen, out to the hall and up the stairs to his room. He was glad to be alone when the tears came, jerking themselves painfully from his chest, up into his throat and out of his eyes; disappointment, sorrow and despair gave raw and sharp edges to his grief.

If only they knew. He and Rosalie had decided to wait until they married.

By the time Rosalie knocked on Henry's door, his tears had dried and he sat staring at the carpet.

"Come in," he whispered.

"Hi, it's only me," she said lightly, peering around the door, noticing immediately the glum look on his face. She had only exchanged a brief "Hello" with Nora downstairs, who had told her to help herself to lunch and, if she didn't mind, to make something for Henry and take it up to him. She was not told about the shenanigans that had upset him. "Are you *having a moment*?" she asked as she carried in a tray of sandwiches, tea/coffee for Henry and a mug of ordinary tea for her. He looked up, his eyes blank. "That's what George asks me if he thinks I've gone all miserable on him." She set down the tray, and sat beside him. "And then he lets me either tell him how I feel, or he just gives me a brotherly hug – you know, crushes my shoulders, bruises my ribs – then leaves me be."

Henry extended his arm and Rosalie slipped under it, snuggling up closely.

"I don't want you to leave me be, though." Henry murmured.

"Happy birthday," she whispered and kissed his bristly cheek; she caught a taste of salt from his tears and wondered if anything specific had caused his *moment*. But before she could arrange the words in her head to ask the question, she thought of something else.

"Hang on a minute," she said, as she vanished then quickly reappeared. "Here." She handed him a package and an envelope before sneaking back under his arm. The present was roughly-wrapped and quite heavy for its size.

"What is it?" he asked, laying down the card and trying to undo the wrapping paper with one hand while Rosalie held the other.

"You'll see," she said, reluctantly removing his arm and relinquishing his hand.

"Wow! Where did you get *that*?" he exclaimed as he stood up and held a plate to the light to inspect it.

It was really quite an ordinary plate, ceramic rather than porcelain or china, and like the mugs, cream with the underside unsigned. On the front, a colourful and belligerent cockerel had been hand-painted; the body was of orange and yellow, the comb and wattle bright blood-red, and the wing and tail-feathers shining black with shades of iridescent green and blue reflecting through.

The plate was very similar to the two mugs they had bought at their first car boot sale, and Henry wondered if they were all part of a set of some kind. And, if there was a set, then he wanted to collect all the pieces!

Rosalie watched hungrily as he studied the plate, turning it in his hands and running his fingertips over the textured relief of the brush strokes. He seemed fascinated by it. She felt a frisson ripple through her as she watched his hands, imagining he was caressing her.

"Happy birthday, Henry," she whispered, standing up beside him and wrapping her arms around him.

Chapter 32

Alice Childs was standing in the kitchen of her cottage in Pepper Hill, waiting for Max Podgrew. She thought she heard his car approaching, and the engine sounded angry. This upset her. Everything upset Alice. But the car passed. It wasn't Max.

Alice turned to the draining board beneath the south-facing window and looked down at the thirty carrots lying there in three rows of ten. She couldn't believe their physicality – after all, they were *vegetables*.

She winced in shame, but didn't understand why. Embarrassment? Yes, she had been extremely embarrassed, surreptitiously selecting the most suitable ones in Poskett's shop.

"If you need that many carrots, why don't you just buy a couple of bunches – at least with the tops on they'll stay fresher longer," Poskett stated irritably as he polished his glasses. How could she tell him she did not need the greenery?

Outside her kitchen, the sun stepped out from behind a cloud and shone onto the steel draining board, glinting sharply, painfully, into her eyes. She reached out her hand to turn the nearest carrot over; with the exception of the part lying on the metal, the skin was a dry, dull and grainy orange. She preferred the bright shiny, damp side, and proceeded to turn all the carrots. They made a heavy thud as she replaced each onto the surface. The action was soothing: grip, lift, twist, replace; grip, lift, twist, replace. But then she remembered what they were to represent, and suddenly to touch them was most disdainful, especially the one at the end; it had a knobble half way down, from which sprouted two stringy roots!

As Alice Childs had grown up she believed that, with her name, it was inevitable she would become a teacher, although her father was a coalman and, as far as she could remember, her mother had never worked. She was a shy person, but clever, and went to a teacher training college when she finished school. Afterwards, she had to return home to look after her parents, who were not particularly well by then, and found a classroom assistant's job nearby.

When her parents had passed away, she applied for and secured a post at Cliffend High as a supply teacher. The position basically meant that she filled in when others were absent, covering every subject taught at the school. She felt she was not really qualified for this, and lived her working life in a state of constant stress. Her home, here in Pepper Hill, was her antidote: after a busy day with rowdy, ill-mannered school children, she valued her peace and privacy. Her only vice – if it could be called that - was a flutter now and then on the horses. She did not consider this to be gambling, and neither were the church raffles, or the bingo sessions she attended on a Monday evening at the village hall.

Because of her duties towards her parents, Alice had not married. She'd never even had a boyfriend. In recent years, however, following a chance encounter at the local bookmaker's, Alice had formed a friendship with Max Podgrew, whom, she quickly learnt, lived only a mile or so down the road in Ashfield.

A knock on the front door broke into Alice's thoughts. The hand holding the carrot was shaking. She replaced it, tutted as she surveyed the others, then wiped her palms down the hips of her skirt.

She opened the door and found Max in a very agitated state standing on the step.

"Come in. Come in quick," she urged as she hustled him inside; she peered first left, then right along the road. Satisfied that no one had seen her visitor arrive, she quickly shut the door and turned the key in the lock.

"Did you get them?" she asked.

"Yes, and a right load of trouble it caused me too!" Max was still angry with Polly for interrupting him. And for making fun of him.

"I really am grateful, Max. There's no way I could have gone into the chemist and bought twenty-five condoms. Thank you. Actually, did you get any spares?" Max did not have a chance to reply before she continued, "Never mind, I'll give you the money anyway. How much were they?" She squeezed past Max in her tiny hall and led the way through to the kitchen. Her bag was on the table; she rummaged inside it and brought out her purse.

"I'm not particularly worried about the money, although, since you ask." And he told her the amount. Alice tried not to wince; she had no idea these things were so expensive.

"Did you get the...?" Seeing the carrots lined up and scrubbed clean on the draining board he stated, "Oh yes, I see you got them okay."

"Yes, I went into Poskett's. Twice. Once Friday morning, when I managed to get about half, well, twelve to be precise, and I went back for the others yesterday, by which time he said he would have had a delivery. He was really angry when saw me sorting through them. I got a few spares – thirty in all. Thirty carrots, that is, not thirty spares. That would be ridiculous. Not that the whole thing isn't ridiculous!"

"You didn't tell him what they were for, did you?" Max asked abruptly.

"No, no. Oh, God, no." She clasped her hands to her face in horror. "I would've died if I'd had to say anything. As it is, I don't think I can ever go in there again. I've never been so embarrassed,"

"Well, I have! Just now, if you must know."

"I'm so sorry. Why were you embarrassed? I thought you said it would be easy; you'd just get them out of the machine in the Gents' at the pub. What happened? Tea?" Max nodded and began to empty his pockets.

"I had to get some of each kind..."

"What d'you mean *kind*? I thought they were, er, just...condoms. I didn't know they had different sorts. Why would they have different sorts?" Alice always babbled whenever she was anxious or nervous: she was surprised she had stopped herself telling Poskett the whole story when she'd purchased the carrots. She tried to distract herself now by reaching for the kettle, filling it with water from the tap and setting it to boil. She could feel her face still blushing.

"Don't ask me for details," Max said, with more than a little annoyance in his voice. "Here, take your pick." He pushed the packets around with his finger, trying not to let his interest and intrigue show.

"Oh, I don't want to look at them," Alice cried. "I don't want to think about it at all!"

"I still can't see why it's been left to you to do this. I mean of all the ridiculous things – teaching teenagers to put condoms on carrots. What on earth is the education system coming to?" Max's voice had risen, and the final phrase came out a lot louder than Alice felt comfortable with. She was conscious that her kitchen, and that of her neighbour, had a thin adjoining wall: she was sure every word spoken could be heard next door.

"Well, Mrs Small, the regular teacher," she said quietly, "is away at some kind of course, according to Mr Morsley who rang last week to tell me. He's been in school sorting the new timetables, apparently." Alice had already explained all of this to Max, but he listened patiently anyway. "And as Supply, I've got to give Year Ten their *Personal Development* lesson on Tuesday."

She swallowed hard, thinking the more times she said the words out loud, the easier their implications would seem. It had taken about ten minutes the first time to explain everything to Max and to ask for his help. In the end, she had handed him the sheet of instructions Mr Morsley had sent, barely giving him time to finish reading before bursting with the request for him to buy twenty-five condoms for her.

"Make it a couple more," Alice had expanded. "Say thirty – because I'll have to practice on my own first. Even so, I'm bound to mess it up in front of a class of children. Teenagers," she had corrected her last word, then blushed scarlet at the thought.

Today, here in her kitchen, when she had composed herself, she continued, "I have to stand up in front of twenty-five pupils, boys *and* girls, I hasten to add. And show them how to…show them…" Alice's face was so red that she could have boiled the kettle without electricity. "And I don't even know how to do it myself! I'll have to practice. That's why I bought more carrots than I needed. How many condoms did you buy?"

Max shrugged, "I didn't have time to count them; Polly walked straight into the Gents' as I was getting them, and I left in a hurry."

Alice lurched forwards and tried to count them, but her hands were shaking and the packets kept slipping from her grasp.

"Argghhh!" she finally screamed, not caring by now whether or not the neighbours could hear, or what they might think.

"They'll sack me if I don't do it, I know. They've been talking about cutting back on staff, and I haven't got all the posh qualifications some of them have. I'll be the first to go, you mark my words." She stopped and drew breath. More rationally, she stated, "No, I think I'll retire. Go off sick, then retire – through ill health! I'll stay at home between now and Christmas, and leave in the New Year. That'll mess their little schemes up! Others have done it! Why shouldn't I? Then I can think about myself for a change. Go on holiday. Have some fun!"

Max stood up quickly and moved towards Alice, not really sure how to handle this situation. All he had wanted from their friendship was a few hours' company a week to share racing form and choose likely winners: he didn't want this hassle.

"Well then, in that case," he suggested playfully, trying to lighten the mood, "you had better learn how to…"

But Alice screamed again, then covered her face with hands to hide her mortification, realising Max was probably not the best person to have asked to help her. But she had no one else. Hot tears of anger and frustration ran down her cheeks and she dug her fingers deep into her eye sockets to stem the flow. Yes, she would definitely retire, go on a cruise. God, how she hated her life!

Max tentatively stepped closer to her again. He brought his arms up then placed one around her shoulders, while the other found its way to her waist. She seemed to stiffen for a moment, then abandoned her resistance and leant against him. She relaxed and, to her surprise, found it was comfortable and reassuring to be this close to another person. And a tiny piece of her mind asked if this was how it was meant to feel, to be being held, cherished even.

"How old are kids in Year Ten, then?" Alice heard Max ask, his voice muffled above one of her ears. She shrugged herself free, searched her cuffs for a handkerchief, found nothing and stretched across to pull a square of kitchen tissue from the roll in the holder attached to the wall.

"Fourteen, fifteen. Definitely not old enough to be learning how to put a condom on a carrot, if you ask me. Or on anything else, for that matter. And, as for Mr Morsley telling me that I have to show them. I ask you, honestly. I have to use a *carrot*!"

"I bet half of them could probably tell him how to do it," Max mused, tactfully at the last minute deciding against saying that they could probably show Alice. He didn't think she had heard, because she immediately continued,

"And, when I questioned having to use carrots, he said they were cheaper than bananas! And then, when he thought I couldn't hear him, he said *"You couldn't exactly use the real thing, could you?"*

The pitch of her voice reached hysterical again. She was shaking her head and trembling violently. "I mean, why pick on me? There are other supply teachers who could fill in who would know about this stuff."

She had turned towards the window and was staring down her back garden. All the resentment that had built inside her over the years for the hours she spent teaching ungrateful kids who did nothing but disrespect her was about to erupt.

But then the fight suddenly, instantaneously, disappeared and she whispered,

"They're going to make a complete fool of me, Max." She turned to face him. Even as she stood, resting the small of her back against the sink, she was aware of the carrots on the draining board behind her, some leaning slightly this way, some that; all orange and rigid; mocking her. "No, that's wrong; I'm going to make a complete fool of myself, aren't I? Oh God, what a mess!"

He looked away from her red eyes and her flushed and swollen cheeks. He was angry on her behalf, and secretly thought her best course of action was just to phone in and say she wouldn't be coming into work next week, either because she was sick, or because she was handing in her resignation.

"It could be seen as constructive dismissal, if they got rid of you because you refused to teach something that you thought was unreasonable," he suggested.

"They don't think it's unreasonable – when I said it was hardly appropriate, the Head laughed at me and told me to *get with it*. Apparently, *it's nineteen eighty-eight* and, because of *HIV* and *AIDS* and *STDs* and taking responsibility for their *sexual hygiene,* kids need to know this stuff."

"Oh, nothing to do with girls not getting themselves pregnant then," Max commented sarcastically.

Chapter 33

Monday was the first morning of the autumn term at Cliffend High School. Usually, terms started on the Tuesday, with teachers going in on the Monday to prepare. But this year a new initiative had been implemented: start at the beginning of the week.

Mr Morsley, the head teacher, arrived at the school at 7.30. He was unrefreshed from his break, having spent most of the five-week holiday working on the new curriculum, sorting timetables which allowed pupils to swap between streams for the core topics while juggling all the other subjects with suitable teachers, as well as maintaining staff training levels and offering opportunities for each to further their own careers. In fact, his mind was so full of clichés and jargon that he was dreading the first day back probably as much as most of the pupils.

He parked his car in his designated bay, and approached the front entrance which was reserved for staff only; it was strictly forbidden for pupils to use.

"Good morning, Miss Urquhart," he greeted his secretary, trying to sound cheerful, but probably failing miserably.

"Good morning, Mr Morsley. There's a parcel for you in your office. It was delivered really early, apparently by a chap from Ashfield. There was no one else about, so the caretaker took it and put it on the desk. It's marked for your personal attention, so I haven't opened it."

"Thank you," Mr Morsley said with a puzzled expression. He hurried into his office and, much to Miss Urquhart's pique, closed the door behind him.

Mr Morsley picked up the large and lumpy parcel. It had been wrapped in brown paper, and the contents seemed to move as he handled it. There was a long white envelope stuck with Sellotape to the front. Underneath the words FOR THE PERSONAL ATTENTION OF MR MORSLEY was the school's address; he recognised the handwriting as belonging to a member of his staff, but he could not immediately place which one. He tore the envelope off, ripping some of the wrapping in the process.

Inside was a letter from Miss Alice Childs, stating that, because of the unpleasant nature of the first lesson she had been ordered (*requested, would have been a better word,* thought Mr Morsley, so used to correcting students' prose that he could not prevent himself affording every piece of writing he came across the same scrutiny; *or even scheduled*) to instruct Year Ten, and the extreme anxiety the thought of such a task was causing her, she intended to make an appointment with her doctor at the earliest opportunity. She ended the missive by informing him she would forward her sick note (*medical certificate – use the proper terminology,* Mr Morsley thought unkindly) in due course. But (*never start a sentence with a conjunction – where did this woman gain her qualifications? Perhaps I ought to take a look at her file!*), she continued, as she did not wish to leave him in the lurch *(huh!)* she had had the enclosed delivered to the school in time for the start of the term. She had also sent the receipts from the purchase of these items.

In his hurry to open the parcel, Mr Morsley ignored the dockets clipped to the letter and continued to rip at the brown paper. Inside were carrots, topless, dry, whisker-ridden and flaccid – definitely not fresh. The noise of these being tipped out onto the desk top prompted Miss Urquhart to tap on the door and look in.

"Is everything all right, Mr Morsley?" she enquired, intrigued to see a pile of floppy and faded orange carrots on top of the desk. Mr Morsley grunted, shook the package one last time and dislodged another parcel from within.

Miss Urquhart placed her hand over her mouth, but could not quite stifle the giggle bubbling up. The headteacher scowled in her direction, but she refused to leave his office. This parcel was more heavily bound with tape, as if the sender was trying to convey the message that its contents were most distasteful.

Eventually, Mr Morsley broke into the wrappings and a number of individual foil packs, rectangular in shape with a central oval blister, fell untidily out on top of the carrots.

"Oh dear," Miss Urquhart commented as she approached the desk and ventured to pick up a carrot in one hand and a foil pack in the other.

"Christ," Morsley swore, when he realised why this parcel had been delivered. He glared at the clock, then sat down and tried to unlock the top drawer of his desk. He was so agitated that he couldn't even line up the key properly. He stood up again and hoisted his wallet out of his back pocket and opened it out. "What time do the shops open, Miss Urquhart?"

"Supermarkets? Er, eight–ish, I think. I don't really know. They're open when I come to work at my usual time," she could not resist the opportunity to remark on her enforced early start. "I do all my shopping on a Saturday afternoon."

"Well, could you go and buy, er, however many carrots there are here, please? Same size as these, er... you know what they're for, obviously!" He felt the scarlet heat of rage flowing through him. And, as he looked down at the disgusting vegetables on his desk, he felt his stomach heave. "This should cover it." he stated as he handed a banknote to her, trying to be calm. "Please, Miss Urquhart, if you could hurry. They are needed for Year Ten's Personal Development lesson second period this morning."

The secretary left, closing the door quietly after her. Mr Morsley wiped his forehead with his handkerchief. In his fury he replaced the contents in the parcel, clasped it with disgust and threw it in his waste-paper bin. He then sat down at his desk, picked up Miss Childs's letter and re-read it, snorting contemptuously.

"Bloody woman! She doesn't know the meaning of *extreme anxiety*," he spat, thinking about the hours he had spent working throughout the summer. He turned his attention to the receipts clipped to the back of the letter. One was a hand written note for the packets of condoms, with a *nota bene* that they were purchased from a vending machine. The other consisted of two receipts taped together: the carrots had obviously been bought on consecutive days, but from the same shop, Poskett's in Pepper Hill.

Chapter 34

George caught the bus from Ashfield to Cliffend High. Today was the start of his two-year GCSE course. When the bus arrived at school, he disembarked and joined his classmates as they walked in through the side entrance and down the familiar corridors; these now seemed smaller and more crowded than they had at the end of last term.

The school smelt of polish mixed with a hint of fresh paint, over-ridden by the spirit of new clothes and fresh beginnings, and a trace of inciting perfume worn by some of the older girls. The slanting sunshine from the high windows striped the pupils' heads as they ambled along the corridors to their designated places.

Inside the classroom, George took his seat at a desk somewhere in the middle of the group and waited. After registration, the first period of the new term was always dedicated to assigning timetables and ironing out any discrepancies or queries. The head oversaw this period at the beginning of Year Ten, on the pretext that he could immediately authorise any changes that might be required.

George looked at his watch; he would have been hard at work by now if he had still been at Tarskers.

The longer they waited, the more noise the excited young teenagers made – scraping chair legs, slightly adjusting desk positions, dropping bags onto the floor. General scuffles began to take place as they produced various books, paper and writing implements.

George felt hot; he removed his jacket and straightened his tie. He glanced around; most of his mates looked as if they had been hastily stuffed into their uniforms this morning and, in the course of their journeys to school, shirt tails had been pulled out of waistbands, new shoes scuffed and laces loosened, ties either skewed or half undone; blazers mostly too big, or too small, already bore the ravages of having been used as goal posts with blades of cut grass and traces of mud clinging on. Almost every boy looked as if he had been marched into the barbers last week for a haircut, the razor-sharp edges still evident. He did not even dare to scrutinise the girls.

George felt increasingly uncomfortable and out of place; he had grown too much over the summer holidays, working each day, taking some of the responsibility for looking after Rosie, helping Nora and Henry at the pub. His knack of being able to concentrate on the job at hand helped him not be overwhelmed by his circumstances; the disadvantage to this being that he now felt too big for the compartment in his life in which he dealt with school. The teachers treated Year Ten students (over the holidays which ended Year Nine, they had transformed from *pupils* into *students*,) with greater respect than the younger years, but the youngsters themselves were still acting like children, even though some were nearly fifteen years old. George was fourteen, his birthday was in

February. But he felt so much older and more mature than those around him; he felt he missed out the juvenile phase of his growing up, even before his parents had died; maybe he had only been trying to keep up with his older sister. And the classroom this morning was making him restless, claustrophobic and impatient.

He thought about Rosie. She was starting her course at Clifftech next week, studying accounts, economics, shorthand, typing and word-processing – computers were now taking over from typewriters. She also had the option to sit her exams from last summer. But George knew she wouldn't cope with it all: to succeed, she needed to want to go there, do the work and pass the exams. And, at the moment, she didn't. She just wanted to be with Henry – which, in a way, was understandable. They seemed happy together, especially when they were visiting car boot sales and charity shops looking for anything cockerel-related.

"Right you lot," Mr Morsley said as he burst into the classroom, his voice relaying his annoyance. "In your seats."

The majority of the students quietly slipped onto their chairs and made an attempt to look as if they were ready. Two of the lads, however, decided to ignore the instruction. George felt a flutter of irritation ripple through him; he thought, if they had to be here in school, they might just as well get on with it. And if these two were playing up now, what kind of tricks had they planned for the supply teacher whom, they had been informed in advance, was taking the lesson after break.

Personal Development. Whatever was that supposed to mean? In his mind, he tried to compare himself today with the person he had been at the beginning of September last year, and concluded that would be a good way to measure *personal development*, in all senses of the words.

"Tillinger, stop day-dreaming and answer your name to the register," George heard Mr Morsley bellow over the noise from the two idiots in the corner.

"Sir," he replied with anger. He was not a child, and yet here he was answering his name to confirm his presence, the same as he had almost ten years ago when he first started school.

"Right, as you know, the first period this morning is given over to sorting out your timetables." He turned to the roller black board behind him, on which he had drawn up the general class schedule, but with certain periods left blank. "Copy this out, everyone. Then come and see me individually, and we'll fill in the missing sections."

This was the part of the first day back that Mr Morsley absolutely dreaded; no matter how many hours he slaved over the timetables, somehow, somewhere, something went wrong: lessons, classes, teachers and/or class rooms would be double booked. His headache was worsening. He wanted to open one of the windows a little, but he knew at least one of the students would complain of a draught.

And, yes, there were anomalies, but none were too difficult to resolve. He sent the class out when the bell announced the mid-morning break, telling them all to be back promptly.

Twenty minutes later, the students returned. George was still in the corridor when he heard laughter erupt from those already in the room. As he walked through the door, on the teacher's desk at the front, he saw two supermarket carrier bags filled with large, straight, shiny, fresh orange carrots. A plastic container was placed beside them and, through the clear sides George could see foil packs of condoms.

In disgust, George turned around and left Cliffend High School. He quickly walked the short distance to Tarskers Engineering.

Two hours later, in the foreman's office, Mr Boston finally persuaded the teenager to talk. But when George started to explain, nothing made sense. Eventually, though, and because he knew the family's history, he pieced together the reasons the lad had suddenly appeared at his works this morning when he should have been back at school. He immediately rang Nora Stickleback, who had already been contacted by Mr Morsley.

"Thank you for letting me know, Mr Boston," Nora said, relieved that George was safe. "They rang and told me he had vanished from lessons. I was a bit worried, but I assumed he would come home at some point."

"It's okay. I tell you what, if you sort out the school, I'll keep him occupied here. I think he just needs adult company, rather than being sent back into the classroom – he may have outgrown school."

"Well, if you think it'll be okay. But that won't solve the problem long term, will it? He's got another two years before he can leave and get a job. He'll have to go back tomorrow."

Still holding the telephone receiver, Graham Boston looked up towards George. He was sitting in the outer office, hunched over a cup of coffee. Derek Tillinger and Graham had been mates as well as colleagues, and he wished there was something he could do.

"Well, I'll make sure he gets back to Ashfield when he's ready," he said, thinking that he would give Personnel a ring when he'd finished speaking with Nora. The main problem was that George was only fourteen - he was too young for any of the training courses on offer. But Graham had promised to sort something out, hopefully in conjunction with his GCSEs.

When the call ended, Nora went through to the lounge-bar from the kitchen; she found Henry cleaning the fireplace. She explained what had happened, finishing with, "So when he does arrive home, don't make a big thing of it, although I expect Rosalie will have something to say about her little brother absconding from school."

"Yeah, I bet she will," Henry confirmed. "Sounds more like something she would do rather than George."

"I know. But at least it solves the mystery as to where all the condoms Max bought from the machine in the Gents' might have gone."

"Well, yes. But not really, though," Henry replied thoughtfully. "I mean, if they are the same ones, obviously he wasn't going to use them to demonstrate to a class full of kids himself."

"No, apparently it was a Miss Childs – Alice? Do you know her?"

"Yeah, she used to fill in for teachers who were away at Cliffend High School. Supply teacher or something, she was called. Not really the kind of person you would expect to teach that sort of thing, though; she's quite quiet, someone's old maiden aunt you would think to look at her."

Nora frowned before asking hesitantly, "So, did anyone ever make you put condoms on carrots? Henry blushed deep crimson, but finally admitted that he had skived off those lessons.

"Well then," Nora continued. "if Max bought the condoms for Alice, what's the connection between Alice and Max?"

"I told you he had a girlfriend, didn't I?" Polly interrupted mother and son's conversation. They hadn't heard her arrive. "I thought I'd better warn you, Rosalie's just got off the bus. Looks like she's been back to the Old Police House. She's carrying a big bag, probably full with her clothes and things."

"You'd better go and help her, Henry," Nora suggested. "And, when you tell her about George, be tactful, please."

"I'm always tactful, Mum," Henry stated grumpily.

Chapter 35

The rain began to fall as Henry and Rosalie set off for Cliffend College on the third Monday in September. Henry was still using Nora's car, but harboured dreams of buying his own soon.

Rosalie did not speak a word for the entire journey. She clutched her brand new bag tightly to her chest; it was filled with fashionable student requisites, plus her Walkman and spare cassette tapes purchased the previous week; George had even lent her his latest tape of *The Pythons*.

Henry scowled as he drove, wishing he had thought to buy Rosalie a gift to cheer her up – a little something to have with her while they were apart, to show he was thinking of her. He realised, however, that no amount of trinkets or fancy objects would take away her loss or make her feel better at times like these. And the further they travelled towards Cliffend, the deeper the frown on Rosalie's face became; she dreaded the thought of college and all the new people she would have to meet.

"It'll be okay," Henry reassured her as he drove into the students' car park. "There's bound to be someone here that you know."

"But they won't necessarily be on my course, will they?" she retaliated harshly. Henry's smile vanished. He was becoming adept at absorbing her outbursts, but somewhere deep inside he was still only a teenager who missed his Dad. He had to live with the memory of discovering Woody on the floor, agonisingly incoherent, vomiting and soaked in blood. And he watched him die. He swallowed back the image that would not quite be buried.

Then he felt ashamed because the situation was as bad for his Mum as it was for him. Henry worked as hard as he could to make things easier for her. But he was also experiencing his first love, at least he thought he was and that alone should have been a momentous episode in his life.

Last week Mr Boston had driven George back to the pub on the first day of school term.   Luckily, George had settled back into school; Mr Morsley having told him, if he studied hard and gained decent grades in the core GCSE subjects, he could transfer to a trainee course sponsored by Tarskers at the end of it. But, it was impressed upon him, he had to do his exams first. In the meantime, Mr Boston had arranged for him to work at the company on Saturdays, and during holidays. George seemed content with this outcome.

"I'll be alright, Henry," Rosalie eventually responded. For a few moments, they had both been lost in their own thoughts, and this seemed to have calmed her. "Thanks for giving me a lift," she said, when they arrived.

"Right," Henry replied, smiling. The pair leant towards each other and kissed on the lips, as if they had been this close for a long while. But this was, in fact, the first time it had happened. And they were both relieved that it was spontaneous.

"Remember, if you want me to come and pick you up early, let me know – you said there's a public phone box near the canteen, didn't you?"

"Refectory," she corrected him. He furrowed his brows as he stared blankly back. "It isn't called a *canteen* in college, it's a *refectory*!"

"Oh," he said, obviously unimpressed. Then he remembered George had taken her to a *refectory* at Mattingburgh cathedral the day of Woody's funeral.

"Anyway, yes there is," Rosalie confirmed as she opened the passenger's door and climbed out. "But I'll be fine, I promise. Now, go – you're blocking those two spaces." Rosalie pointed to the marked bays in front of them. Henry nodded as she closed the door. He reversed up then set off for the exit, returning her wave as he watched her in his rear view mirror.

But Rosalie wasn't fine. She walked with trepidation into the cavernous foyer of Clifftech, which smelt almost the same as school. The space in the middle was noisy and crowded with milling students, chattering and laughing – mostly in groups, some in pairs; Rosalie saw no one else on their own. Various tables had been erected around the walls, and on these lay folders which she later discovered were registers for the various departments. Banners had been erected above each table to advertise the different courses offered. She tried to make her way to the stand marked *Business and Commercial Courses*, but a rowdy group in front of her suddenly started jeering. They turned around and blocked her way before they surged towards the front entrance. Someone knocked into her. Although she prevented herself from falling, she dropped her bag. Her books and pencil case, the Walkman and her cassettes spilled out.

"Now look what you've done, Col!" one lout called to his mate. Rosalie crouched down, mortified that her personal belongings were on display to so many strangers.

"Sorry," a voice that held no contrition muttered above her head. Then three pairs of trousered knees plummeted to the floor and hands began to scrabble at her things.

"What's going on here, boys?" a voice boomed out, causing the lads to stand up in response.

"Nothing sir, we were just helping," the jeering lout stated unapologetically.

"Right then, off you go now. I'll see to this young lady," he ordered. Grudgingly, they accepted their dismissal and left. But the foyer remained crowded and Rosalie could still feel many pairs of eyes watching her. At last she managed to gather everything and crammed them back into her bag.

"Are you all right?" the man asked, holding her elbow to steady her as she stood up.

"Yes, thank you," she replied, her face burning with humiliation. She blinked several times, but could not look directly at him; instead her eyes rested on the name tag suspended on a length of faded red tape from his neck; *Mr Roy Hoppen, Head of English*, it read.

"You look a little confused," he observed. "May I help you? Which course are you on?"

"Secretarial with 'O' levels – I mean, GCSEs,"

she replied.

"Okay, well I think you need to register over here," he said, steering Rosalie to a stand at the rear corner of the foyer adjacent a set of stairs. "The tutor on duty will direct you from there."

Chapter 36

Steady rain fell throughout the week following Rosalie's first day at Clifftech. Today the sky remained heavy with dark grey clouds bubbling their way across from south-west to north-east, and the autumnal chill had caused Nora to light the fire in the lounge-bar at The Fighting Cock.

She tidied the hearth, dismayed at the increasing number of cockerel items that had appeared on the mantel piece, window sills, shelves and anywhere that had previously been a blank space. And they all now required daily dusting, especially when the fire was in use and the ash needed clearing. She sighed as she inspected her grubby hands, then set off towards the kitchen to wash them.

Recent days had been difficult and not only because of the drab weather. Rosalie had left her first day at Clifftech early and, although she insisted she had no lectures scheduled for after lunch, Nora suspected there was a deeper problem. On a lighter note, she reflected that maybe it was just a Tillinger trait; they didn't like the afternoons of first days.

When Rosalie returned last Monday, she had ensconced herself in her room, placed her Walkman earphones on her head, switched on the cassette and lay on her bed humming and singing along to songs that only she could hear. Fortunately, Henry had been at home, working his way through a mug of his tea/coffee concoction, which he drank almost as if it was a penance. He sat with her for a while, explaining later that they were making a list of the books and things Rosalie needed for her course.

This morning, Henry had cleaned and changed the pipes on the barrels, brought up crates of drinks from the cellar and refilled the shelves behind the bar. He and Rosalie had made breakfast, then Henry drove to Cliffend, dropping George off at the high school and Rosalie at college. However, it was now mid-morning and he had not yet returned. Nora cleared the kitchen, not bothering with breakfast for herself, then tidied up around the bar before picking up the local newspaper. She took this to a table near the fireplace in the corner; the flames in the grate were an invitingly warm yellow and orange colour. As she sat down heavily, she was thinking that they reminded her of Henry's infernal cockerel mug, and of the picture on the plate which Rosalie had found for his birthday.

The Cliffend Herald had been delivered on Friday morning, but so far Nora had not had time to read it. Now, she needed to relax for a few minutes, so she placed it on the table in front of her. She was thirsty, but her legs ached too much for her to bother to walk through to the kitchen and make a cup of tea. She looked at her watch, ten-thirty. Polly would arrive soon; they could start the day with a drink and a chat.

Nora glanced at the front page of the newspaper, but found that the print was too small for her to read without her glasses. She remembered using them in the kitchen at some point, and thought she had probably left them in their usual place, next to the kettle. If she got up now, she could boil the water to make the tea...

"Morning, Nora," Polly's bright voice broke into her dreams. She realised she had fallen asleep.

"Hello, Polly." She looked at her watch again. "Good grief, I must have dozed off!" Over an hour had passed.

"Yes, I thought as much." Polly touched the landlady's shoulder kindly. "Don't worry, we can soon get ready. Henry's done all the heavy lifting – he's a real treasure, you know, Nora. You should be proud of him."

"I am," Nora confirmed, a little annoyed at having this pointed out to her. "I'm proud of them all!"

Polly smiled before replying, "Right. Tea first. Then we can open up." She turned to walk away, but spun back again. She opened her mouth to say something, but then changed her mind. "Tea," she repeated.

A few minutes later, she returned with a tray laden with the teapot, cups, saucers, spoons, sugar, milk, and a plate containing two cheese sandwiches.

"I bet you haven't had any breakfast yet, have you?" Polly asked as she bent down to place the tray on the table, and in doing so revealed far more of her bosom than Nora wished to see. Not waiting for a reply as she handed Nora the sandwiches, Polly continued, "By the way, the red light is blinking on the telephone answering machine, I think you've got a message."

"It might be Henry," Nora said, unnecessarily, as she replaced the plate on the tray and slowly stood up. She walked stiffly to the bar and into the kitchen. Pressing the button on the machine, she winced as Henry's detached voice started to speak.

"I'll be another hour or so, I just want to have a look in that new second-hand shop on the retail estate on the way home."

Nora laughed to herself at the description *new second-hand shop*. There was bound to be a clever name for it. She would ask George later, or Max or Quinny when they came into the bar.

There had been a lot of controversy about the new retail park being built on the outskirts of Cliffend, but planning permission had been granted by the local authority on the condition that the developers allowed half a dozen local businesses to rent units at reasonable rates. These were now all taken, whereas many of the larger shops remained empty.

"Henry's looking around junk shops again," Nora advised Polly when she returned to the seats around the table near the hearth. The fire had burnt down, but a warmth glowed red from the remnants of two large lumps of coal.

"What on earth is he going there for?" Polly asked.

"I think he's developing a magpie complex, or a cockerel complex – look at all these bits and pieces he's been buying. And they're all *cockerels*, in the shape of cockerels, or they show cockerels!" Nora exclaimed, but with an exasperated smile.

Polly had to admit that this was true. A black,

cast iron cockerel-shaped door stop was ready and waiting to prop the front door open. Most of the ash trays along the bar and on the tables had been provided by the brewery, but dispersed here and there were various others either shaped as, or depicting, cockerels; an ancient and faded painting had appeared on the wall by the side of the chimney breast featuring two fighting cocks, complete with barbaric spurs and head irons.

"And he was complaining the other day that someone had stolen a rather nice vase with farmyard-type scene on it – a cockerel and several hens and their chicks," Polly said.

As Nora looked around, she felt her eyes droop, and the fingers of the hand holding her plate relaxed. Polly reached over and retrieved it, then sighed as she watched the landlady's eyelids flutter then fall.

A few moments later, when Nora jolted herself awake again, she said,

"I'm a bit tired today, Polly. I think I'll ring Craig in a little while and ask how he's fixed to come in and help."

Chapter 37

"Oxymoron," Quinny stated sagely as he supped his pint. Today, he had one manila-coloured rubber band on his left wrist, almost disappearing beneath his watchstrap, and three on his right; the two outer ones were dark brown, and the middle one faded red. The bands were clearly visible as he raised his glass to his lips. "The word for something that seems to contradict itself – oxymoron."

"Clever-sod-type moron," Max commented, thinking if he were still seeing Alice she would have known that. She had said she would send a post card when the cruise docked at their first port, but he had received nothing as yet. He grunted meditatively to himself. His trips to the bookies had been less eventful since she had decided to go away. She had never seemed the spontaneous type but, within a couple of days of what he now thought of as the carrots and condoms' incident, she'd handed her notice into the school and booked herself on a world cruise.

Max had wondered if Alice had expected him to go with her, or do something to make her stay – offer to marry her, perhaps. He chuckled at this as he raised his pint to his lips, thinking even Alice would not try that – or, if she did, her plans had gone awry. Even so, he was eagerly awaiting the results of the 2.45 race in which he had backed a three year old filly, *Evening Alice*, at 15 to one.

"That's it," Nora replied.

"That's what?" Polly asked, having just returned to the bar carrying four glasses in each hand, clasping them individually with her long fingers and thumbs.

"When Henry said on the answerphone earlier that he was visiting that new second-hand shop."

"Yeah, but it's the shop that's new, not the stock," Max stated, determined not to be up staged.

Max's formal education had ended abruptly when he was fifteen: his father, who had been forced to leave school at fourteen, insisted he found a job as soon as he could. George was now fourteen and Max saw the irony: George wanted to leave school but couldn't, Max had wanted to stay on but had to leave.

But Max did not really know George, who, as this conversation unfolded in the bar at The Fighting Cock public house, was in the lounge at the Old Police House in Pepper Hill.

George had Games that afternoon at school, followed by Music; he wished to participate in neither of these subjects. He caught the bus lunchtime and travelled from Cliffend, past Ashfield and on to Pepper Hill. On the way, he saw the poster on the notice board outside St Jude's Church. *Autumn Bazaar*, the advert stated, with a date in four weeks' time. *Bric-a-brac, Jumble, Craft products, Prizes for Raffle. All items to be left in the Church, at Pepper Hill's Village Hall or the Rectory* up to three days before the event.

George looked around at the pictures, photos, ornaments, furniture and knick-knacks. No one else would want these, they were too personal; the blanket Rosie had crocheted when she was twelve: miss-matched, misshapen squares made up of nylon, acrylic and wool, some now stretched, others shrunk. The colours clashed in places, and stitches were splitting: trebles, George remembered her calling them, because to make one, the yarn had to be passed round the hook on three occasions. It had been their mother's favourite blanket: no one else should have it, or anything else belonging to their family.

But George didn't think his future included remaining in PepperAsh or Cliffend, or even Mattingburgh. He would make his home elsewhere. He would have no need for these things.

Rosie would marry Henry – everyone could see that! But he hoped this would be right for them both, not just a way of coping. He wanted Rosie to be happy. He wanted Henry to be happy. He wanted to be happy.

He sank down onto the chair with the crochet rug, and pulled it around him.

Chapter 38

"The bishop said I should promote the church more, be active in the community, socialise and show an interest in people's goings on," Quinny was explaining to Nora, Max, Polly and Henry in The Fighting Cock on the evening of the last Wednesday in September. Max spluttered into his pint at the rector's last comment.

"*People's goings on?*" he queried incredulously.

"Yes, people's goings on! They were his exact words." Quinny set down his pint, wiped the back of his hand across his lips, then absentmindedly fingered the faded red elastic band around his wrist. He looked at Max and continued, "Should I have poked my nose in to find out why you were buying up all the condoms a while back?"

Henry turned away, thankful that other customers needed serving. Business didn't really warrant three members of staff on duty, but Rosalie was upstairs supposedly practising her shorthand and he was at a loose end.

"I could come downstairs and try to take down people's conversations," she had offered earlier, her pencil hovering menacingly over a blank page in her shorthand pad.

"No, no," he had replied briskly. "Just stick to the tapes they've given you. Lucky you've got your Walkman, so you won't be distracted by anything else."

Now Henry was thinking it was a good job she was not noting down this conversation; he knew it would end with lewd comments about carrots. Rosalie was adamant her class had not been subjected to the lesson that had been planned for George's group.

By the time Henry had served and tendered change to the last of the waiting customers, the talk had turned to a Christmas Fayre and the need to raise money for the church's fabric fund.

"Thought you were saying at one point about an Autumn Fayre," Max stated. He didn't like the idea of people asking him for money; nobody had ever given him any charity, nor had he wanted it. At the moment, he was building up quite a nice stash from his winnings; he liked to think of this as a shrewd investment, betting every so often on horses, greyhounds or football match results – but only backing the ones that really stood out to him. His job earned him just enough to live on. Agricultural wages had always been minimal: for luxuries beyond a couple of pints in an evening, he relied on his gambling.

And this made him miss Alice again. In the smoky atmosphere of the lounge-bar, he felt his stomach constrict; he looked downwards and studied his work-boot resting on the brass rail secured along the bottom of the bar.

"Well, if you do go to the bazaar/fayre thing, Henry," Nora said, thinking it was a shame to miss the opportunity of donating that enormous but ugly brown bear she still had stowed in the back of her wardrobe as a raffle prize; it was still in its clear wrapping, so it would be nice and clean for the next person, "please don't come back with any more *cockerels!*" She exaggerated her complaint, but everyone nodded agreement that the place was beginning to look like a chicken coop.

Henry's latest acquisitions were two tall book-supports, which he had positioned at either end of the mantel above the corner fireplace. There were no books held between them, and behind each bird was a flat back, to be placed against the wall. The fronts each depicted a fierce-looking cockerel; they faced each other, and both were highly coloured with their iridescent tails feathers fanned, and wings spread defensively. Their bodies were a mix of orange, yellow and crimson feathers, which mirrored the flames in the fire-grate below. Their toes tapered to long black talons; their beaks were open, above which black eyes with white rings glared.

"What? You mean you don't like Morris and Mortimer?" Henry teased.

"And what makes it worse is that you name the bloody things," Nora exclaimed, then apologised to the rector for swearing.

"Oh, don't worry about him," Max stated, moving his empty pint glass across the bar top towards Polly. "He's used to hearing worse! Huh, what am I saying? He's used to using worse!"

Quinny grunted, slid his glass next to Max's and said, "Same again, please Polly. Max's paying; and if he complains, I'll deduct it from his donation to next Sunday's collection."

"You miserly old bugger…"

"That's enough, Uncle Max," Polly chastised as she started to pour the drinks. Max did not like being called *uncle*.

Nora quietly left the group and Henry also seized his opportunity to escape, moving quickly out amongst the customers and tables to collect glasses; he returned a few moments later to wipe the surfaces and distribute new beer mats. He stood for a moment when he reached the table by the fireplace, looked up at his two fine specimens on the mantel-piece, and smiled. When he glanced down at the beer mats remaining in his hand, a vivid memory flooded his mind.

Henry did not think about Woody if he could prevent it and, when his father did intrude on his thoughts, he usually tried to push these aside. But today the memory refused to be dislodged.

"This place is unique, son," he had said. "Every other pub with a similar name is called The Fighting Cocks – plural, you see?" It was one of the few occasions that Woody was sober. "But this one's The Fighting Cock! Singular. Oh, I know what they say about me being able to pick a fight with myself and not needing anyone else around. But that's not true, son. I need people. I need your Mum. I need you. And I need this." He had gestured to the pub. "Never forget, Henry, this is the only one of its kind. And one day I'll buy it for you and your Mum."

Henry was still replaying this conversation, when he realised Nora was speaking to him. She had to repeat herself,

"I'll finish here, if you want to go and see if Rosalie's okay. It's nearly ten o'clock and she usually comes to join us before this. Make sure she isn't working too hard up there. It isn't busy now; Polly and I can manage." There were seven customers in, including Max – Quinny had left at the same time as old Poskett, who had offered him a lift back to the rectory in the shop's van.

"Right, well. If you're sure," Henry replied enthusiastically.

"Go on, before I change my mind and make you stay 'til closing time," Nora teased. Henry looked tired; she felt exhausted herself, but she thought it would be good for him and Rosalie to spend some time together.

Nora sat down behind the bar again and fanned herself with an advertising leaflet she had been reading earlier. She decided that, if she didn't stop feeling so hot and tired soon, she would make an appointment to see Doctor Thorne. She had experienced the menopause a few years' ago, barely noticing the slow decline of her monthly periods at the time. But now she was burning up with one hot flush after another.

"I'll take her a coffee," Henry said, then offered, "Would anyone else like one?"

"I'll do ours in a minute," Polly stated. "You just go and see if Rosalie's okay."

Chapter 39

Upstairs, Rosalie had worked on her homework until she felt herself begin to doze, taking the recent happenings in her shorthand classes with her into her dreams.

Yesterday, they had undertaken a short recap from the beginning of the course. Now, her subconscious was hearing the sentence *Stow the oats in the base of the boat and tow it to the bay* whilst her fingers twitched to make the correct pencil strokes.

"What's *tow*" the girl sitting next to her had asked the tutor. Teachers at college were called either tutors or lecturers, Rosalie had discovered on her first day, and lessons were lectures; pupils – as in Year Ten and onwards at school – were students.

The shorthand tutor's name was Mrs Handly, a short Northumbrian lady with a thick accent.

She stood up and demonstrated the outline on the board behind her, enunciating the word slowly in order to allow the young, mostly indigenous East Anglians in the group time to understand. The students found dictation especially hard because of this. Mrs Handly failed to realise that she was only accentuating the consonants; her vowels still sounded very flat and foreign to them.

"It will stand you in good stead for the world of work," she had explained when one particular student complained that she couldn't understand. "Not all bosses will speak perfect English." She was acutely aware, of course, of how broad some of the students' accents were, even if they themselves didn't realise. "Anyway, if you stopped chewing that disgusting gum, you might be able to hear more clearly. Here," and she tore a piece of paper from her own shorthand note pad, walked over to the offending student and placed it on the desk. "Put the gum in here, and then throw it in the bin."

"Not bloody likely," the girl replied. The remainder of the class perked up at this response, and were watching with interest, hoping for a drama to unfold; for some of them, college was proving every bit as boring as school. The girl inhaled sharply as if she were about to speak again. But in doing so, she sucked the chewing gum to the back of her throat and started to choke.

Mrs Handly patted the student hard between her shoulder-blades. The gum flew out of her mouth and, surprisingly, landed on the piece of paper.

"There," Mrs Handly said in a calm and patronising manner, "That's what happens when you chew that revolting stuff! Now go and put it in the bin, before we lose any more time from our lesson."

"Lecture," a voice from behind Rosalie corrected.

"Not bloody likely," the gum chewer replied a second time. Student and tutor locked into a glaring match.

After a few minutes of silent battle, Mrs Handly triumphed. Still glowering, but blushing deeply, the student grabbed the piece of paper containing the gum, scrunched it up, marched over to the wastepaper bin and hurled it in. It made a remarkably loud sound, considering its small size.

"Right, now you can leave," Mrs Handly ordered.

"What?" the girl scoffed. "I've done what you frigging well wanted me to! What's your problem now?"

"Your attitude," Mrs Handly replied. "Unlike school, you do not have to be here and I do not have to teach you. You don't want to be here. I do not want you here. Go."

"Are you chucking me out?" the girl asked incredulously. She shrugged her shoulders and looked around at her fellow students, expecting their support. Although everyone had all been watching, they – as one – turned their eyes downwards and studied their notes, their books or whatever else was on the desk in front of them.

"You are disrupting the other students, who are all here to learn. You obviously do not want to learn…"

"What, just because I was chewing some bloody gum? For Christ's sake!" shecursed.

"Because you were being insolent." A challenging and stern silence followed. The girl then snatched up her bag, leaving her books and pencil case on the desk, and stomped out. She pulled the door behind her, intending to make it slam, but the automatic closure mechanism drew it sedately shut.

"Right, girls," Mrs Handly had returned to her desk at the front from which she now addressed them. "Shall we get on?"

Rosalie had not mentioned this episode to Henry or George, or to Nora: Nora looked fraught when they had arrived home, and Rosalie had cooked tea for them, shepherd's pie, using minced lamb, and a secret mix of herbs for the gravy. She always grated cheese on top and browned it in the oven, because her Mum had done so. But Annie's cheese had been red Leicester; it had a pleasing colour and a tang to its taste. Nora only had cheddar, which neither she nor George liked, but she did not have the heart to ask for anything different.

Rosalie almost awoke, but was still too sleepy to continue with her homework. She removed the headphones and scratched at her scalp where the top had been resting. She roused herself enough to discard her Walkman, together with the boat that had oats stowed in the base and was being towed to the bay – the tape in the cassette had finished anyway. Instead, she wrote Henry's name on a clean page, intending to learn how to write it in shorthand. But she had forgotten what to do. She wrote her own name, then experimented with signatures. And after a while she tried again to write shorthand.

Break it down, like spelling, she told herself. *The first soft vowel sound will give the line position – e, heh.* She fumbled with her text book and found she was wrong; the correct vowel 'e' sound was shown as a light dot. She told herself to go back to look for H. But as she flicked through the pages, she saw so many exercises and short-forms, phrase drills and test pieces that the entire subject overwhelmed her and she just wanted to cry. She flopped backwards onto her pillows and desperately searched her inner reserves for a solution.

"When you start to panic," her wise, younger brother had told her after the exam debacle in the summer term. *"Stop. Put down whatever you are doing. Relax. Close your eyes. Breathe in. Breathe out. Concentrate just on that. Nothing else matters. When you start to feel better, think of warm sunshine. Think of nice things."*

On the third occasion, he'd had to repeat this advice to her, she had wailed, *"But I always end up thinking about Mum and Dad!"*

"Then think about me instead," George had responded. *"Think about how irritating and annoying I am when I call you* Rosie!"

It worked, and she was imagining hiding his underpants in the freezer when her pencil slipped from her hand and she fell properly asleep.

Henry left the bar and went through to the kitchen. He made a cup of coffee for Rosalie – decaffeinated, because she sometimes had trouble sleeping. He also made a mug of his tea/coffee concoction in his special ceramic pot. Henry was not worried that the caffeine in three heaped teaspoons of coffee plus a tea bag, or the amount of sugar he heaped in, would keep him awake, he could sleep whatever, whenever, wherever.

He held the tray of coffee and a plate of biscuits in one hand and knocked quietly on Rosalie's bedroom door with the other. When there was no reply, he tapped again and called her name. Still there was no answer. He carefully opened the door and peeped in. Rosalie lay on her side on top of the bedcovers, her notepad and pencil in one hand and her abandoned Walkman and headphones just beyond reach of the other. She moved slightly when he placed the tray on the dressing table. He didn't like to disturb her, and stood watching her as she slept.

After a few moments, though, Henry realised Rosalie would be startled if she suddenly awoke to find him staring down at her. He bent over, gently lifted Rosalie's hand and removed the notepad from underneath; the wires on the spiralled top had dug into her fingers and turned the soft flesh a harsh pink.

He straightened up and studied the hieroglyphics on the page. Underneath each statement were indecipherable squiggles and strokes. Further down, Rosalie had written the name *Rosalie Stickleback*. A squiggle she had previously used for her name was under Rosalie. But there were several attempts to write *Stickleback* by the side of it; the last one was struck through with an angry, dark line.

She had also practiced her imagined signature several times, each one differently, with extra or exaggerated flourishes; the one Henry preferred was in her own small, neat, slightly forward sloping handwriting: it was as unique as she was.

Chapter 40

In early December, the Fighting Cock was already being prepared for the festive season. Henry and George strung fairy lights around the car park perimeter and amongst the bushes close to the door. In the lounge-bar an enormous Christmas tree had been erected in the opposite corner to the fireplace: it looked real, but was in fact an artificial one. Extra baubles and other decorations seemed to have been added over the weeks; Rosalie enjoyed looking out for unusual trimmings and such during her lunchtime trips into Cliffend from the college. The overall effect was probably a little garish, but the customers commented that it felt festive and bright. A few then regularly asked when the mistletoe would be hung up. The landlady ignored them.

As Nora had anticipated, Christmas Eve had been very busy. They had opened at six o'clock and within an hour the bar was crowded. The cigarette smoke hung thick in the air, and the flames from the fire reflected brightly on the red, silver, gold, green and blue tinsel decorations all around.

By eight-thirty in the evening, Nora was exhausted, and hardly able to remember the orders, let alone draw them, add up the cost and return the correct change. New customers were replacing those leaving. Max sat on his stool at the bar resolutely not moving, but downing a pint approximately every half an hour.

"What's happened to the new chap?" he asked Nora as she prepared yet another round.

"Craig's in for New Year's Eve, so it's just us, tonight," Nora said. Everyone still referred to Craig as *the new chap*. He was a pleasant young man, a disillusioned Psychology student from Mattingburgh University, who still lived with his parents in Cliffend. He explained that he had realised less than a month into the first term that he had chosen the wrong subject to study. He had reapplied for Law starting next year, but was still awaiting a response.

"Your mate not with you?" Stan, another regular, asked Max above the rising noise of chatter and laughter.

"You mean Quinny? The rector?" He received a nod in reply. "No, I expect he's busy down at the church. This and Easter is probably about the only time he actually earns his keep."

"Now, that isn't fair," Nora stated defensively. "He does a lot of good work – things that you don't necessarily see or know about."

"Oh yeah? Like what?"

Nora stared at Max. Although no one really knew how long his affair with Alice Childs had been going on, the longer she was away, the more bitter and cynical he seemed.

"Like," Polly reached over the bar for the ashtray which was now overflowing, not only with ash and cigarette butts, but also cellophane and the dull silver paper from packaging; "he'll be preparing for Midnight Mass – you know, the *biggy,* when baby Jesus is born?"

Max grunted, and pretended not to notice that Polly, deliberately or otherwise, had shaken a sprinkle of ash into his pint. Nora had to look away; as licensee, and the person responsible for health, safety and hygiene throughout the establishment, she should have mentioned the contamination to the customer and reprimanded her employee. But she was just so damn tired, she couldn't be bothered, and didn't care if Max went down with some kind of stomach bug over Christmas and New Year.

"Actually, he was very good to me, you know, when Woody died, especially when the holiday company and the police contacted me about Annie and Derek as well." Her voice had grown quiet and she turned to watch Rosalie and George collecting glasses, tidying up, chatting with the customers and generally just helping.

"It's doing them as much good as it is you," Polly commented, tracing Nora's line of vision and following her thoughts. "What would they be doing if they weren't in here?"

Nora sighed. "Henry should be taking Rosalie out for the evening, spending time with people their own age. And George – well, I'm not sure what he would be doing, maybe out with his mates as well?"

"Well, they aren't! They're all here, where we know they're occupied, safe and – hopefully – relatively happy."

"Anyone want a drink?" Henry asked cheerfully as he returned to the bar.

"Are you offering soft, alcoholic, or hot?" Polly

asked, teasing the lad.

"Mine's a pint," Max stated, hoping no one had noticed him quickly finishing the beer, despite the flakes of ash.

"I thought you were pacing yourself," Nora commented. "You aren't due the next for another – oh, what – quarter of an hour?"

"I'll make an exception, 'specially if it's on the house – you know, to compensate for the ash," he said, pointedly.

"Beer for *Uncle* Max, and coffees for Nora and me," Polly replied, bending forward in front of Max; despite the avuncular reference, she ensured his imagination was left with little work.

"On the house," Nora stated as Polly placed the frothing glass on the beer mat in front of him. "Right, I suppose you want your usual mix, Henry?" she asked as she slid off the stool. As her feet took her weight, she stood still for a second; despite her choice of sensible court shoes, her toes, ankles and calves immediately began to ache. "Won't be a minute," she said as she turned towards the kitchen.

The room was quiet in comparison, even though the door to the lounge-bar was open. Nora sat for a while at the table as she waited for the kettle to boil. This was her first Christmas without Woody, and she twisted her wedding ring around her finger. It was loose now; she didn't wear her engagement ring because the weight of the diamond – not particularly big or impressive, but still heavier than the rest of the ring – turned it around to the underside of her finger and she was concerned in case she lost it: one of the claw fixtures was already damaged.

She placed four ordinary mugs onto the tray, plus Henry's pint pot depicting his famous cockerel. Rosalie's mug – the companion to his - was upstairs on display in her room. Nora   had made his drink several times, but was not completely confident – nor was she sure of the wisdom of him drinking it.

Henry, Rosalie and George had talked earlier about going to Midnight Mass when the pub closed: they were not especially religious, and had never been to the service before. Polly and Nora had also been invited; Polly had declined, saying she needed to get home to Susan, her partner; Nora said she would think about it, see how she felt closer to the time.   But she knew – as, no doubt, they did – that she would just want to go to bed as soon after closing time as she could.

When the last customer had been shooed out, Henry said to his mother, "We'll clear up, if you want to rest for a while."

"Thank you, son. I think I'll just go up now, if that's okay." She wasn't asking his permission, but she should have been the one who ensured that all the jobs were done - that the doors were locked, the till was emptied, the money totalled and put away, and the float returned; that the bar was cleared, and the glasses, if not all washed up and replaced on their shelves, the machine was loaded and switched on. Restocking could wait until the morning. "I won't come to the service with you, I think I'm bit too tired."

"Okay," Henry said and kissed his mother's cheek. "Good night. We're still planning on going, but we'll try to not to disturb you when we get back."

"'Night, Nora," Rosalie said, hugging her. She then followed Henry's lead and kissed her cheek.

"'Night," Nora echoed. George felt a little awkward and was uncertain as to what to do: he was not as demonstrative as his sister. Nora saw his confusion and reached out her arm, patted him on his shoulder and said, "I'm relying on you to look after these two. Make sure they don't stay out too late."

"We're only going to *Midnight Mass*, Mum," Henry protested. "We'll be back after about an hour or so, I would imagine." He looked at his watch and asked, "By the way, what time does it start?"

Chapter 41

Quinny sat in the vestry pinging the elastic band on his wrist. The air smelt of damp stonework, and his breath condensed into mist as he exhaled. Three bars glowed from the silver-backed electric fire by his desk, but he still felt cold; the heating was on in the church, but some of the congregation were bound to complain about the chill.

He reminded himself to thank the good people of the parish who had prepared the church for this festive tide. The interior of the nave was lit only by white lights decorating the enormous Christmas tree on the sanctuary – a real one, not like the one at the pub – and the many, many candles that had been placed upon window sills, side tables, plinths and, of course, on the altar. Vases of chrysanthemums were displayed around the church, with blooms of gold, bronze, maroon and violet; the crib scene was central, placed at the top of the aisle; and the empty manger awaited Jesus – a 1950s plastic baby doll, clothed in swaddling bands.

At this moment, he thought it was all so pointless and, as if to agree, the first twinges of arthritis twisted their white hot pin points into the gaps between his joints. He stopped fiddling with his elastic bands, heaved himself to his feet, opened the tiny north door, and slipped outside.

The night was black, studded only by gleaming silver stars shining so far away. The vastness of the heavens highlighted Quinny's loneliness; there was no one with whom he could share the magic of tonight's Nativity, or the peacefulness and relief of Christmas morning. This was a time for families, and he had no living relatives that he knew of; he just baptised, married and buried other people's.

There would be the odd gift for him from members of the congregation, and he did appreciate their kindness. But he realised how much he would have loved to have seen his own children – maybe, by now, grandchildren – opening their presents. But the thought of toys brought back the memory of the wooden, yellow train with red wheels that he had left in the garden. Even in the darkness, he could picture it, and he reached out his hand towards it. It wasn't there.

Suddenly, he even lost the impetus to ping his elastic bands.

He walked a few paces to and fro, listening to the crisp, frosty grass crackle beneath his feet. He decided there would be no sermon tonight: he would simply wish everyone a Happy Christmas, telling them to attend on Sunday if they wanted a prosperous New Year.

He tutted to himself. As if that would happen! Attendance at Sunday services had been down by at least a quarter during this Advent compared with last year. All in all, it had been a bad twelve months. There had been the deaths of three parishioners, the non-event of either an Autumn or a Christmas bazaar; Bishop Clement's intermittent threats to retire him, relocate him, or add additional parishes to his burden. And the taunts and arguments between various people that he used to see as harmless now felt malicious and spiteful. He exhaled deeply, and a pall of mist plumed out in front of his face.

Mr and Mrs Ervsgreaves would soon be here, one to wind up the congregation's charitable spirit, the other to crank up the organ; both attempting to be humorous, neither actually achieving it.

And this thought alone gave him the energy to snap his rubber bands. Again, and again, until his skin was red and his wrist sore.

Now he was ready to start Christmas!

Chapter 42

Nora thought she could hear voices downstairs. She looked at the alarm clock on her bedside table; it showed a quarter past two in the morning. She sat up and her head swayed for a moment. The room felt cold; the heating went off automatically at midnight.

Midnight. She remembered the youngsters had said they were going to Midnight Mass at St Jude's. She had never known any of them to show any interest in religion before, other than engaging with Quinny in the odd conversation. He was not exactly an evangelist, but perhaps some good had rubbed off after all.

She swung her legs out of bed, wriggled her feet into her slippers and wrapped her dressing gown tightly around her. She walked quietly along the landing and down the stairs, and was greeted by the aroma of warmed mince pies and mugs of hot chocolate.

The whispering voices of the three teenagers grew louder as she reached the door to the kitchen. She was about to speak, just to let them know she was there so they wouldn't be startled by her sudden appearance, when she heard her name mentioned.

"I didn't think your Mum would come with us to church, Henry," George said. "She looked really tired again. Are you sure she's okay?"

"Yeah, I think she just has a lot on," Henry replied, a little defensively. "Here, have another mince pie."

"Won't these be missed?" George asked, picking one up and studying before taking a bite.

"Not really," Rosalie said. "We made loads, and I think I was meant to put these in the freezer, but I forgot. Besides, they are supposed to be eaten, aren't they?"

Nora smiled as she rested against the door jamb, too exhausted to stand properly, but unable to reach a chair without drawing attention to herself.

Henry, George and Rosalie were all sitting on low stools in front of the fire, which had been roused into flames again. The Christmas tree lights were on, creating a soft and magical atmosphere. The two lamps, either side of the main door, gave the only other light. And the youngsters had provided themselves with an impromptu feast. There were plates of mince pies and biscuits, packets of crisps and bottles of cola resting on the hearth. Each had a mug of hot chocolate, including Henry who, for once was not using his tall cockerel pot.

Rosalie was sitting in the middle, with Henry on one side and George on the other. She also accepted a mince pie. George took another, immediately stuffed it into his mouth – which was only big enough to accommodate half – and reached out for a third.

"Hey," Rosalie reprimanded. "Greedy!"

"I'm hungry. Tea was a long time ago, you know. And we've been running around in the bar all evening."

"Not to mention sitting in a cold church for an

hour," Henry added.

"I thought it was a lovely service, with us all singing the carols by candlelight. And there were lots of people there! I didn't think there would be so many."

"You didn't warn us they'd have a collection, though did you, Rosie?" George complained spraying pastry crumbs from his lips. "I only had a fiver!"

"I didn't have anything," she replied quickly with a smirk.

"I had a few odd coins; they made quite a clatter when I put them on the plate," Henry stated.

"It was a bit shiny, wasn't it?" Rosalie commented, not expecting a reply. "Was it brass or copper?"

"Brass," Henry said. "Copper was what I gave them. I even heard old Ervsgreaves complain..."

"Who?" George asked.

"Ervsgreaves – church warden. He was the one with the plate. His missus was playing the hymns."

"Carols," Rosalie corrected him.

"Carols – whatever. Anyway, they come here sometimes – usually only in the summer though, when they can sit outside. She doesn't like cigarette smoke."

"She doesn't like music either, judging by the way she was playing that organ," Rosalie concluded. "Anyway, lucky you two had some money on you."

"Yeah, I noticed you indicated that my contribution was for both of us," George said.

"Well, I'm sure you don't mind, do you?"

Nora smiled as she listened from her vantage point, concluding that they really did seem to all get along with each other, despite being – or because they were – three very distinct and individual characters.

"Oh, stop whingeing, George." Rosalie was scolding her brother again. "Have another mince pie – oh no, you've already had two."

"Three," Henry corrected. "But, who's counting. You have another one, Rosalie."

"I ought not to," she replied hesitantly before adding quickly, "But I am hungry."

"And I'll have the last two," Henry stated.

"No, no. You can't eat them both," Rosalie cried. "We've got to leave one out for Father Christmas!"

"You what?" Henry and George said in unison. Realising their voices had risen in volume, they 'shushed' each other and glanced up to the ceiling. Satisfied that they hadn't disturbed Nora – who they thought was upstairs in bed asleep – Henry continued, "You are not seriously going to leave a mince pie out for Santa Clause, are you?"

"Yes," Rosalie replied innocently. "And a glass of sherry. And something for Rudolph."

The boys both tried not to laugh; for Rosalie's sake they played along.

"Okay, well, I can manage the sherry," Henry said standing the plate carefully on the table behind them. "Er, d'you think he'd prefer sweet, medium or dry?"

"Anything. The stuff out of that blue bottle near the till is nice," Rosalie said, thinking she was being helpful.

"How d'you know which sherry is *nice?*" George asked, pretending to be shocked.

"Nora needed some to put in the Christmas cake about a month ago, so I took a bottle through, and we both had a sip to check it was all right." Rosalie realised half way through her explanation that she was not being very tactful. But a drop of sherry couldn't be condoned as a crime in the circumstances: it would certainly not make her into a raving alcoholic.

Henry did not react, but Nora blanched; she had not thought about it at the time: it was part of the tradition and she could remember tasting sherry when she and her own mother, Elspeth, made their Christmas cakes years and years ago.

Henry simply stood up and walked over to the bar. He returned after a few minutes with a schooner of dark golden liquid that glowed in the firelight. "And here is a sherry – a large glass because by the time Santa reaches here, he'll be knackered and in need of sustenance…"

"Should've left that second mince pie, Henry," George interrupted, belching coarsely and being elbowed by Rosie to say, "Pardon."

"You can talk," Henry rebuffed. "Anyway, what have we got for Rudolph? What do reindeer eat anyway?"

"Carrots," Rosalie announced triumphantly before all three began to giggle; at first they tried to do so quietly, but found it impossible. Just managing to lay down any plates or mugs they were holding, the teenagers lost themselves in a helpless bout of laughter.

Eventually, George regained sufficient self-control to say, "I can't look at a carrot now without thinking of Max and the condoms – not even when they are sliced and cooked on my dinner plate."

"What, the condoms sliced and cooked?" Rosalie queried.

"No, you idiot. Carrots," he retorted before sitting upright. "Come on, we'd better tidy up a bit. I'll dampen down the fire – I just hope the chimney isn't too hot for when Santa climbs down!" He glanced mischievously towards Rosie, who was still trying to muffle her giggles, before continuing, "Then we need to get to bed. We all said we'd help Nora cook Christmas dinner tomorrow."

"Today," Rosalie corrected him.

"Okay smarty-pants. Today. Is the pub open at all, Henry?"

"Yeah, just for a couple of hours later – six 'til eight, I think."

In the darkness and chill of the hall, Nora turned and crept stiffly back up the stairs to her room. She knew she was wrong to be eavesdropping like this. But, in some ways, it had set her mind at rest. Henry, Rosalie and George all seemed as happy as could reasonably be expected. They were sensible youngsters, mature but still able to have fun; and Nora hoped they would raid the bunch of carrots she had in the pantry, and leave at least one out for poor Rudolph.

Chapter 43

The first anniversary of the Tillingers' deaths fell on a Wednesday. Rosalie was a little subdued leading up to the date. All year, she had studied towards sitting her exams this June – academic subjects which she should have taken last year, and business and office-skills qualifications. Her tutors thought she was coping well. Her mock exam results were encouraging; she was not predicted to achieve distinctions in anything, but it was hoped she would pass with reasonable marks – as long as she continued to study and revise.

"I don't think I'll go into college today," she told Henry and Nora at the breakfast table; George had already caught the school bus, and Henry was waiting to drive her in to Cliffend. "I won't be able to concentrate."

"Okay, I know I can't make you go, sweetheart. But don't mope about all day," Nora advised kindly but firmly. "Try to find something positive to do."

"Well, if there were graves I could visit, I would go there – take some flowers or something," she replied truculently. "I wish Aunty Shirley had asked us what we wanted done with Mum and Dad's remains. But she never gave us the chance."

"You can come down to Dad's grave with me later," Henry offered. She leant across and hugged him.

"Yeah, it's a year since you two lost Woody, isn't it?" she replied quietly. "Maybe I will – later. But first..." She didn't finish her sentence. Henry and Nora could see her mind was chasing an idea around her head. "Er, I think I just want to be on my own for a while," she announced as she stood up from the table.

Henry looked over towards his mother. Nora gave a slight smile of encouragement, but shook her head to advise him not to persist.

"We'll be here when you get back," she told Rosalie. Henry watched her go, then started to gather the breakfast crockery.

"Leave that, son," Nora said. "Come and sit down and talk with me for a few minutes."

"Okay," Henry said then returned to his seat. "What do you want to talk about?"

"I just wanted to ask if you were all right. We all seem to be focussing on Rosalie and how she is dealing with the anniversary; maybe we are forgetting that we've all lost someone."

"I'm okay, Mum. Honest. I just want Rosalie to be happy." He looked at her as if searching for an answer. "And you. I want you to be happy too. And, well, you seem to have been really tired for a while."

"Oh, I'm okay really. Just getting old," Nora tried to reassure him. "I'm a lot better now that Craig is here full-time – well almost, anyway."

"How is having to pay another wage affecting the profits, Mum?" Henry asked.

"It's okay. We're doing really well. You know I invested some of the money from my life assurance and your grandmother's legacy into the refurbishment, so there's no loan outstanding.

And, the brewery has confirmed that as soon as we have held the tenancy for fifteen years, which we will have in September, they will sell the place to me, and at pre-refurbishment value – which I was very surprised about."

"Wow," Henry exclaimed, showing uncustomary enthusiasm. "That's brilliant."

"Yes, I must admit, I'm very pleased. It gives us something to look forward to. But there's no reason why we can't celebrate today – let's make it a landmark for you and me, Henry, not just a sorry reminder."

Henry paused for a moment. His life changed so much on that day; before Woody, Annie and Derek had died, he did not have Rosalie. Now she was here, but his Dad and her parents were not.

"Can I tell Rosalie," he asked impulsively, "when she gets back? About buying the pub, I mean."

"Of course. And George," Nora reminded him. "Don't forget to share the news with George."

Rosalie had gone upstairs then crept quietly back down as Nora and Henry were talking at the kitchen table. She left the pub via the lounge-bar and she walked across the car park. She then set off towards Pepper Hill. She thought the bus might come along soon – she looked at her wrist, only to find she had forgotten her watch. She shrugged, and steadied her pace, wanting to enjoy the experience as much as reach her destination. She smiled as she remembered Henry's birthday last September when she had returned to Pepper Hill to wrap his present. But today, she had a different destination in mind.

As she walked, she looked around; the sky above was clear and, despite the early hour, the sun felt hot and strong. The hedges were heavy with leaves of various greens; white blossoms fluttered and let their petals go with the breeze. Bluebells on the verges rocked back and forth amid the luscious grass where the Lords and Ladies were hiding. A wren scolded her from the hedge as she walked too close to its nest.

Shortly after this, she heard a vehicle approach from behind. It drew level with her. She turned around to see the post van. Jim opened the passenger window, leant across and said,

"Hi Rosalie. Do you need a lift anywhere?" He knew her circumstances and, like everyone else, would do anything to help.

"No, thanks. I'm fine. I just wanted some fresh air," she replied politely. Jim smiled and thought maybe the sun would put a little colour into her cheeks.

"Okay then, if you're sure. Look after yourself, now. Bye." And he drove away.

At approximately the midpoint between St Jude's Church and Pepper Hill, there was a length of the road known locally as *the tunnel*; the tree branches on either side met each other across the top, and sunshine did not penetrate the leaves which not only darkened the way, but chilled the atmosphere. A footpath led from the road, through the woods, down to the marshes and across to the River Potch. And a little further along was Ashfield Staithe.

Rosalie had not visited the staithe since her parents moored that night. In fact, she had never been there at all. Now, it was the only place she could think of where she could say a final goodbye. And she wanted to leave something with them. She pulled her hand out of her pocket and unfolded her fingers. Tucked neatly inside a tiny, delicate silk drawstring bag was Annie's gold locket, complete with a heart shaped photo each of her Mum and Dad secured inside.

Rosalie followed the footpath into the woods; she found the atmosphere cooler here. The trees were a mixture of young and sinuous, mature and thriving, old and decaying. The leaves formed a thick, lush-green canopy overhead, through which the sun sparkled and swayed with the breeze.

As she was glancing upwards, her foot caught on something and she nearly stumbled. Looking downwards again she could see a web of roots from the trees all around her; these stood proud of the ground where the soil had been worn away, leaving the path uneven and difficult to walk. She continued carefully, avoiding the hazards and wishing she had worn sturdier shoes.

Within ten minutes, however, Rosalie had reached the slope that took her down onto the marshes. Here the brightness contrasted sharply with the density of the woods, and she smiled at the pleasant view in front of her; patchwork pasture spread out, dotted with cattle and horses. She remained on the path which led by the side of a marsh and up onto the river wall. This raised bank had been built to protect the open and very low-lying marshes from flooding. A flight of wooden steps had been built to give access from the marsh path to the footway on top, and a boarded walkway led directly to the staithe.

Breathless, Rosalie realised she was unfit and needed to take more exercise. As she approached the staithe, she could see two vessels had been moored there: the first was a rowing boat, used by local fishermen; the other a holiday cruiser – much the same, Rosalie surmised, as Peach Dream, the one her parents had hired. She could hear voices close by and shied from approaching. Instead, she walked around the staithe; it was a pretty place with tubs of brightly-coloured flowers and a picnic bench similar to those at The Fighting Cock. A steel meshed pen with a strong lock on the gate had been built into the corner; it held stocks of bottled gas, fuel drums and the like.

By now, Rosalie was hot and thirsty. But she felt exhilarated – as if she were finally achieving something positive. Calmly but with more than a little excitement, she looked around for a suitable spot.

Behind a particularly large trunk among a clump of trees on the approach to the staithe from Ashfield, Henry watched Rosalie stoop down. After chatting with Nora earlier, he had wanted to talk to Rosalie, but she had not said where she was going. Something she had mentioned, however, about not having anywhere to visit made him wonder whether she might wander down here. He knew a quicker way to reach the staithe than walking along the road then taking the path through the woods and over the marshes. He had crossed the road, slid through a gap in the hedge and strode down the side of Tidal Reach's land, just as he, Bloo, Hopper and Sidney used to do when they were children and wanted to go fishing in the Potch. He then picked up the track that ran westward from Cliffend to the staithe. He had reached the trees just as Rosalie climbed up the river bank steps.

Using a piece of flint that had been lying nearby, Rosalie scraped at the ground just beyond the biggest of the flower tubs before digging a hole. Then she took something from her pocket, placed it inside and pushed the earth back over. She stamped it flat, looked around then stared back downwards. Henry had flinched as her gaze swept by, but she obviously did not see him.

She stood reverently, feeling she had offered a sacrifice, a ritual letting go.

"'Bye Mum. 'Bye Dad. I love you both," she whispered. And the wind stole her words from the air and carried them away.

After a few minutes, she turned and retraced her steps from the staithe back onto the river wall, her figure in silhouette long before it disappeared down onto the marsh path.

Henry stayed amidst the trees until he could not see Rosalie. He then walked quickly up onto the walkway and over to the largest flower tub. The patch of disturbed but compressed soil was not difficult to locate. He stared at it for a moment, aware that the sun was streaming down and burning the back of his neck.

"Hello there," a voice from the cruiser called across to him. "Are you waiting for the supplier to open up for gas?" asked a middle-aged man, who was wearing shorts, polo shirt and a floppy floral summer hat.

"No. I, er, I lost something when I was last here. I was just having a look round," he improvised.

"Oh. Anything I can help with?"

"No, no. It's okay. I don't think I'll find it now. Thanks anyway."

The man waved an acknowledgement. When Henry thought he was no longer interested, he bent down. Reaching for presumably the same flint that Rosalie had just used, he removed the earth. It came away easily. Buried about six inches down was a small silken drawstring bag which now had dirt clinging to it. He carefully picked this out and, wiping his hands on his jeans first, he opened it. Inside was a beautiful golden locket, complete with a delicate chain attached.

Henry stood up and turned to face the sun. The light glinted on the gold as he studied it. Using his thumbnail to prise the two halves apart, he could see two tiny, heart-shaped photos inside. He was surprised, and yet unsurprised, to discover that these were of Annie and Derek Tillinger.

Chapter 44

The Christmas preparations for 1989 followed much the same pattern at The Fighting Cock public house in Ashfield as they had the previous year, with one exception. Three days before the big day, Henry had confided in Nora that he intended to ask Rosalie to marry him.

"Not so that I give her an engagement ring as a Christmas present, Mum. I thought I'd propose on New Year's Day."

"What, when you expect she'll be hungover and not notice that she'll be committing herself to you for the rest of her life?" Nora joked. She was overjoyed, and relieved; she had been expecting something like this to happen for a long time.

"No, Mum," the ever-serious Henry replied. "So that the *New* Year will be a *new* start – you know, the first day of the last decade of the twentieth century!"

"It's a bit clichéd, isn't it?" George commented. They had not noticed him join them.

"Well, no. I mean, I suppose it could be seen like that," Henry struggled to explain. "But…"

"It's okay," George said, leaning towards his pal and extending his hand.

Nora compared the two young men. Henry was now twenty years old, no longer a teenager; George, five years his junior was not quite as tall as her son, but broader across the shoulders and chest, and a little thicker around the waist. But Nora knew the extra weight George carried was not puppy fat or flab. It was pure muscle.

George still worked for Tarskers in Cliffend, although an apprenticeship was no longer guaranteed because they were about to be bought out and rebranded by MaCold, a multi-national company, specialising in this part of the country in offshore oil and gas drilling platforms. The name was an acronym of Maintenance and Construction of Offshore to On-Land Direct. Mr Boston, George's mentor and sponsor, was due to retire shortly after the take-over was complete, but had secured a place on a training scheme for him as an interim solution; it would then be George's responsibility to prove his worth, and he was confident the young man would.

"And, if you want my blessing – as the head of the Tillinger household, mate," George said to Henry. "You have it!" They shook hands enthusiastically.

"Thanks – you'll be best man, won't you? I mean, if she says 'yes' when I propose."

"Of course. And of course she'll say 'yes'."

"Well, there you go," Nora stated, pleased and proud of both of them. "And, Henry, don't let Rosalie hear you talking about it before you actually ask her!"

On Christmas Eve morning, Nora had deliberately made extra mince pies and two dozen sausage rolls, stating loudly that she was sure she had over-estimated how many were needed.

"I just hope they'll all get eaten," she concluded.

"Oh, I expect they will – especially if we offer them around the bar during the evening, like we did last year," Rosalie answered as she stood at the sink washing up the crockery, pans and utensils that Nora had used in her final baking session before the big day. Even with her back to her, Nora could see the girl's figure had filled out, with slender curves and a firm softness; she understood why her son had fallen in love with the young and beautiful Rosalie Tillinger. Rosalie then turned around and smiled, still wiping dry a mince pie tray.

Rosalie had been experimenting with different styles for her hair; luckily, it took to being twisted, curled, pinned up, anchored down, flicked and fastened, then glued into place with hair spray, and little harm resulted. Her locks were blonde, slightly frizzy and wiry. And, of course she wanted it to be exactly the opposite; straight, fine brunette and silky. But no amount of potions, treatments or styling would change it for long.

Nora returned the smile and, despite the extra work looking after Rosalie and George had caused over the past eighteen months, coupled with her constant tiredness , she was glad they had decided to stay at The Fighting Cock with her and Henry. Even she felt the cold emptiness at the Old Police House; it was no wonder neither Rosalie nor George wanted to return.

"Are you all going to Midnight Mass again?" Nora enquired casually as she admired the wire rack of golden-topped, delicious-smelling mince pies. Her mouth watered but she had already had one, and there was now a casserole cooking in the oven for their lunch.

"Yes, I think so," Rosalie replied. "Craig is working tonight as well as Polly, so we'll be able to slip away early. Er, would you like to come?"

"No, no, that's fine. Thank you. I expect I'll be tucked up in bed long before you get back. I'll put some pies and things out for you to have – you know, to set you off in the holiday mood." She wanted to add that there were plenty of carrots in the pantry, but the incident in question seemed to have been forgotten.

"Thanks, that's very kind." Rosalie responded and kissed Nora's cheek.

Polly arrived after lunch, and Nora slipped away upstairs to her room. The weather was clear outside, and Nora could just see Ashfield Staithe from her window. She shivered and drew away. To distract herself, she thought about the forthcoming wedding. Realisation dawned that she would be the one who organised the entire event. She knew Polly and Rosalie would help, as would anyone else she might ask. No doubt there was money in the Tillingers' trust fund to cover the cost, and Nora had her own little nest-egg, even after the purchase of the pub was recently completed.

Nora's mind skittered restlessly onward, oblivious to the possibility that Rosalie might not agree to marry Henry. The next question was where would they live? The obvious place would be here at The Fighting Cock, but she thought perhaps she, and maybe George – and even the new-weds themselves – would find that difficult.

Rosalie and Henry might want to make their

home at the Old Police House in Pepper Hill, but that property belonged equally to Rosalie and George. And there would be too many memories there for the bride. Plus, of course, Henry would be spending most of his time at the pub, so it made sense that they stayed here.

The smallholding opposite the pub, Tidal Reach, had been withdrawn from the market last year because either no one could afford it, or it was not suitable for their needs. It was too small to be farmed, and had the wrong type of soil, apparently, sandy heathland that drained too quickly for horticulture without a massive investment. The lower pastures sloping down to the marshes had, at one time, been licenced for slurry tank emptying, the incline of the land and its sandy filtration quality making drainage ideal. Both hamlets of Ashfield and Pepper Hill lacked mains' sewerage, and residents were reliant upon cess pits and soakaways for their domestic foul waste disposal; the tanks also needed the accumulated solids to be pumped out occasionally.

On impulse, and hoping she remembered which estate agents had previously been dealing with the property, Nora used the telephone extension in her bedroom to enquire if it was still for sale.

"If you could bear with me a moment, madam, I'll just check," the young lady who answered the phone responded. In the background, the firm's Christmas party sounded a joyful affair. "Yes, it's still on the market. Would you like me to send the details to you? Viewing is by appointment, but I'm sure we can fit you in between Christmas and New

Year."

Nora thought *viewing is just across the road*, but said, "Yes, please send me the details. Then, when I've had time to study them, I'll contact you again – possibly not 'til after the holiday period, though."

"Do you know the property at all?" the young lady enquired.

"Yes, actually, I live opposite." And she gave her address, name and contact number. The price had surprised Nora – much less now than the vendor was originally asking.

The envelope containing all the relevant information arrived the day after Boxing Day. The photograph showed the cottage as gleaming white in bright sunlight, and Nora suspected the photographer had stood in the entrance to the pub's car park to take it.

Tidal Reach had three bedrooms, but the third was rather small, and an upstairs bathroom. Downstairs comprised a kitchen/diner and a separate lounge, second toilet and storage cupboards. There were several outbuildings and a barn, set on three sides of a large concrete central area. Details of fields and accesses were included, but Nora found some of this information difficult to understand. She kept the leaflets upstairs in her room, but returned to them several times a day, and a scheme unfolded in her mind.

Chapter 45

"She said *yes*," Henry bounded into the lounge-bar in an uncharacteristic display of emotion. "Mum, she said *yes!*"

A few minutes earlier Henry had called Rosalie over to the corner of the kitchen and Nora silently slipped away, thinking now must be the moment. She then deliberately made herself busy, noisily clearing out the ash-pan from under the fire grate and tunelessly singing along to a Christmas song playing on the radio.

"Come here, son," Nora said as she stood up and held open her arms, ignoring the fact that her front was covered in dust. "Rosalie," she called through. "Come on, you too."

Rosalie approached, blushing and self-conscious. She was brimming with excitement and apprehension. Henry stooped to enclose them both in his embrace. Nora was the first to break free. Stepping back, she asked,

"Well, where's the ring?"

"Ah, er..." Henry stammered. "I thought I'd better let Rosalie choose one herself."

Very wise, Nora thought. She said, "Well, that's good." Her mind was chasing its own thoughts. "I have an idea. Only if you want to... Wait here a moment."

Nora looked back as she strode through the door on her way upstairs. Henry and Rosalie were holding each other tightly; Rosalie's head rested on his chest, and his bearded cheek lay on the crown of her head. They looked comfortable together, and Nora swallowed down a sliver of jealousy that they had found the love and companionship and passion that she no longer had – indeed, which had not been hers for many, many years.

In her bedroom, Nora retrieved her jewellery box, and took out her own engagement ring. One of the claws holding the diamond in its clasp had finally broken and the gem was slightly loose. It wasn't a very big stone, the cut was not spectacular; without tipping and tilting it, the colour was plain and transparent, but blues and reds and greens blazed with the movement against the light. And it was a link with Woody. Henry would understand. But would Rosalie?

"I don't know if you would be interested," she said when she returned. "But this…" and she held it out. Rosalie's smile was fading. "…is the ring Woody gave to me when we got engaged." She faltered, suddenly wondering if her own marriage was a good example. She stumbled on anyway. "It needs repairing, look." And she showed them the broken claw. "But, what you could do, if you wanted, you could design another ring to incorporate the diamond, and have someone make it up – and I'll help pay for it."

"You don't have to do that," Henry said, as he picked up the ring. He was a little concerned about Rosalie's reaction: sometimes she did not appreciate this kind of gesture, and a second-hand diamond that represented a dubious association with happiness might not meet her exacting standards. He held it reverently in his hand and then gave it to Rosalie. She studied the ring intently and, after several long moments, took it from him and slipped it onto the appropriate finger.

"Well?" Nora interrupted the protracting silence. "What d'you think?"

"It's lovely," Rosalie said quietly. But it was obviously a little too big. Henry watched her face, the sparkle in her eyes reflecting off the diamond's many facets.

"Have you got any ideas?" Nora asked, with the presumption that Rosalie had accepted both the ring and the plan. They waited a few seconds before she responded.

"And I could have it made up however I like?" she asked Henry.

"Of course," he stated, exhaling his relief. "If you draw up some ideas, we can take a trip to the jewellers…"

"There's a place that specialises in personalised pieces in Mattingburgh, near the university – Craig can tell you the address, I'm sure," Nora ventured.

"Actually, I've just had a brainwave," Henry said brightly. He gently grasped Rosalie's shoulders and turned her to face him. "D'you trust me to do something really special with the diamond? You can have a ring as well." Rosalie gazed into his face, a slight crease appearing between her eyebrows. "It'll be great, honest. I promise you," he added.

"Well, okay. I suppose so. As long as I have a ring of some sort, though."

Chapter 46

During the week following the New Year, Nora telephoned her solicitor, Ambrose Brideman, and made an appointment to discuss the possibility of purchasing Tidal Reach for Henry and Rosalie as a wedding present.

Three days later, Nora sat on the chair facing him in his office; her back was straight and she grasped her handbag tightly on her knees. These interviews were becoming routine; first Mr Jones at the bank, then here, twice, with Mr Brideman for the purchase of The Fighting Cock. And now, for Tidal Reach.

Mr Ambrose Brideman thought he was very important, and showed this by making people wait in his presence until he was ready to deal with them. His new computer had been delivered, but he would not countenance such a monstrosity on his desk; it remained in its box on the floor by the window while he stayed faithful to fountain pen and paper.

"Well, Mrs Stickleback, may I clarify what exactly it is that you wish to do? I am right in thinking that you own the public house, The, er, Fighting Cocks ..."

"Fighting Cock," Nora interrupted and received a very stern glare over the top rim of Mr Brideman's glasses. But she was not going to be intimidated. "It's called The Fighting Cock, singular." She too had been lectured on this point by her late husband.

"I stand corrected. The Fighting Cock public house."

Nora nodded. "Yes, that's right, I own it outright now. You dealt with the purchase."

Mr Brideman nodded, then lowered his eyes to the sheet of paper in front on him and continued, "And your son, Henry, will eventually take over the business?"

"As far as I am aware," Nora replied. "I haven't actually discussed things with him to any great extent – it isn't that long since his father, my husband, died. But Henry's now talking about getting married."

"He's very young to be thinking of settling down. How old is he now?"

"Twenty. He's very sensible. And Rosalie…"

"That would be Rosalie Tillinger?"

"Yes," Nora replied defensively. Mr Brideman's tone suddenly irritated her. "Rosalie has been through a lot. I know they are both young, but they are…"

Nora found it difficult to explain to this very old-fashioned, formal gentleman in his pin-striped suit, starched white collar with bow-tie, gold cuff-links, liver-spots on his arthritic hands, grey hair and bushy eyebrows that her son and his girlfriend were very much in love. "They are in love," she eventually said aloud, "And I think they would benefit from the stability a place of their own would give them."

Mr Brideman nodded, made a note on the paper in front of him, and asked, "How are you proposing to purchase the property – er, Tidal

Reach?"

"I still have capital from a life assurance policy, enhanced by a tidy sum bequeathed to me by my mother. She died a couple of months before my husband." She purposely did not mention the expensive refurbishment she had also paid for. "This seems an ideal thing to do for Henry and Rosalie, but I thought I would ask your advice first, as to the feasibility."

"It's your money, Mrs Stickleback. If you wish to purchase Tidal Reach for your son and his bride-to-be, then there is nothing and no one to prevent you."

Driving home later, Nora thanked her mother, wherever her soul now resided, for her thriftiness and acumen. She was looking forward to telling Henry and Rosalie. Her only worry in the plan was what George would think and do. He and Rosalie each owned half of the Old Police House in Pepper Hill, but they would have to wait until they were both eighteen until they could decide the future of the property. In any case, she hoped George would continue to live at The Fighting Cock with her, at least until he finished his studies.

Chapter 47

Quinny and Max were the first customers in The Fighting Cock on the second Saturday in March. Both were contemplating the froth on their beer when the door behind them opened. The new carpet muffled the approaching footsteps.

"Good morning," Polly greeted the arrival pleasantly. "And what can I get you?" She did not recognise the woman who was now standing only a few feet behind Max.

"Well, you could get that chap there," and she prodded Max's side, "To get his face out of his pint and say 'Hello'."

Max did indeed raise his eyes, turn and look directly at the woman. She wore a tailored skirt suit which looked expensive, and her make-up had been skilfully applied. Her shoes and matching handbag he thought were hand-made. A navy hat with red trimmings sat perched on top of her hair, which was now coloured a light brown instead of the previous grey. She removed her gloves and revealed manicured crimson-red nails, the fingers were adorned with several extravagant rings. Even through the stale cigarette fug of the pub, Max could smell perfume. She laughed and slapped his forearm.

"It's Alice, you idiot."

"Alice?" Max asked. "Alice Childs?"

"Alice of the condoms and carrots fame?" Polly asked tactlessly. Then, in aside to Alice, she explained, "Don't worry, he's my uncle. I know all about *him*. Good to see you, anyway."

"I am *not* her uncle," Max protested. "And she doesn't know *all* about me!"

Quinny leant back against his elbow on the bar, a wide smile creeping across his face, the elastic bands on his wrist completely forgotten.

"Have you finally agreed on the design for your engagement ring?" George asked Rosalie as they walked towards the washing line at the back of the pub. Rosalie removed the clothes, folded them and laid them in the basket that George was holding, along with the peg bag.

"Yes. And Henry's taking me to Mattingburgh next week, so we can go into the jewellers there and get it made up." Rosalie explained. "Nora's given him the diamond from her engagement ring – you know, because the claw is broken, and she said she'll never wear it now. She told me to be careful not to let the stone fall to the underside of my finger so that the setting can get damaged – she says that's what happened to hers."

"Good," George responded barely concealing his boredom. He pulled a face. Rosalie threw a tea-towel at him, he flicked it off and it floated on top of the pile. "And I'm sure it will be fine."

"I'm so pleased I can use Nora's diamond," Rosie said softly. "It'll make a kind of special connection, if you know what you mean."

"Yes, Rosie, I know."

"And don't call me Rosie." They both shouted at each other at exactly the same time.

Chapter 48

"I don't want to end up looking like a *meringue!*" Rosalie stated petulantly as she browsed along the rails of wedding dresses. This was the third bridal emporium, as they insisted on calling themselves, that Nora and Rosalie had visited since arriving in Mattingburgh around ten o'clock that morning. Henry had driven them here, promising not to peek at anything they might buy; he had his own mission to undertake in the city.

The shop displayed a sea of gowns in chiffon, voile and silk in colours described as ivory, cream, white, pure white and – at the very end – silver, which to Rosalie just looked grey.   The different fabrics created a cottony smell of shiny cleanliness and white tissue paper which transported Nora back to the time she and Elspeth had bought her outfit. She knew that scent would for ever remind Rosalie of this day.

Rosalie reached the rack of outrageously wide crinoline-styles, which contained so many layers that she imagined she would have to sit on top of the wedding car to ride to church, because she and her petticoats would never all fit inside.

Dismissing these, she moved along, passing a mannequin displaying a super-slender and sparkly dress in shiny satin with a slit up one side from the hem to beyond the thigh; Rosalie was sure this would show the bride's knickers and, although she liked to think she was up to date and trendy, this style was not for her. She sidestepped to the next rail where the dresses were again of a slim design, and the skirt lengths ranged from maxi, midi to mini. Another mannequin set into an alcove modelled something that looked more like a kiss-a-gram costume than an outfit in which to make solemn wedding vows.

Rosalie scowled. She was confused – grateful that Nora had agreed to accompany her, but annoyed that she couldn't seem to find that *special* dress.

"No, that's fine," Nora replied to the meringue statement. She was beginning to need a cup of tea to revive her; they were meeting Henry for lunch at one o'clock, but she did not think she could wait that long. "You chose which ever one you want, dear. We've got time for it to be altered before the big day, if need be." As she spoke, she tried to disguise the sound of her stomach rumbling – there had not been time for breakfast.

Rosalie struggled to unhook one of the gowns, and eventually held it up in front of her, amazed at the weight. "What about this one?" she asked.

"Sorry," Nora replied, her mind thinking of finding a coffee bar, or a restaurant. Or even a pub. "That one? Yes, it's er…its quite like the first one you tried on in the last shop, isn't it?"

Rosalie turned angrily around. Tears were forming, and every gem and sequin and pearl that was sown into the dresses' intricate patterns and decorations simply reminded her that Annie was not here to help her choose.

She slowly replaced the dress, needing the time to compose herself: she knew it was not fair of her to take out her temper on Nora. Nora had helped to care for her in those dark days of her worst grief; she had not forced her to do things that other people told her she should: get on with life, look to the future. She had just left her alone, allowed her to be with Henry, opened her home to both her and George, made them all one big family. And now she was snapping at her.

She turned slowly around and saw a similar sorrow to her own in Nora's eyes.

Nora held open her arms and Rosalie stepped into them, sobbing and clutching her.

"Is everything all right in here?" the assistant started to ask before she fully entered. "Oh," she said when she saw whom she presumed to be the bride-to-be and her mother having an emotional moment. "Oh. Shall I come back?"

"No, no, it's fine. I think our beautiful bride here," Nora said, looking straight at Rosalie as they still held each other, "is a little sad that her own Mum isn't here to help." Then added quietly, but loud enough for Rosalie to realise an explanation was necessary. "She sadly passed away a couple of years ago."

"Oh," the assistant repeated. "I am sorry to hear that."

"But, as I already think of Rosalie as my daughter, it's a privilege to help her choose the outfit in which she will marry my son." Nora, who was not usually expressive or sentimental, was pleased that she had managed to explain the situation so clearly. "But, whichever dress you chose, my dear," she told Rosalie, "I think you will need high heels because Henry is somewhat taller than you, and you need to look him straight in the eye to let him know who is the boss – although I think he already knows!" With that statement, both she and Rosalie began to laugh. The assistant nervously joined them, ranking these customers in her own private scale of 'normal' to 'ridiculous' at somewhere around the 'barmy' region.

After a few more minutes, Rosalie's hand hovered in the folds of a beautiful, expensive – they were all expensive, and she was reminded of the suits at Knatwich & Tacks in Cliffend – dress with chiffon shoulders supporting a lace and applique bodice. The assistant helped her to try it on. It was the one, but would need shortening, even with the high-heeled, plain white satin shoes they chose to match. The ensemble was completed with a veil and Juliet cap.

And then they sought the nearest restaurant to have that cuppa Nora dreamt of earlier, which happened to be in the department store a short walk from the bridal emporium, where they had arranged to meet Henry later.

"I daren't think how much…" Rosalie began to say as she rummaged through one of the long-handled branded carrier bags on the seat next to her; there were five bags in all – and that was without the dress, which would be delivered to Ashfield after it had been altered.

"Well, we haven't finished yet," Nora reminded her. "You have to get your undies and nightwear and a going-away outfit – what used to romantically be called the bride's *trousseau*…"

"Oh, I thought that was just household bits and pieces, you know, sheets, embroidered pillowcases, table cloths. Mum used to call it a *bottom drawer*." Rosalie's face had blushed a brilliant red when Nora mentioned undies and nightwear. "Anyway, I don't know about you but I think I've had enough for one day. Maybe I'll ask Jayne to come with me when I get the, er, rest."

"Jayne?" Nora questioned. "Oh, Jayne from Clifftech. Yes, that might be a good idea," she said with relief. Rosalie was frowning deeply as she peeped into the bag again.

"Is anything wrong? You know you can change any of it if you don't like it when you get home."

"It isn't that. I love everything. It's just that, well, everything was so expensive and I'm a bit concerned." Rosalie stated timidly.

"Well, don't be," Nora informed her kindly. "It's all sorted out – I'm going to make you and George wash up every day for at least ten years to cover it!"

"Thank you," Rosalie whispered as she held Nora's hand and enjoyed the joke.

Nora saw tears gathering in Rosalie's eyes again. She knew today would be bitter-sweet, as would their wedding day. "Your Mum and Dad were good and kind and thoughtful people; they loved you and George very much…"

"But I was mean to Mum the day they went on holiday!" Rosalie cried, her heart still full of remorse, even though she and Annie had made up before her parents left.

"We're all *mean* to our parents at some time,

sweetheart. They know it doesn't mean we don't love them. It's all part of being a parent – which you will find out when you have your own children!"

"D'you think we will? Have children, I mean."

"I sincerely hope so!" Nora exclaimed, disturbing the two ladies on the opposite table. "I want at least two grandchildren. A little boy and a little girl – I don't mind in which order they come – I just want to spoil them!"

Rosalie smiled, and joked, "As long as they don't come in eggs that hatch to look like a cockerel and a hen, I don't mind." Then she added, in a more serious tone, "Did you spoil Henry?"

"Not enough," Nora said quietly. "I wished I had spent more time with him. But I was running the pub, and his father… Well, you know about his father."

Rosalie squeezed Nora's hand. Her soon to be Mum-in-law looked really tired. They still had half an hour to wait before Henry joined them. She poured another cup of tea for them both.

"Henry and I have got to meet with Quinny – I mean the Reverend Boyce – again tomorrow, to sort out the reading of the banns," Rosalie said, her mind jumping quickly from guilt at Nora having to help her so much, to the excitement of preparing for her special day.

"Oh, right," Nora said, thinking proudly that Rosalie was polite enough to say *Henry and I* instead of the modern tendency to put oneself first and say *me and Henry. Oh God, I'm so old-fashioned,* she thought, then reprimanded herself for blaspheming. But then, Quinny's language wasn't exactly pure at times. This brought her mind back to the reverend gentleman. "Right, well, it's traditional for the bride and groom to go to church and hear the banns being read, if not all three times, then at least once."

"Why?" Rosalie asked, and Nora heard echoes of a child-like inquisitiveness. Taking a deep breath, Nora realised she was now really looking forward to returning home and having a quiet afternoon and evening to herself. Craig and Polly were opening up for her, and George had said he would help later.

When she had explained the traditions of hearing the banns, she closed her eyes, but then thought about all their purchases and realised she would, in fact, be very busy for the rest of the day helping Rosalie to unpack everything. She would want to try everything on. Then she would go through it all again when the dress was altered and delivered.

Henry arrived at the allotted time and asked, "Have you been waiting long?" He kissed his mother's cheek before sitting next to Rosalie and kissing her lips.

"A while, but we were early," Nora said. This seemed to alarm him and he asked,

"Is everything all right? Did you get what you wanted?" He glanced at the numerous carrier bags and grimaced.

"Yes, we're fine. We found most of it in one shop. We're lacking one big box, though: the dress has got to be shortened."

"Gosh," Henry exclaimed. "I hear so many nightmarish stories from customers at the pub about buying everything for the wedding, then it all having to be returned. I thought we would need at least three visits to the city. D'you think they'll get the hem straight?" he mocked, and received a side-swipe from Rosalie. She then said,

"I'll come over with Jayne for the rest of the things I need another day."

"Good," Henry stated. "Well, I've got to collect something next Saturday, I could give you a lift again. But now, if you're hungry, are you ready to order lunch? And I'm parched, but I bet they won't do a mixture of tea and coffee for me."

"No, I don't expect they will. And don't even ask!" Nora threatened.

Chapter 49

"I publish the Banns of Marriage between Rosalie Andrea Tillinger, spinster of Pepper Hill, within the parish of PepperAsh, and Henry Thomas Stickleback, bachelor of Ashfield, also in the PepperAsh parish. If anyone knows of any reason in law why these persons may not marry each other, you are to declare it now. This is the first time of asking."

Quinny looked up as he closed the register and moved it aside on the lectern. In the second pew from the front Nora sat nearest the aisle next to Rosalie, both smart in their Sunday best; George was between his sister and Henry, looking as if he was eagerly awaiting the end of the service so he could dash away to something more interesting; and Henry had squeezed his tall physique into the wall end of the pew, and was brushing the white powder from the paint-wash off his dark sleeve.

The last time the rector had looked down on the family in church was at Woody's funeral. But that was two years ago and they weren't all there then anyway. *Life goes on*, as the cliché says, he thought; and now the youngsters were getting married. Quinny pinged the elastic band on his wrist – not because he was agitated, but because he was pleased for them.

And he felt happy for himself, in a strange, inexplicable way. Not that he took any credit for Rosalie and Henry's forthcoming nuptials, but weddings had been in short supply in the

PepperAsh parish recently and, hopefully, this would be an auspicious event.

Nora half listened to the sermon – something about turning water into wine at a wedding, and the first miracle. She thought her customers were more adept at turning wine, or more likely beer, into water; she remembered she must arrange for a plumber to come and check the flush to the Gents' urinal again. Something wasn't right, and Henry had not been able to fix it; George had also tried, bless him, and so had Polly – more by frightening the clientele into not using the facility than by employing any mechanical remedy. Nora and Rosalie had made it their rule to stay out of the Gents' if at all possible, although it was not always so; sometimes, when Mrs Mawberry wasn't able to come in, someone had to clean in there.

Suddenly, everyone was standing up, turning to each other and shaking hands. Shocked, Nora followed suit, engaging an equally surprised Rosalie beside her.

Chapter 50

On the Thursday night before Rosalie's wedding, the bar at The Fighting Cock was full; there was a mix of customers, locals and tourists, older and younger. Nora recognised the lad in the corner with his girlfriend as Bloo, one of Henry's pals from school. She sent Henry over to sit and talk with them, replacing their drinks after a while as a goodwill gesture. George had joined them, totally at ease in the company of people older than himself, but still respectful of the fact that he was underage; he was drinking cola and Henry was nursing his cockerel mug still half full of tea and coffee.

Rosalie had caught the bus into Cliffend earlier; a group of her friends from college were taking her out. Nora suspected they would probably spend the evening visiting most of the pubs in Cliffend and finish up at Boxie's nightclub which closed at 1.30 a.m. She had offered to collect four of them – one of whom was Jayne who had indeed accompanied Rosalie on the second shopping expedition to Mattingburgh. The girls all lived on this side of town, and Nora said she would taxi them to their various homes before driving Rosalie back here. She suddenly felt very tired again. But, she told herself, she could not afford the time to be weary; there was so much to do in this coming week.

Nora turned her attention back to the conversation around her. She and Polly were behind the bar, Craig was due in soon, and Max and Quinny, as usual, were propped up in the corner near the opening that led through to the kitchen.

"So, a general invitation has been issued to everyone in PepperAsh," Max asked.

"That's right, Quinny replied. "I gave out the good news from the pulpit after reading the banns these last two Sundays, reminding everyone that they are welcome to attend both the ceremony at St Jude's Church first, and the reception here afterwards. Mind you," he added, "every service that's held in church is a public event, and nobody can be prevented from attending anyway."

"Oh, yeah?" Max queried, "Then why's there a lepers' squint-hole built into the west wall centuries ago to give the *excluded* a view of happenings on the sanctuary?"

"Them were different times," Quinny replied enigmatically.

"So, you won't object to my partner attending, then?" Polly asked provocatively.

"Not in the slightest," Max Podgrew replied lecherously. "What's she like?"

"It isn't 'what's she like?' but 'who does she like?'" Polly answered acerbically. "And it certainly wouldn't be you!"

Polly moved away from the bar and a few moments later, Nora followed her.

"Her name is Susan and, I know you've known me for a couple of years or so now and not yet met her, but it's very hard for us to be accepted as a couple – even our neighbours won't speak to us."

Nora touched Polly's forearm and said, "She'll always be welcome here. And if Max gives you any trouble, I'm sure you'll know how to handle it! And don't spare the brutality on my account – it's about time he was taken down a peg or two; now that he's with Alice again, he's unbearably smug."

"Yes, but where is Alice?" Polly asked.

"She's gone back on a cruise ship. She said she had been asked especially because she is so accomplished at the roulette wheel. But I don't believe her – she talks as if she's now the chief croupier." Nora and Polly giggled like school-girls. Then Nora added, "She asked me why I don't go on a cruise – you know, when Henry and Rosalie get back from their honeymoon. Have a bit of a break."

"Well, why don't you? You deserve it."

"Oh, I don't know. I'd feel I was deserting them."

"Don't be silly," Polly assured her. "I'll be here to help, you know that. Craig doesn't seem to be in a rush to get back to studying, so I expect he'll be glad of a few extra shifts. And, as Tidal Reach…" Polly was privy to Nora's planned wedding present, "…won't be ready for a while for them to move into, you could give them some space, let them have the place to themselves. And, you never know, you might meet a handsome gentleman who'll sweep you off your feet and take you away from all this."

Nora smiled at this idea, then dismissed it as nonsense. But it kept returning to her, at least the part about having a holiday, not so much the thought of meeting a handsome gentleman – although anything was possible.

"Anyone serving?" they heard called through. Raising their eyebrows at each other, they returned to their duties.

"Here," Polly said, trailing foam as she set the second pint down. "Who's paying for these?" and she held her hand out, palm upwards, across the bar.

"Him," Max and Quinny both chorused, pointing at one another.

"Here, let me," their postman, Jim, offered. The rector scowled at him and, when he'd moved away, he nudged Max and asked,

"Who was that chap?"

Max looked around, then laughed, "He's the bloody postman. You ought to know him, you cadge enough lifts off him!"

"Well, I didn't recognise him out of his uniform. He looks very different, doesn't he?" Quinny huffed indignantly, feeling more than a little silly.

Jim stepped back and bought cigarettes from Polly. He opened the packet and was about to light one when Quinny stated,

"Isn't it about time you packed that filthy lark up, lad?"

"Isn't it about time you bought yourself a car and stopped thumbing lifts everywhere?" the postman snapped; he was tired of being told that smoking would kill him. "Better still, retire!"

"He can't retire yet," Nora interjected. "He's got a big wedding to conduct next weekend."

"You make it sound like I'll be in charge of a

load of bloody musicians."

"No, there'll only be one musician there," Max stated. "Mrs Ervsgreaves on her organ."

"Sounds like a good do – that's Henry and Rosalie you're talking about, right?"

"Nothing gets past the postman," Max stated, saluting with this glass. "It's an open invite. Everyone's welcome. Bring your missus and get to know your neighbours."

"Not married," Jim said sulkily.

"Girlfriend, mum, budgie – anyone."

"Okay," Jim turned and blew his smoke out to the side. "What time and where?"

"Oh, maybe posties don't know everything after all!" Max was feeling particularly belligerent this evening: he was missing Alice.

"Two o'clock at St Jude's Church, and then afterwards, here." Polly volunteered.

"So, is your Susan coming?" Quinny asked with a mischievous innocence, picking up on Max's tone.

"Shouldn't think so," Polly said as she finished wiping the beer taps. "She doesn't believe in religion. She thinks all the churches should be pulled down, the stones used to repair the roads, and the parsons stuck in the verges and used as mile-markers!"

Quinny had laughed as heartily as everyone else at Polly's joke. But inside he was deeply hurt. He couldn't decide if it was the fact that his calling was so badly regarded by other people that cut him so deep, or the reference to rubble. As he finished supping his pint, he tried to clear his throat of the gritty brick dust suddenly lodged there. He placed his glass on the bar's polished surface and withdrew his hand. His opposite fingers immediately started to fiddle with the elastic band on his wrist.

"Right," he stated as he carefully stepped away. "I've got some paperwork to do."

"D'you want a lift?" Jim asked, sensing the sudden change in the rector's mood. He had only taken a couple of sips of his own pint, and knew he was still within the legal limit; he might give unauthorised lifts as he went about his rounds, but he wasn't stupid enough to drink and drive – his job depended on his licence. "It won't take a sec, will it?" He stubbed out the remainder of his cigarette and retrieved his car keys from his pocket.

"No, no, don't trouble yourself. I could do with the walk. And it isn't dark yet." Quinny said with his eyes firmly studying the floor. He took his leave without bidding anyone farewell. Nora and Polly looked at Max, who said defensively,

"Well I didn't tell him he was useless, did I, Polly?" Polly shrugged; she was still smarting from comments about her choice of partner.

"Honestly, you two. *Like niece, like uncle* is all I can say." Nora said.

"I am not his niece," Polly stated at exactly the same moment as Max chanted,

"I ain't her uncle!"

"Well, whatever. I just hope you haven't upset next week's wedding, that's all!"

Chapter 51

Henry left George talking to Bloo and his girlfriend, and slipped quietly past the group at the bar. Polly and Nora were chatting to Stan and his wife, who had joined Max and Jim. Henry rinsed his cockerel mug in the kitchen sink and left it upside down on the draining board before making his way upstairs to his bedroom. He closed the door and listened to the silence – almost silence; there was still a faint murmur of voices from downstairs.

He looked at the digital clock by his bed; it said 21:05 in bold white letters against a circular black background. He took a deep breath in; only a few more hours to go – forty-one, to be precise. Less than two days, more than a day and a half. Everything was ready. George already had the two ring boxes. His suit fitted; as promised to Rosalie over two years ago, he had returned to Knatwich & Tacks, and purchased a brand new, made to measure one for this monumental occasion. After a little persuasion, he had also bought George his suit. And Nora was still undecided as to whether or not to wear a hat with her outfit.

Henry looked at the suit-carrier hanging from the wardrobe door, and the holdall on the floor. He and George would be spending tomorrow night at the Old Police House; Nora had organised Mrs Mawberry to give the place a good dust and clean up. Although she had grumbled, she worked tirelessly, even making up their beds – George in his room and Henry in the spare room. They would get ready and leave from there.

He felt his legs begin to shake. He hoped Rosalie was not as nervous as he was. It was the bride's prerogative to be anxious. The groom was supposed to… Henry did not know *what* he was supposed to do. He had no one to ask: neither Quinny nor Max were married; his own father was gone, as was who would have been his father-in-law; Craig had a different girlfriend each time they spoke; Bloo was going steady, and Henry didn't know anything about that side of Jim's life.

He sat down heavily on the bed, then reached forward and pulled open his bedside cabinet drawer. He took out a small box – flatter than a ring box, but still bearing the jeweller's insignia. Reverently, he opened the lid.

Snuggled inside was the locket he had retrieved from Ashfield Staithe. The two photographs, of Annie and Derek, had been removed and were now stored in a custom-made sleeve slotted into the box lid lining.

Henry extracted the two-pronged pin which secured the locket onto the padded cushion, and gently lifted it up, his fingers almost too big to handle such a delicate object. Prising the front half away from theback, he opened the locket to reveal, fastened into a specially installed setting, the diamond from Nora's engagement ring.

Henry smiled. This was his special present to Rosalie. He wrapped his hands around it, held it to his mouth and blessed it with a kiss.

Chapter 52

The big day arrived, Saturday, 28th July 1990. Polly walked into the pub at eight o'clock in the morning, ready to start decorating the lounge-bar and organise the caterers – she had insisted Nora bring in professional help; they could not cope with this on top of everything else.

But, before anything else, she tied a pinny over her wedding outfit – a lemon-yellow, customarily low-cut dress – and made tea. She carried three mugs upstairs to Rosalie's room where Nora was setting Rosalie's hair in large curlers. Rosalie was facing the dressing table wearing a light cotton house gown while her wedding dress hung on the hook behind the door. Her eyes were drawn to the white of the flowing skirt, the lace of the bodice, and she could not believe she was special enough to be allowed to wear it in only a few hours' time.

"I thought these might be needed," Polly said as she handed a mug to both Nora and Rosalie. "How are you feeling?"

"Nervous, excited, apprehensive, a little sick at times," Rosalie replied truthfully.

"Normal for a bride, then," Polly said, glancing at Nora.

"Yes, but I keep seeing shorthand outlines going through my mind as I either think or talk – I've got whole conversations in my head awaiting transcription and typing up. It's very distracting. What happens if I'm still doing it when we're in church and I'm making my vows?"

"Well, I would imagine you'll be okay, as long as you can read it back later, and check that you didn't make any wild promises you've no intention of keeping – like to *obey*!" Polly laughed. She too had tried to learn shorthand, but had given up after the first term.

"Have you heard from either Henry or George?" Rosalie asked anxiously. She was glad that Nora had organised for them to spend the night at the Old Police House so that she could stay here at the pub with Nora, who had promised to help her prepare.

"No, there's been no word from Pepper Hill," Nora said. "At least I haven't heard the phone ring."

"The red light wasn't showing on the answerphone when I came past it a few minutes ago," Polly confirmed.

"What if something has happened?" Rosalie suddenly leant forward, pulling the strand of hair that Nora had been preparing to wrap around a curler, away from her hand. "What if there's been an accident?"

Polly crouched beside Rosalie and, looking straight into her eyes, explained, "There hasn't been an accident. They are probably both still asleep, it's only eight-fifteen and they have five and three-quarter hours to get ready."

But Rosalie's eyes filled with tears. Nora knelt on the other side of her, gave her mug to Polly then took her hands and said,

"Every bride has doubts – doubts as to whether they are marrying the right man, or if they even want to get married at all! It's only natural to feel nervous and unsure."

"I miss Mum," Rosalie suddenly sobbed. "And Dad. I want them here."

Nora gathered the weeping bride in her arms and rocked her back and forth, thankful that this had happened before Rosalie was wearing her wedding dress, or had had her face made up. Nora knew it was no use trying to stem the tears; they had to fall. They might wash out some of the sorrow, and then allow Rosalie to enjoy her day. In time, Nora thought, the pain would diminish. But today Rosalie clung onto Nora, feeling more like an eight year old than an eighteen year old.

Polly stood up, and placed Rosalie's mug on the dressing table. She looked around at the outfit hung and strewn around the bedroom – dress, veil, shoes – and a sadness washed over her that she would never be a bride.

"Oh, that reminds me," Polly suddenly said. "I'll be back in a minute." She rushed down the stairs and retrieved a box from her bag under the counter near the till – the same shelf that had hidden Woody's secret bottle of whisky. As she returned, she glanced at the answerphone; the red light was not shining: Henry had still not rung.

"Here," she said as she held the box out to Rosalie, who was now wiping her eyes.

"Thanks," she said as she pushed the paper handkerchiefs into her pocket and took it. She opened the lid. Inside, nestled against white tissue paper, was a garter trimmed with light blue lace and decorated with slightly darker blue ribbon bows. Rosalie lifted it out and held it up to the light; one of the curlers, having been dislodged as Nora held her earlier, finally slipped out and onto the floor. She stretched the garter, then slipped it over her wrist.

"No, no, don't do that to it," Polly cried in horror. "It reminds me of Quinny's rubber bands." All three stared at the garter, stark and loose against Rosalie's narrow wrist. Then in unison, they laughed out loud. Rosalie was still giggling when she carefully lifted the hem of her dressing gown, slid it up her leg, over her knee and placed it on her thigh.

"Right," Nora stated. "Is that something *new* or something *blue*?"

"Make it *blue*," Rosalie replied. "My whole outfit is *new*. This bracelet is *old*," and Rosalie picked up a delicate golden expander bracelet. "Mum gave it to me when I was thirteen." She gazed down at it, pinching the sliding ends until it was tight against her skin. "It was a bit of a struggle to get it on, but I wanted something of Mum with me today." She suddenly looked up, her eyes wide in horror, "You don't think *this* looks too much like Quinny's rubber bands, do you? He won't think I'm taking the mick, will he?"

Nora and Polly exchanged glances, before vigorously shaking their heads.

"No, of course not!" Polly reassured her.

"Anyway, you could say that the diamond in my engagement ring is old, it being the one from your ring, Nora." She held up her hand with the fingers straight, her nails neatly trimmed to a sensible length and prettily enhanced with a pale, pink pearlescent polish. They all bent over to examine and admire the jewel set so beautifully in its surround, with curved and curlicued decorations which Rosalie had designed herself and Henry had commissioned.

"It's gorgeous," Polly admitted. But you'll have to put it on the other hand for the ceremony, won't you?"

"That's what I did, anyway," Nora added, thinking back to her own happy day. And it had been a very happy day, despite Elspeth's cautions and warnings.

"Right then, let's get back to the business in hand," Polly stated; after all, they now only had just under five hours left in which to prepare. "That's the *old,* the *new* and the *blue* dealt with. *Borrowed.* What have you got with you that's *borrowed*?"

"Nothing," Rosalie answered hastily. "I forgot about *borrowed.*"

"Here," and Polly took off her watch. It was gold and stylish. "Susan gave it to me for my birthday, so you'll have to let me have it back. But you'll need something to tell you how late you are when you finally arrive at the altar."

"So," Nora said quietly and calmly, thirty minutes before the car was due to arrive. She was wearing a smart, light pink satin effect dress with a jacket of matching background but with lilac and purple squares; these shades matched her shoes and handbag. Her hat (Henry noted later that, yes, she had decided to wear the hat) replicated the pink of the dress, with flowers of the two contrasting colours.

Rosalie had decided not to have a bridesmaid; she was closest to Jayne, but she hadn't known her very long; all her friends from both school and college had been invited anyway. The only other person who had really helped her, besides Polly, and she had outright refused, was Nora.

And so, fulfilling two roles, Nora thought – no make that three - Groom's Mother, Foster-mother to the Bride, and Matron of Honour – Nora looked at Rosalie. She acknowledged that she was not the only one discharging several sets of duties; George had doubled up as Best Man and the one *who giveth this bride.*

Tears welled in Nora's eyes as she saw the beautiful young bride, her soon to be daughter-in-law, adorned in white – whether it was appropriate or not. The brightness of the skirt shimmered as Rosalie moved and, although the veil was not yet fixed, she looked delightful. The little roses in the posy she was holding ranged in colour from lilac to palest then darkest pink. Pink roses were Annie's favourite flowers, Rosalie preferred lilac, but they were both bright happy colours for a wedding.

The moment was broken, however, when they heard a pair of size ten shoes thundering up the stairs towards them. A single knock sounded before the door burst open and George entered, smart in his new suit.

"Cor, Rosie," he exclaimed as he stared at his sister. "You don't half scrub up well!"

"Don't call me *Rosie,*" she screeched back at him,

trying to reach past Nora to clout him.

"Now, now, you two!" Nora tried to calm then distract them. "How's Henry, George? Is everything all right with him?"

"Yes, he's fine - well, as fine as he can be. And yes, I've got the rings – Oh…" And he patted all his pockets in turn, and mimed a frantic search. "Now where did I put them?"

"He was just as bad at the rehearsal last week," Rosalie said to Nora.

"I know. I was there!"

"What about the guests' button holes?"

"They're at the church, I think. I'll pick mine up when I get there – you've got your flowers, so…"

"Didn't you call in on the way and check? Who drove you here?" Rosalie demanded.

"Calm down, sis."

"Don't call me *SIS*,"

"Right you two," Nora exclaimed. "You," and she pointed to George. "Out. It's not seemly for a gentleman to be in a lady's boudoir just before her wedding."

"Even if he is the annoying little brother of the bride!" Rosalie added.

"But I'm the best man, and I'm giving away the bride, so I should have access to all areas today."

"Don't you believe it!" Nora stated. "My pub. My rules. You, out!"

"Okay, okay," George laughed as he raised his hands in surrender and retreated. "I'll tell Henry not to bother getting done up too smart as the bride hasn't really made that much of an effort!"

Rosalie swung the door shut angrily. It

slammed. They heard the shoes jaunt back down the stairs, accompanied by a nonchalant whistle.

"Quinny said we didn't have to have the part in the service where someone gives the bride away," Rosalie said. "But George wanted to do it; he said he was going to say something along the lines of *'I've had to look after her for long enough, it's someone else's turn now!'*"

"Well, let's just hope he's sensible about it and just does what he's supposed to do," Nora replied.

"Oh, he will be. He's acting all brash, but deep down, I think he's quite nervous about today as well."

Polly then wandered in again; this time she was carrying a tray with three glasses of champagne. They each took one.

"Here's to you, Rosalie. And Henry," she toasted. "Cheers."

"Cheers," Nora and Rosalie repeated, then they all clinked glasses and sipped.

"Oh, I'll be squiffy before I leave here," Rosalie squealed.

"I told you that you should've something to eat," Polly said. "Wait here…"

"I'm not going anywhere – except church – in this get-up," Rosalie responded.

"…And I'll get you a sandwich."

A few minutes later she reappeared. "Here, eat this – it's just ham, no mustard, mayonnaise, tomato or anything to dribble down your dress. Sit down," she ordered.

"Wait, I'll get something to put over your lap," Nora said, dashing off and returning with a clean towel.

"But I'll have to brush my teeth again if I eat anything now."

"You'll probably have to visit the bathroom a dozen times before you leave anyway!" Polly advised her knowingly. "So, sit, eat, digest, brush your teeth and whatever. Then sit again. Then we can go," Polly commanded.

"Gosh," Rosalie uttered as she obediently sat down and raised the sandwich to her mouth. "I'm glad you weren't one of my school teachers!"

Chapter 53

The sun was shining as the chauffer-driven wedding car, bedecked with pink, lilac and white ribbons, left the car park of The Fighting Cock public house.

George was already at St Jude's Church and Polly said she would follow on; she wanted to park her car so that she could escape as soon as the ceremony was over and return to the pub to make sure the caterers were following her instructions.

Rosalie sat in the back seat of the limousine next to Nora, her veil already over her face *("So that you don't accidentally wipe your fingers in your eyes and ruin your make-up,"* Polly had instructed before they left). The white diaphanous fabric made her feel as if she were peering at the world from behind a screen, separated and excluded from reality. It also made her very hot.

The entire day was taking on a detachment from reality and, despite sitting next to Nora, she felt very alone. She looked down and realised she was clutching the bouquet of roses a little too tightly. She concentrated on relaxing as she breathed deeply, her eyes falling on the watch Polly had lent her. The hands on the face told her there were two minutes to go before she was on time; George had asked her not to be too late, just a minute or two would do. She grinned slightly as she tried to imagine Henry quaking, as surely he must be at this very moment.

She saw the second hand on Polly's watch move

stiffly onward. Her gaze then flowed across to the golden bracelet on the other wrist, and finally rested on her engagement ring, which she had obediently transferred to the third finger of her right hand for the duration of the ceremony. The diamond in the ring shimmered and sparkled its bright colours in the sunlight and she twisted and turned her hands fractionally to make it sparkle.

A gust of wind from the open car window worried at the bottom of her veil. She breathed deeply again, then looked up and ahead, now full of poignant emotion: although the jewellery she wore connected her to Annie, Nora and Polly – the latter two being the people to whom she could turn in times of crisis – she suddenly missed her Mum and Dad so much, and she was troubled that she was too young, and still in too much turmoil from her bereavement, to marry.

But she loved Henry. Yes, above all, she loved Henry.

Sensing the bride's nervousness, Nora whispered, "You look beautiful."

Rosalie smiled at her and mouthed the words "Thank you." Her voice seemed to have disappeared. And she feared that she would not be able to make herself heard when she made her vows – words that, if she thought about them, were again replaced with shorthand squiggles that suddenly she could not transcribe.

"You're all packed to set off on your honeymoon tomorrow? And you've got everything for tonight?" Nora tried to distract her by asking.

Again Rosalie nodded. This time she tested her

voice. "Henry's being a bit cagey about where we're going this evening." Although she heard the words being spoken, they did not sound as if they came from her.

Nora smiled. She knew the honeymoon was to be spent in Inverness. Henry and George had been sneaking around for a couple of weeks, nudging, whispering and plotting but, despite various bribes and threats, she couldn't prise tonight's destination out of them. Arriving at St Jude's Church gate, Rosalie was surprised at the number of cars parked at the entrance, in the rectory garden and on the verges along the roadside. The sun gleamed from the polished and sparkling chrome, the glass and metal surfaces, striking sharp points of light into her eyes. She moved her head into the shade and smiled as her brother stepped forward from a waiting group. He first opened the car door for Nora to climb out, then walked around the rear and opened hers. He offered her his hand and she took it before gently easing herself onto her brand new, uncustomary high heels. As soon as she stood up, she felt the warmth of the sunshine, and she realised she was trembling with anxiety and excitement.

Nora busied herself with Rosalie's skirt and, when they were all ready, George curved his elbow towards her and said,

"Come on then, Rosie. Henry's waiting for you. Max is trying to keep him calm, but I'm glad you weren't late otherwise I think he would've had a heart attack, he's so nervous – Henry, that is, not Max, he's just as crotchety as ever!"

Rosalie ignored George calling her Rosie and hooked her hand into his arm. She then turned around and held out her other hand to Nora. The sun was in her eyes, and she felt blessed to have George's support on one side of her and Nora's on the other. Pushing away the shorthand strokes and the jagged, flashing colours chasing each other behind her eyes, she urged them forward and, together, they walked from the car to the church door.

Before they entered, however, Nora whispered as she removed Rosalie's hand and settled it firmly around the bouquet, "Unfortunately, I don't think the aisle is wide enough for all three of us to walk up side by side." She took her place behind George and Rosalie; an enormous swelling of pride filled her and squeezed out a tear.

"Are you ready?" George asked. Rosalie looked up at him. He winked and nodded towards the cool and inviting interior of the church.

Nora signalled to the usher standing just inside and he, in turn, raised his hand to Mrs Ervsgreaves. Five seconds later Wagner's *Bridal Chorus* thundered out of the organ. After the initial octave F fanfare, the lower Bb pedal notes rumbled through St Jude's very foundations.

Chapter 54

Bride and groom were standing just inside the bar of The Fighting Cock public house. Rosalie's smile radiated happiness, and she held her left hand in front of her, palm downwards, so that she could inspect her new wedding ring. As they had travelled from the church to the pub, she had transferred her engagement ring back onto the correct finger. Now they sat side by side, golden, glinting and perfect against her skin. She reached up and kissed Henry. He was also smiling, now relaxed and happy.

Rosalie's veil was thrown back and, amid the pins and grips, her straw-like blonde hair spiked a little in protest at being forced into an unfamiliar style. Luckily, it had remained relatively well-behaved for the photographs, the taking of which the newly-weds thought lasted longer than the actual ceremony.

Quinny believed the same; towards the end, he had crept back into the rectory to discard his robes. Although retaining the dog-collar, he changed into a lighter, more casual suit. He noticed the elastic band on his wrist was about to split, and so he replaced it before walking back to the church to find Max and George waiting for him.

"Where have you been?" Max asked grumpily. Officially in charge of lifts for George and Quinny, Max was in a hurry, firstly, to rid himself of his tie which felt as if it were choking him, and secondly, to find himself a beer. He knew there would be champagne on offer as soon as they arrived, but he didn't like that insipid, fizzy stuff; he needed a good old pint of bitter. Unlike the groom, he thought, who looked as if he could do with a stiff whisky – or a mug of that revolting tea/coffee combination that he drank.

"Congratulations Rosalie, Henry," two of the indomitable ladies who kept the church and parish running said almost in unison; Rosalie recognised one as Mabel, but could not recall the other one's name at all.

"Thank you," she said accepting a kiss on the cheek from each, her face now burning from nervous exhaustion and the heat. "And thank you for the gorgeous flower arrangements in church." Rosalie was aware that Nora had paid for the flowers – begrudging Smithy, the florist in Cliffend, every single penny and checking each bloom and stem individually when they had arrived.

"You're quite welcome," Mabel said. "And may I say how beautiful you look." She turned to Henry and continued, "And you look so smart, young Henry; all grown up now, and tall and handsome."

Henry did not know how to react. He just wanted to get out of his suit and into his jeans and T-shirt; he would much rather have been serving behind the bar than here welcoming his wedding guests. He smiled, held out his hand and shook hers, repeating his new wife's gratitude. He did wonder if he ought to be thanking people for their gifts, but he couldn't remember who had given what; Rosalie said they would write formal *thank you* notes when they returned from their honeymoon.

"D'you fancy slipping away for a moment?" Henry whispered.

"Why, Mr Stickleback," Rosalie said in mock modesty, placing her hand dramatically on her throat. "What are you suggesting?"

Henry blushed. "No, I just mean, oh – you know. Out into the kitchen for a few minutes' quiet?" There were now so many people in the lounge-bar that Henry was feeling very claustrophobic. Plus he had just witnessed someone's child – he didn't actually recognise who – pick up a large cockerel ornament. He wanted to go around the room and retrieve all his treasures, but knew that would make him look paranoid. But he had found that particular cockerel, highly coloured and fantasy-styled, at the end of a long Sunday morning's search at the weekly car boot sale, and he did not want it broken. As he drew in a sharp breath, the mother removed it from the child's hand. He knew he would have to miss tomorrow's sale, and this made him whisper again to Rosalie.

"Don't you want to know where we're off to tonight?"

"Well, it must be somewhere close as the car hire firm are taking us." She smiled, her lips, eyes and cheeks all reflected her bliss. And Henry was incredibly happy.

"Oy, you two," Max shouted. They turned to greet him. George and Quinny were with him.

"Hi Max, Quinny," Henry said, automatically extending his hand and shaking theirs in turn.

"George. Thank you all for today."

"Yes, thanks," Rosalie echoed.

"No problem," George replied. Craig, dressed in a waiter's uniform, hovered laden with a tray of champagne. The catering firm had commandeered his services, and Henry saw him watching a very short-skirted young waitress as she walked past. Quinny and Max shook their heads at the champagne and indicated towards the bar; Henry also declined but Rosalie helped herself. George looked longingly.

"One glass, and save some of it to toast your sister and brother-in-law's health later," Nora's voice suddenly sounded in George's ear. He grinned.

"No problem. Cheers," he said as he raised the glass before taking a drink then walking away.

"At least we know where he is and what he's doing," Nora stated sadly, watching him walk over to another group of people. "And where to collect him from with his hangover!"

"I don't imagine that's his first drink, do you?" Rosalie said, resigned to the fact that her brother looked and acted very grown-up.

"I don't think I want to know," Nora stated. Henry grunted and said,

"If all the guests are now here, I'm going to slip into the kitchen and make myself a proper drink."

"Here you are, Henry," Polly suddenly appeared with his special cockerel mug; it was standing on a delicate white paper doily, on a silver tray. "I've done my best – been watching you make this stuff for ages, so I hope it's the right mix."

Henry looked dismayed: no one else could make his specific concoction. But, good-heartedly, he said,

"Thanks, Polly." He took the mug, prising the paper doily away from its bottom, and raised it to his lips.

"Cheers," he said as he took a tentative sip. A smile crept across his face as he wiped a drop from his top lip, then drank more deeply. "That's brilliant, Polly. Just right."

"Blimey," Rosalie exclaimed. "That's the first time he's ever liked his brew made by anyone else. I suppose I'll have to learn to do it properly now!"

"Well, not for a couple of weeks. And now I have something for you," Nora said as she stepped in front of both of them. "I think it's the time to give you your wedding present from me." She handed an elaborate envelope to Rosalie. Henry's hands were occupied with his mug of tea/coffee.

"What is it?" the young bride asked, her veil flowing down behind her as she leant forwards.

"Open it and see," Nora advised. Polly was hovering beside Nora with a broad smile on her face. Henry guessed she had been party to the secret, Henry himself having only been told yesterday morning.

"It's a key?" Rosalie held it up with a puzzled look. "What's it for?"

"It's for the cottage across the road, Tidal Reach. I've bought it for you. You can live in the house and rent out the land if you want…"

"Wow," Rosalie exclaimed. "Thank you, Nora. Thank you so much. Oh, Henry. Our own home. I thought we decided we would be staying here for a while. But this is... Oh, I'm so pleased. Thank you, Nora. Thank you." Rosalie broke free of the group and tottered, impeded by her high heels, to the door. Several of the guests paused in their conversations and turned around to watch. She tiptoed to the car park entrance and peered across the road; the sun streamed down on the cottage. Her smile widened as she imagined the home she would create with Henry - the décor, the furniture. Raising her gaze to take in the surrounding land, bordered by green hedges, she was disappointed when the sun was blocked by a dark cloud. But smiled again as the wind quickly drove it past.

Rosalie hurried back inside. "Can we go over and have a look?" she asked, her eyes wide with excitement.

"Later maybe. Not yet," Nora cautioned. "It hasn't been lived in for a while; you'll have a lot of work to do before you can move in."

Chapter 55

The early evening of Henry and Rosalie's wedding turned hot and sticky, and the wind blew itself out. Later, more dark storm clouds pushed the sun down over the western horizon; George, Quinny and Max stood in the pub car park and watched it disappear, leaving trails of smoky violet and vivid pinks dripping colour onto cotton wool clusters. The gentlemen then turned their heads towards the coast, and Max asked George,

"D'you know where they're off to tonight?"

"Yeah. A hotel, but I'm not telling anyone where, just in case someone tries to play tricks on them. Cans tied to the back of the bumper is just about acceptable – anything else isn't," the young man warned. "Anyway, the car's gone for now, the driver'll be back later."

Quinny chuckled. Max snorted, "Talk about a load of bloody spoil-sports."

"Wow, look at that!" George shouted, pointing at a jagged fork of lightning streaking from the middle of a black, bubbly cloud and down into what he thought would be the sea. The shafts of light remained visible on their retinas for several moments after vanishing from sight. They couldn't actually hear the thunder, but Quinny thought he felt it resonating through the ground.

"And they're off to Inverness tomorrow?" he asked.

"Yes, they have to call in here to pick up their suitcases, then catch the bus and train – it'll take 'til

Tuesday before they get there," George chuckled; he was glad he did not have to make that journey. But, then, maybe he wouldn't mind, if it was for his honeymoon.

By the time the storm reached PepperAsh later, angry shafts of white lightning were spearing their way downwards. At first, several seconds passed after the lightning and before the roaring, ground-shuddering thunder sounded. The rumbles brought folk out of the pub to have a look. The happy couple had been driven to their destination, and Nora was trying to persuade the hardy hangers-on to go home. The lightning and thunder grew closer together, and eventually were almost simultaneous. Then the rain began to fall.

The drops were large and round, and they pounded the ground, slowly to begin with, before pausing slightly as if to apologise for what was to come. Then they powered earthward with a force that knocked green leaves from their hold, flattened plants, dislodged moss from roof tiles and guttering, and cleansed cars and window-panes of their summer dust.

Poskett, who had remained sober for the entire celebrations, offered Max and Quinny a lift to their respective homes – the new van he had purchased for his shop and post office businesses had two passenger seats in the front. The gentlemen were grateful for the ride, but not as much as Nora was to finally see them leave.

By the time Poskett reached Pepper Hill, the wind was lashing the rain almost horizontally, and the sky lit up with beacons of lightning skittering in each and every direction across the otherwise black sky. The thunder was both heard and felt; the sonorous pounding vibrated people's diaphragms and unsettled every part of every being.

The storm seemed to have abated by the time Nora and Polly finished a preliminary tidy up in the lounge-bar and kitchen.

"The rest will have to wait until the morning. The rain is easing a little now," Nora commented as she held back the curtain and peered out of the window.

"Gosh, I feel tired," Polly announced. "These heels make my feet ache." She eased one foot out of her bright lemon shoes – purchased especially for the occasion to match her dress – and wriggled her toes.

"They are lovely, though," Nora remarked enviously. "I wish I could wear such elegant things!"

"You wouldn't say that if you had my feet and legs at the moment, though." They both laughed as Polly removed the other shoe and shrunk at least three inches.

"Yeah, well, they'd only bring out my varicose veins," Nora admitted, wringing around to look at the backs of her calves. "Come on, let's make a pot of tea, then we can turn in. If we have any customers tomorrow lunchtime, they'll have to take us as they find us!"

Nora checked the pub's front door was locked. As she flicked off the final light switch in the lounge-bar, another, fainter flash of lightning lit the room. She shrugged her shoulders before joining Polly in the kitchen.

"It isn't as bad now," Polly said. "Let's hope we've seen the last of it."

"My grandad used to tell me this old folk tale," Nora reminisced as she boiled the kettle and made the tea amid the debris on the kitchen table and work tops. "That if a thunderstorm was gathering out at sea and the tide was coming in, it would follow the magnetic pull of the water to the nearest river. Then, if the storm carried on following the river when the tide turned, the storm would be hauled back again and return out to sea, meaning the poor people underneath its path got a double-dose."

"Oh," Polly said stifling a yawn. "I don't think I've heard that before."

"I think it was just a popular tale around here because of the Potch being affected so much by the tides – the whole of Ashfield marshes used to flood several times each winter before the river bank was built up. There are high-tide markers down near Perrona Dawn's resort where that area of Cliffend was regularly underwater. It wasn't just the tides rising and bringing in the sea, though; storm water regularly brought flash floods from off the land behind as well."

"Oh well, let's hope everyone got home okay. The love-birds won't even notice the weather tonight," Polly added playfully.

Nora grimaced, "Ah, er, no. I don't think I want to think about that, thank you." They both laughed.

"I was glad when Poskett offered to take Max and Quinny," Polly added.

"Yes, I thought they would both be sleeping on the sofas here in the lounge-bar." Polly was actually staying the night because Susan was away and she knew the evening would finish late. Nora continued, "Thank goodness this storm held off until now – it would have been a disaster if it had broken during the wedding." They were sitting down now, sipping their tea.

"Yes. But, oh, didn't Rosalie look wonderful? And Henry, God, he's a handsome chap, your son, you know! I can't wait to see the photos. That photographer was a bit bossy, wasn't he?"

"Yes, well, I guess he has to deal with some awkward customers sometimes."

"Uh! Don't we all?" Polly exclaimed. "George was good, though. He really is a very grown-up young man, isn't he?" Nora nodded agreement as she continued to drink. "By the way, where is he?"

"He went up to bed about an hour ago. I found him sitting through here in the kitchen, looking as if he couldn't keep his eyes open any longer. I don't think he and Henry got much sleep last night at the Old Police House – Henry let it slip that they sat talking for a long time." Nora fiddled with a plate of sliced wedding cake covered in film-wrap. She offered it to Polly. "Would you like some?"

"I really shouldn't but…"

Mrs Ervsgreaves had made the cake, and several pictures were taken of it before the newly-weds cut into it. It comprised two tiers, and in keeping with tradition, the top one was to be stored away safely for Rosalie and Henry's first child's christening party. Most of the bottom layer had been eaten – it was delicious, the royal icing spread perfectly smooth and pristine white, the shells piped around the outside alternately pink and lilac to match Rosalie's flowers and Nora's dress, and the fruit cake inside was luxurious and crumbly and light, releasing a slight aroma of sherry. It was that mouth-watering smell that greeted Nora as she peeled back the clear film.

"That isn't Henry's prize cockerel plate, is it?" Polly asked.

"Yes," Nora admitted guiltily. "It was the only one I had spare."

"He'll have a fit if he finds out you're using it," Polly smirked.

"Well, I won't tell him, so please don't you either!"

Polly giggled, then shrugged before taking a slice. As she bit into it, the icing melted onto her tongue and she had to quickly catch a few falling crumbs. "Ummmm," she said with a full mouth. "That is delicious."

"Isn't it just!" Nora concurred. "And if you were anything like me, you didn't actually have time to eat much earlier," Nora stated.

"No, it was busy, wasn't it? Still, the caterers worked hard. So did Craig, didn't he? What time did he go?"

"I don't know. I wouldn't be surprised if we find him asleep here somewhere in the morn..."

Nora did not finish her sentence. The pub – along with the entire hamlet of Ashfield was plunged into darkness as thunder split the sky and shook the ground, seemingly taking a safe, comfortable world and placing it into the precarious hands of wrathful gods.

A flash of lightning lit up the interior of the pub, followed immediately by more thunder, which had not stopped by the time another bolt of lightning and more thunder boomed and exploded – almost breaking apart the night and ripping open the earth. Nora, even in her flurry to find torches, was reminded of Quinny's words earlier: *"Those whom God has joined, let no man put asunder,"* He had said as he bound Henry and Rosalie's hands for a moment with the ends of his stole.

Safely ensconced in the Honeymoon Suite at the Thrimbale Hotel in Cliffend, Rosalie and Henry barely noticed the storm.

George, thanks to an illicit tipple or two during the afternoon and evening, slept soundly through all the noise and disruption.

Nora lay in her bed listening to every creak and groan of the structure around her, as it answered the fury of the wind and rain outside.

Polly, unaccustomed to the softness of the mattress in The Fighting Cock's spare bedroom, was unable to sleep. She had not spent a night apart from Susan since they made their own vows to one another many years ago, and her thoughts were only for her partner, and how lonely life would be if they were not together.

Quinny listened to every explosion of lightning, and every unending roar and rattle of thunder, praying that St Jude's would not be struck, and pinging his rubber bands until they broke. He did not realise the electricity had failed until he tried to switch on a light to fetch more.

Max wished he was with Alice on board a luxury cruise-liner. He had already sustained damage to his roof and chimney in a previous gale, and did not want to make another claim on his insurance quite this soon. Then he thanked his lucky stars that he was not on a ship, because being tossed around on the seas in a storm such as this would be more that he could endure.

Poskett slept soundly in his room above the shop and post office in Pepper Hill. Jim, the postman, was up all night with a turbulent stomach after eating and drinking too much. Stan's wife tossed and turned, then got up to watch the storm from the bedroom window; Stan's snoring easily matching the thunder outside.

Craig had fallen asleep in his car outside, alone; in the morning he did not know which was the greater miracle – that he had slept at all or that he had done so on his own.

Chapter 56

"Did I dream it, or was there a second storm last night?" Rosalie asked Henry as she poured tea. Room service had brought a pre-breakfast trolley, with tea, coffee, grapes, and other fruit, toast, and a handful of wrapped chocolates artistically laced beneath a bouquet of pale pink roses. A full breakfast was to be served mid- to late-morning in the dining room as part of their Bridal Suite package; no one expected a young, newly married couple to be downstairs early.

"I think it was the same one that turned back on the tide and went out to sea again," Henry replied, trying to devise a way of making at least one cup of his tea/coffee concoction.

"You don't believe that old yarn, do you?"

"Of course I do," Henry said as he supped. "Urgh! Can't wait to have a proper brew." Rosalie threw a pillow at him and he only just managed to save the bed from a spillage.

"By the way, I have something here for you," Henry announced as he slid away and replaced his cup and saucer onto the trolley.

They had not unpacked last evening, and their wedding outfits had been strewn across any piece of furniture that was able to catch them. Before Henry reached the wardrobe, he stumbled on one of Rosalie's shoes – they were the first items to be discarded.

"I had this delivered here yesterday especially for this morning. I hope you like it." Henry looked apprehensive and Rosalie enjoyed his uncertainty; it made her feel empowered. But George had warned her not to manipulate poor Henry, even if she felt entitled as his wife.

Henry dragged out of the wardrobe a large, roughly wrapped parcel.

"I know it isn't a conventional wedding gift, but… Well, it's just supposed to be a fun present."

Rosalie had climbed out of bed. She slipped into her gown and was tying the belt around her as she accepted the package. "What is it?" she asked.

"Open it and find out," Henry encouraged.

Rosalie noisily ripped the paper off and drew out a large brown teddy bear in a clear loose wrapper. It wore around its neck a golden, heart-shaped locket.

Rosalie froze in horror. Then she began to tremble. She snatched at the covering, which crinkled then finally gave at the point Henry had slit and resealed it in order to slide the locket in and over the bear's head. Not bothering to even look at the sad-faced bear, Rosalie lifted the locket to examine it.

"Mum said her friend in New Zealand sent the bear when I was little, but she only recently gave it to me. I thought you would like it. Rosalie, what's wrong?" Henry watched in horror as his wife's face grew paler.

Rosalie glared at him as, with shaking hands, she attempted to unfasten the catch on the chain. Eventually she pulled it apart and discarded the bear. She ran across to the window and fumbled in the light to un-snack the front of the locket.

Inside, instead of seeing the treasured photos of her beloved parents smiling at her, she saw two plain red backgrounds. And, set a little off centre on the back half, was a diamond. Nora's diamond. She looked at her engagement ring. She'd thought that was the diamond. She suddenly felt afraid. Then furious.

"The locket is the one you lost at Ashfield Staithe. I found it just after you left," Henry tried to explain. He was bewildered at the sudden change in Rosalie's mood. She turned her full glower onto him. Her eyes became wide as her lips compressed and narrowed. Henry withdrew a step, totally confused. "I thought you would be pleased," he repeated. "And the diamond is the one from Mum's engagement ring. I know you thought it was the one in your ring, but that's a different one. I bought that one from the jeweller's when he made up the ring…"

Henry could hear his own voice babbling. But he was so confused. He didn't understand why Rosalie was reacting like this.

"How did you know I lost the locket at Ashfield Staithe?" Rosalie growled.

"I happened to be there when you arrived," Henry explained. "But you looked as if you wanted to be alone, so I didn't come forward, I stayed in the trees."

"You were spying on me?"

"No, no. I knew it was the anniversary of your Mum and Dad's deaths. It was the anniversary of my Dad's death too, you know. And I've still got the photos, in the locket's box at home, you can have them back!" He stopped. They had never argued before. In fact, Henry had never argued with anyone. His heart was hammering and he felt a little faint: he had not eaten much the previous day; prior to the wedding he had been too nervous and afterwards, he thought perhaps excitement and relief had taken away his appetite. For food, anyway.

"I didn't lose the locket. I left it there for them. Aunty Shirley refused to have Mum and Dad buried so I had nowhere to go and visit. I buried the locket so I could go to them." Rosalie's voice had started at a reasonable level, but was increasing in both volume and hysteria. "So I've been going there and talking to them. It made me feel better. But for over a year, they weren't there. HOW COULD YOU BE SO CRUEL, HENRY? HOW COULD YOU?"

It was not the first time the staff at the Thrimbale Hotel had overheard newly-weds arguing the morning after their wedding night. Sometimes the couples didn't even make it through until the morning. But it was the first time the bride had stormed down the stairs, barefoot, clutching a large teddy bear, and with just a negligee wrapped around her. The receptionist later told the chef, who happened to be her boyfriend, that she was sure the bride was not actually wearing anything underneath.

Rosalie had run out of the hotel's front door, and stood at the top of the steps, gasping and glaring frantically around her. Luckily a taxi had just dropped off a fare. She sprinted towards it and pleaded with the driver to take her to Pepper Hill.

"No, I haven't got any money on me," she exclaimed, almost letting go of both the gown and the enormous teddy bear. "But my brother will be there, and he will pay you. Honestly. Please," she implored.

"Okay, okay. Jump in, love" he said. When the door was shut, and he was beginning to drive away, he looked in the rear view mirror and asked, "That wouldn't be your old man, now coming down those steps, would it?"

Dear Reader

If you have enjoyed reading my book then please tell your friends and relatives and leave a review on Amazon.
Thank you.
Franky

More **PepperAsh** stories coming soon

Acknowledgements

I have scribbled stories for years, but it was not until I joined the Waveney Author Group that I achieved my ambition to be published. I would like to say an enormous thank you to Suzan Collins for all her kindness, support, and practical help. Thank you, also to the other members of WAG, and to the staff of the Coconut Loft in Lowestoft. I would also like to thank Pat for proofreading my novel.

And finally, the biggest thanks of all goes to my dear husband, John, for all his hard work.

Editor: Jo Wilde
Cover: John Sayer
Reader: Pat Vellacott

The places featured in The PepperAsh Clinch story are all fictional, although there may be a passing resemblance to towns and villages around the coastal area of the Suffolk/Norfolk border. The characters, personalities and their predicaments are also completely fictional.

About the Author

Born in Felixstowe, Franky moved to North Suffolk as a small child. She still lives close to the Norfolk/Suffolk border, with her husband, John, and their yellow Labrador, Boris.

Franky trained as a shorthand/typist/secretary, and worked as such in a variety of industries, including a rock and sweet making factory, an offshore oil and gas platform construction company, and as a local government officer. Other employments include music engraving, and over two decades as a parish council clerk.

Her hobbies include music - she plays tenor recorder, guitar, piano and church organ and the last of these led to her becoming the chapel organist for twenty years in a local prison.

Her other interests are artistic roller skating – she is a member of the Waveney Roller Skating Club – dressmaking, walking her dog in the countryside, and reading.

This is Franky's first novel.

If you would like to know more about Franky and to follow her on social media please go to https://www.facebook.com/Franky-Sayer-Author-121619925146482/

26111342R00162

Printed in Great Britain
by Amazon